THE PERSIAN WOMAN

BY
THOMAS BOOKER

www.circlebpublishing.com

ISBN: 978-0-9987736-2-9

Prologue

The two assault boats slice quietly across the surface of the Red Sea. The spray that hits my face is as heavy and warm as drops of blood.

I look from the boat carrying my Navy SEAL platoon to the second boat carrying the British SAS team. I spot Mickey Simski, the U.S. Navy flight surgeon who volunteered for this mission even though he was never trained as a special operator. He looks grim in the oversized Kevlar helmet we scrounged up for him. I put him with the Brits because it is their job to locate Senator DeLong's two daughters in the rambling old compound where they are being held. Mick will be on hand to provide the highest level of medical attention to the girls, if they need it. That keeps our own special ops medic free to deal with any casualties we may incur on our end of the mission. Our job is to neutralize Malaku's so-called Army of Heaven holding the two girls hostage. I have a clear idea as to what neutralize means.

It is after midnight when we cut into the beach near the little fishing village of Mohammed Qol on the Sudanese coast. A low layer of clouds seals the night sky, but even in the extreme darkness the old colonial-era fort on the edge of town where the girls are being held looks like a giant cube of sugar dis-

solving into the desert. Both teams reach the assembly point without incident. I give my final instructions:

"Remember, this is a hostage extraction," I say. "That means we're here under a black flag. No prisoners. The only people we're bringing out of there alive are the two DeLong girls, if they are alive. Whatever happens in there, keep your cool. Don't lose your heads. Now let's roll."

The demolition squad tapes up twice the necessary amount of boomer on the fort's entry doors. We aren't blowing a bank safe; I want a lot of flash and bang to disorient the garrison inside.

I watch as the massive wooden doors disappear in a thundering ball of smoke and flame. My SEAL platoon storms in first, then the Brits. I am the last one in.

There is gunfire, shouting, screaming. Battle stench clogs my nostrils: blood, excrement, the musk odor of men both frightened by death and excited by it. Other men's blood soaks my boots.

A British-accented voice comes through the earpiece of my field intercom. "We have one of the hostages, Commander Quinn."

"Dead or alive?" I ask.

"Alive."

"Where?"

"Passageway under the big stone arch."

I race down the passageway until I come to a room lit by a dim light from a kerosene lamp. In its glow I see two Brits covering the doorway with leveled assault rifles. Two others are helping a teenage girl from a cot by the wall. She is dirty and slightly emaciated, but she is alive. I fumble out two photographs from the pocket of my flak jacket and compare them to the girl. Great! We have one of the girls, the younger one, the one named Teal.

"Take her out to the beach," I say. "Call in the dust-off."

Another British-accented voice crackles through the earpiece, but faintly as though from the bottom of a well. This one belongs to the big sergeant-major who heads the SAS team.

"We've got the second one, Yank."

"Where?"

"Steps leading down from the iron door at the rear of the compound. Watch out, it's a bloody maze down here. Twists around like a pretzel."

"Set out some chem-lights. What's her condition?"

"You'd better come look, Yank."

I find the steps and head down and down, seemingly forever. The underground passageway is dark and winding, a labyrinth where the dread creatures of mythology might wait to devour the unwary. I follow the green chem-light trail to where the passageway dead-ends at a small cell. Its barred door has been pried off its hinges. Flashlight beams are jumping on its walls.

"Hold those damn lights steady," I hear a voice say. It is Mickey Simski's voice.

Three SAS men are half-standing, half-stooping, holding their flashlights shoulder high, pointing them unsteadily at two men kneeling on the floor. One of the kneeling men is the big sergeant-major who had buzzed me. Something dirty and ragged is propped against his wide chest and cradled in his massive arms. Mickey is the second kneeling man. He has his back to me, but I can see that he is working furiously at the object the big Brit is holding. As I get closer I realize that the object the Brit is holding is the second DeLong girl, the older one, the one named Robin. Already I know something is dreadfully wrong.

She is covered only by a torn T-shirt gone stiff with sweat. Her legs are skeletal, the knees swollen to the size of melons. Her skin is the color and texture of melted wax. Her entire body is encrusted with dirt, body salt, and feces. Tangled blonde hair falls like jungle vines over her face. She smells of vomit.

"This one they left for dead," I am thinking.

Mickey is doing something with the girl's right arm. He unwraps a long filthy rag from the arm and throws it on the floor. "Damn," he mutters.

"What is it, Mick?" I ask.

"Just a damn minute," he says.

He un-wraps another long filthy rag and throws it on the floor. "Damn," he says again.

"What is it, Mick?" I say. "We're running short on time here."

He doesn't answer me. Instead, he keeps un-wrapping rags and muttering damn. Finally, he finishes and looks up. "Look at this," he says. "Look at this, damn it."

He holds up the girl's right arm. Only it doesn't look like an arm. It looks like a length of sausage that has discolored and gone bad. Striations of red and purple run up to the elbow. The end is swollen, blackened, and blunt.

Mickey's voice is bitter. "The goddamn goniphs cut off her hand."

Chapter One

The day it all began the hostage rescue in Sudan was five years in the past. Since then my life had been a series of savage storms and angry winds. It was as though a spiteful ancient god had raged the very elements against me. I had been blown so far off my chosen course that I hardly knew where I was or who I was.

First, my wife Lori Ann had been killed when a lone-wolf jihadist opened fire with an AK-47 in a crowded California shopping mall. Barely twelve months later I was sentenced to ten years in the Texas penitentiary for sending a rogue Houston cop to the hospital. My discharge from the Navy followed immediately afterward. I was a man drowning in my own grief.

It was Albert DeLong, the senior senator from Texas, who pulled me out of the depths and dragged me ashore. He pulled some strings with the governor's office to get my sentence commuted to time served, gave me a job, and even guaranteed a loan so I could buy a small horse ranch. He did it out of gratitude, he said, because I had led the raid that had rescued his two daughters, Robin and Teal. Those who knew him best said he never did anything out of gratitude, but I took him at his word. In turn, his kindness sparked a kind of reciprocal gratitude in me to him. I tried to show this gratitude in various ways; one of those ways was to look in from time to time on his daughter Robin. That's what brought me to East Texas that day in June.

"Robin around?" I asked, as if Robin had someplace to go.

"She's out in her garden, Mr. Quinn," the big-haired woman behind the reception desk said. "I'll give you a pass."

I clipped the visitor's badge on the lapel of my sport coat and exited by the metal door that gave out onto the facility grounds. It was like opening the door into a circle of hell; it was oppressively hot and humid, even for Texas in early June. The air felt like damp wool on my skin. I didn't want the contents of the box I had under my arm to melt even before I delivered them, so in spite of the heat I double-timed it along the graveled walkway that twisted through the grounds.

From a distance the facility might have resembled a small college or perhaps a corporate research campus. The one story red brick buildings were carefully spaced, their trim enameled a spotless white, their slab foundations hidden behind beds of daisies and periwinkles. The new mown grass in the open areas was as thick and green as the outfield in Yankee Stadium. Groves of oak, elm, and pine provided periodic shady spots. Through the trees you could see the blue shimmer of a private lake. But this was no college or corporate campus. The bars on the windows never let you forget that you had entered a world of dancing shadows and personal demons that few of its residents ever managed to leave.

I found Robin DeLong on a mild slope that led to a ten foot chain link fence separating the grounds from a state park campground. She was on her knees, weeding out a row of onions in the small vegetable garden I had put in for her that spring. She was dressed in pink coveralls, a floppy canvas hat, and a white men's dress shirt. The left sleeve of the shirt was cut off at the elbow; the right sleeve was left long to cover what she had come to call "her thing."

I started toward her, but then I noticed an attendant in a white uniform and a crushed-up straw cowboy hat slouched on a bench to my left. He was working a toothpick between his teeth, watching Robin work in the sun. Asylum attendants came and went. I hadn't met this one before so I thought I better check in before heading down the hill.

"How's our girl today?" I asked.

He shrugged for an answer, not turning his head.

I tried again. "Any problems with Robin?"

Another shrug.

"Sir?" I said loudly.

Not even a shrug this time. I kicked the edge of the bench.

"Wake up, bud," I said.

He raised his eyes lazily, ran them up and down my entire length, then retrained them on Robin. He was about twenty-five. A two day growth darkened his face and a sour odor rose from his armpits. He spoke without looking at me, still working the toothpick between his teeth. His voice had the kind of nasal twang that sounded as if invisible fingers were pinching the bridge of his nose.

"She nailed herself shut in her room the other night," he said. "She ain't done that before."

"Say what?"

"I'll say it for you slow, big dude. She-took-a-hammer-and-some-nails-and-nailed-her-door-shut-from-the-inside."

"Why'd she do that?"

"Hell if I know. That's the kind of stuff them crazoids do."

"Where'd she get the hammer and nails?"

"Who knows? Crazoids is sneaky, too. She probably snuck 'em out of bungee-low six when they was doing repairs there the other day. There's no tellin' what kind of high-boogery that girl will get herself into."

I was digesting these remarks when he suddenly looked up, a smirk on his face now.

"She's a head case, all right," he said, "but there ain't nothin' wrong with her body. She's tight, bro', even with that grabber on her arm."

I stood perfectly still with my eyes closed, my ears whirring with a sound like that of a speeding train about to jump its tracks. When the moment passed I turned and walked down the hill.

"You going to make me stand here all day, partner?" I said to the kneeling young woman.

Robin hadn't seen me walk up, but when she heard my voice she sprang up, brushing mud off her overalls with her left hand.

"Jeffrey!" she shrieked like a child. "I didn't know you were coming."

"This is a covert operation. No advance warning."

"You sound like a Navy SEAL," she giggled.

"I deny everything. Here, I brought something for you." I handed her the box I had under my arm.

"What is it? What is it?"

"Open it and find out."

She opened the box. "Awesome, Jeffrey, I love chocolate cake."

"I know. That's why I brought it. Made it myself. You should see my kitchen."

"You didn't make it yourself, but I love you anyway." She scraped off some frosting with her finger and held it to her tongue. "Mmmm . . . want some?"

"Nope. It's all for you. Better put it someplace you won't forget."

She nodded. "You're right. Here, I'll put it next to the ship's log you gave me. I'd never forget that."

She bent down and sat the box on a towel she had spread on the nearby grass, placing it beside an inexpensive girl's diary I bought at a Wal-Mart not long after I had put in her garden. The little book had a yellow plastic cover featuring Minnie Mouse in a sailor's costume. This led me to refer to it jokingly as a ship's log since I had once been in the Navy. She had asked that I bring her something in which she might write. In my amateur psychologist way I thought a diary might be good therapy for her. Maybe it was; the asylum staff told me she lugged it with her everywhere.

"How about a hug, partner?" I asked.

She stood back up. "I'm all muddy, Jeffrey."

"I like muddy women."

She smiled, placed her arms around my midsection, and squeezed me gently with her elbows, being careful not to touch me with the stainless steel prosthesis on her right arm. I hugged her lightly. Her back felt frail, as though it were nothing more than tissue paper spread over a wire frame. Her blonde hair smelled vaguely of strawberry shampoo.

She finished hugging me and knelt back down in her garden. I knelt on one knee beside her.

"Has something been scaring you, princess?" I asked.

"Why do you ask, Jeffrey?" She spoke nonchalantly, but her eyes avoided mine.

"That guy at the top of the hill says you nailed the door to your room shut the other night."

"He's a bad man. I don't like him."

"Is that what's scaring you, that guy up there?"

She hesitated. Then she shook her head no.

"What is it, then?"

She didn't answer. Her eyes suddenly focused inward. It was as though she were looking down some dark corridor visible only to her. She began weeding her garden ferociously. Conversation over. I patted her on the head and stood up.

When I reached the top of the hill the attendant was still slouched on the bench, still working the toothpick between his teeth, still studying Robin. I walked over and thumped him hard on the shin with my boot. His head jerked up. The toothpick plopped out of his mouth and hung by a ball of saliva on his shirtfront. His eyes widened to the size of hubcaps.

"What the hell?" he said.

He started to get up. I gripped the top of his head through his hat and shoved him back down.

"Listen up," I said.

"Fuck you, asshole."

"You're not helping yourself."

"I said fuck you," he repeated.

His eyes turned yellow with hate, but he stayed seated on

the bench. I lowered my hand and spoke in the most civil tone I could manage.

"Look, bud," I said, "that young woman down there is a friend of mine. I'd appreciate a little respect for her."

"What do you fucking mean, 'respect', asshole?"

"What I mean is that if I ever hear you call her a crazoid again, I'm going to get on you like a chicken on a June-bug. You reading me on this?"

"Fuck off. Anything else, dickhead?"

"Just one more thing."

I reached down, grabbed his left ear, and jerked him to his feet so that his face was level with my own. I brought him so close that I could smell the mixture of Jim Beam and mouthwash on his breath and see the pain flickering in his eyes.

"If I ever find out you've touched her," I said, "I'll hunt you down and kill you."

I shoved him back down. He started to get up, but again I gripped him through his hat and shoved him back down.

"Don't lose your head," I said.

I walked back to my truck in a dark frame of mind. I'd have to do something about that guy. Robin had had enough trouble. She didn't need some peckerwood sex predator stalking her. I'd think of something.

Meanwhile, I wished she could tell me what was bugging her, but I doubted if she could—or would. That's the way it was with Robin. She could carry on a conversation more or less normally for a twenty-four year old, right up to the point you touched a hidden nerve that sent her retreating far inside herself, not eating, not sleeping, practically catatonic for days on end. She had been that way ever since we brought her back from Africa. Her therapists—and her father could afford the best—had all but given up on her. One therapist, a crisp woman with a PhD from a prestigious east coast university, opined that Robin's lack of progress stemmed from her "lack of intellectual resources." I wondered about that. What amount of intellectual resources could ever help you cope with having your hand chopped off, and then finding yourself cast into a dungeon in the very bowels of the earth?

I got into my truck, started the engine, and dialed the A/C onto high. I slipped a classical piano CD Lori Ann had once given me for Christmas into the CD player and settled in for the three hour drive back to my ranch. I liked the long drive; it gave me time to think.

I made it back to my ranch on the prairie northwest of Houston right around supper time. I skipped supper. Instead, I helped my hired man muck out the high-raftered old barn where I stalled Sergeant Pepper, the pregnant mare that had belonged to my wife. When we finished mucking out the barn we turned to the horse. We took her out to the soft dirt lot adjacent to the barn and brushed her down. Then we ran a curry comb through her mane and tail to break up the inevitable clots of mud that horses accumulate just being horses. We finished by sponging her off with warm water and drying her with a soft sheepskin. We put her up just as the sun was sliding behind a low bank of purple clouds and the evening sky was thickening with night birds. I went to bed early and hoped for a long, dreamless sleep.

I wasn't to get it.

Chapter Two

The knock on the door came at four o'clock in the morning. It was loud, persistent, delivered by the base of the fist with enough force to rattle the door in its frame. It was the kind of knock that doesn't take "go away" for an answer. I knew before I even opened the door that I would find a cop on the other side. Lo and behold, I found two of them.

The first was the ex-Marine type of deputy sheriff: ramrod straight, trim, muscular, hair cut so high and tight that you could see his ears from low earth orbit.

"We interrupt something beautiful?" he asked.

"What do you mean by that crack?" I answered.

"What took you so long?"

"It's my house. I'll take as long as I want. If you're in such a hurry, why didn't you just break down the door?"

"Next time we will. Your name Jeffrey Quinn, the one used to be a SEAL?"

"That's right. What do you want?"

"We want to talk to you."

"Come back during business hours."

"If we come back, it'll be with a warrant, swabbie."

"What kind of judge would give you a warrant for anything, jarhead?" I said.

But before the deputy could answer the second cop stepped up. “I’m sure a warrant won’t be necessary, Alton,” he said. “Mr. Quinn’s a good citizen. Aren’t you Mr. Quinn?”

The second cop was much older, paunchy, and stiff in his movements. He wore a wrinkled blue business suit and white shirt, and a yellow tie that showed spots of soup and ketchup even in the dim porch light. To top it off, he had on the kind of short-brimmed Stetson hat with which Hollywood directors routinely crown the heads of western movie goobers. A gold badge was pinned to his red suspenders. He might as well have had a sign hanging around his neck that said Hick Town Sheriff.

“What’s this all about,” I asked.

“Why don’t you invite us in and find out?”

I weighed my options. No matter what the courts say, when you’re confronted by two policemen in the middle of the night you don’t have any options. I stepped aside and let them in.

The deputy marched past me, flicked on the lights in my dining room, and pulled out a chair at the head of the table for the sheriff. The big man lowered himself ponderously into the chair, like a bull elephant sitting itself down in a watering hole. He hooked his hat on the back of a nearby chair and placed a paper sack he had brought in under his arm on the table before him.

“Thanks, Alton,” he said. “Go wait in the cruiser.”

The deputy left in the same huff in which he had come in. I sat down at the table and folded my hands in my lap. I realized for the first time that I had answered the door in my boxers. I didn’t care.

“All right,” I said, “what’s this all about?””

“Well, my name is Tuck, son. I’m just a country sheriff up in Rusk County.”

“I never would have guessed.”

If he caught the attitude in my remark he didn’t show it, except perhaps for a slight tightening of the skin around his eyes. He went on, wheezing slightly now as he spoke.

“We got a fine little rest home in our county, a special kind of place for folks with nervous problems. Ever been there?”

"Maybe."

"Maybe? The folks at the home tell me you've been a regular visitor for quite a spell. You was out there yesterday, I hear, visiting that young woman them A-rabs got a holt of: Robin DeLong, Senator DeLong's daughter."

"Okay, so what?"

Now his eyebrows drew together and the color rose in his throat. "You're a smart aleck son-of-a-gun, aren't you?"

"I'm never very charming at four in the morning."

He lowered his eyes to the sack on the table, his face clouding with thought. He patted the sack a few times, as though it were a puppy, then looked up and went on.

"Know a fellar out at the home named Boo Hightower?"

"Nope."

"About twenty-five or thirty, wiry, wears a Mexican cowboy hat. Ring a bell?"

"You talking about a guy who smells like he rolls in a pile of dog poop every morning just to start his day off right?"

"He don't smell like fresh-cut honeysuckle, if that's what you mean."

"I met him for the first time yesterday. Why do you ask?"

The sheriff's face turned serious. "He says you assaulted and threatened to kill him, damn near tore his ear off. What do you say to that?"

I knew better than to lie to cops; it only pisses them off.

"It's true," I said. "Want to hear what happened?"

He nodded. I went on to describe my encounter with the man named Boo Hightower. He listened without interrupting. When I finished he leaned forward and exhaled heavily, as though he had been holding his breath underwater. He shook his head.

"I know the Hightower boy," he said, "knew his mama, too. She used to sell out of her pants over on Hines Boulevard in Dallas. I warned the home not to hire him."

"Well, they did. But I made it perfectly clear what would happen to him if he got out of line with Robin."

"Did you have to go and grab his ear?"

"It's a great attention getter."

"I had a deputy once was an ear grabber. He said the same thing."

"Sounds like a man who knew how to get the job done."

"He could do that all right. He once set a prisoner loose so he could follow him to a wanted man still at large. Called the one he set loose his bird dog. Brought both of 'em in the next day."

"Sounds creative too. Where's this guy now?"

"Oh, he ain't in my little county no more. You learn that ear grabbing trick from them folks in the Navy?"

"No, I learned it from Sister Mary Agnes in the seventh grade."

"Why didn't you just tell the folks up at the office instead of taking it on yourself to put the boy right?"

"You mean tell the same pencil-pushers that hired the little dirtball in the first place?"

He didn't respond. He pulled the paper sack off the table and began turning it over and over in his hands, studying it as though it were a grocery item he was considering buying. He spoke without looking at me. "You're still a fairly young man, Mr. Quinn. Thirty-five, maybe? How come you left the Navy?"

"The Navy and I had a falling out."

"They tell me you work for Senator DeLong now."

"That's right."

"What do you do for him?"

"General trouble shooter, I guess you'd say. I spend most of my time as dive master on an excursion boat he bought for his son, Travis."

"Is going to see his daughter out at the home part of your job?"

"No, I do that on my own time."

"Good for you, son. How come you got to be so close to her?"

"We have some things in common."

"Like what, son?"

"I don't know, maybe because we both got a full dose of *jihad*. You hear how my wife was killed?"

"Didn't one of them radical fellars slip in and shoot up a shopping mall or someplace out in California, kill your wife and a bunch of other folks?"

"That's right."

"I was sorry to hear it."

An uneasy silence followed. The sheriff continued to examine the paper sack in his lap. I could hear cicadas chirping in my back pasture and, further away, a dog barking with a ferocity that usually meant a coyote was getting too close to his perimeter. Somewhere in the back of my mind I sensed a disconnect between what was being said and what was happening. I should have been in cuffs by now and on my way to Rusk County in the back of the sheriff's cruiser.

"Sheriff," I said, "are you telling me that you drove all the way down here in the wee hours just because I twisted the ear of some East Texas peckerwood?"

He looked up, a softness in his eyes now. He spoke in a low, gentle tone of voice. "No, son, I'm not telling you that."

"What are you telling me?"

He reached over and lightly laid his hand on my forearm as he spoke. "Your friend Robin . . ."

"Yes?"

"She went and hung herself last night."

"What?" I shouted, springing to my feet so fast that I knocked my chair backward into a glass-fronted china cabinet. The glass and most of the china inside broke with a crash that sounded like two cars colliding at an intersection. A second later the deputy named Alton was storming through the front door, his right hand poised over a holstered .357 Magnum. The sheriff waived him off.

"It's okay, Alton," he said. "Mr. Quinn just had a shock."

I didn't know how long I stood there with my eyes closed—a minute, five minutes. When I snapped to I felt naked and ashamed standing there in my boxers. The sheriff said I could put on some clothes. I went to my bedroom and slipped on some jeans and a khaki work shirt. Then I went to the kitchen and put on a pot of coffee.

While I was waiting for the coffee to perk, I put in a call to the Delong home in Houston. The black housekeeper answered the phone. She told me in a hushed whisper that the family was aware of the tragedy and had gone into seclusion.

"Any idea why she did it?" I said to the sheriff as I put two mugs of coffee on the table, my composure somewhat back in order.

"I was hoping you could tell me."

"No idea, unless Boo what's-his-name didn't believe me when I said I'd kill him if he touched her."

"We don't think that was it. The medical examiner didn't see any sign of sexual contact. Besides, you really put the fear of God in ol' Boo. As soon as you left he asked the office to assign him to another patient. He was never alone with her after that."

"Then I don't know."

"When you was out there yesterday did she say why she nailed her door shut a few nights ago?"

"No, she wouldn't talk about it."

"She ever talk to you about taking her own life?"

"No."

"Nothing in her life right now that would set her off?"

"Not that I know of."

"What about something from her past?"

"If you're talking about her experience in Sudan, that was long ago and far away."

"I don't know, son, the past is never that far away. I was in the Marines during Vietnam. I still remember what I saw and what I smelled, like it was yesterday. Sometimes, when the wind's just right, I can swear I can hear screaming children and smell burning hooches, and in broad daylight too. So, why don't you tell me what happened over there in the desert."

"Not much to tell really."

"Then tell me what you can."

I shrugged and took a sip of coffee. The sheriff leaned forward, splaying his big hands on the tabletop and waited for me to begin talking. Though they were covered with liver spots the size of dimes, they were hands that looked capable of strangling a Cape buffalo.

"The basic story is pretty well known," I said. "Senator DeLong's two daughters, Robin and Teal, were on a scuba diving trip to the Red Sea, allegedly with a marine biology expedition with Texas A&M. Given his prominence in American politics, the Senator should have kept it low-key, but he was always on TV bragging about how his two girls were in a remote and rough region helping out science. Eventually word got out in the Middle East where the kids actually were: in a suite at the Four Seasons hotel in Sharm el-Sheikh. That's a very expensive scuba diving resort on the Sinai Peninsula, at the head of the Red Sea. The Red Sea is considered the primo recreational diving venue in the world because of the warm water and fantastic coral formations. So it really should have come as no big surprise when some ragtag jihadists calling themselves the Army of Heaven seized the opportunity and snatched the two girls. The kidnappers took them down the Red Sea coast to a run-down old fort in Sudan. When negotiations for their return broke off, the President sent in my SEAL team to fetch them out. We went in, together with a Brit SAS team, and did the job. Nasty business, but we got them out. Teal bounced back from the ordeal okay; Robin never got back on her feet. Maybe that's because those nice holy men had chopped off her right hand."

The sheriff interrupted. "How come they was to do that?"

"Robin would never talk about it."

"What'd her sister have to say?"

"Teal says it happened during a time they were being held apart."

"How come they kept them apart?"

"Two people can be brave; an isolated person will break sooner or later, usually sooner. You should know that, Sheriff, you keep prisoners."

"I don't try to break prisoners, son. If I keep prisoners in isolation, it's for their own safety."

"You're from a different tradition."

He leaned back in his chair and massaged his temples with his fingers, his face filling with more questions. I waited for him to ask them.

"As I remember," he said, "them kidnappers had a leader with some kind of funny name. What was that again?"

"Malaku."

"What's that mean?"

"Our operations research team said Malaku is the name of the Angel of Death in the Quran."

"You believe in that kind of stuff, angels and things?"

"Sheriff, I don't believe in angels, demons, ghosts, goblins, ectoplasms, extraterrestrials, leprechauns or anything else I can't touch with my hot little hands."

"You ever catch up with him?"

"I don't know."

"Wasn't he there when you raided that compound or whatever it was where they was holding them girls?"

"Maybe. We never identified him."

"No picture or nothing to identify him with?"

"Nope. He was camera shy, I guess. No known photograph exists."

"Didn't the prisoners you took point him out?"

"We didn't take any prisoners."

His raised his eyes to mine as the import of what I had just said sunk in. "Is that how the SEALS does things?" he asked.

"It's how I do things."

"So you don't know if he's alive or dead?"

"If he was in that compound, he's dead."

He pursed his lips into a "0", ran his eyes around the room, and bounced the little paper sack in his lap. I got up to bring us some more coffee. When I returned he was ready with some more questions.

"You know of any bad blood between Robin and her sister Teal?" he asked.

"No."

"They tell me Robin would never see her or talk to her. How come, you think?"

"I don't know. Robin would never talk about it."

"Don't you think that's a little odd?"

"I don't know what's odd anymore. I was in Abilene a week ago and saw two cowboys walking down Main Street holding hands."

A smile traced across his lips for an instant. His face turned serious again. "You think Robin blamed Teal for what happened to her?"

"If she did, she never said so to me."

"You think she was afraid of Teal, or of what Teal might do?"

"What do you mean," I asked, "what she might do?"

He shrugged as though his question were as innocent and innocuous as an order at the Jack-in-the-Box drive-thru.

"What's your point?" I asked.

"My point, son, is that Teal had quite a reputation before her old man shipped her off on that scuba diving trip. I guess you heard about the oil refinery fire."

"I know that Teal was into all sorts of radical movements as a teenager, like a lot of kids. I heard that there was a fire at a cracking plant in Pasadena that some say Teal and some environmentalist radicals set. Nothing was ever proven."

He shook his head and grinned. "That's because her old man found a way to squeeze the *cajones* of everyone involved in the investigation, from the state arson investigator down to the one-eyed vet who sweeps the floor in the DA's office. Meanwhile, he sent Teal and Robin on that trip to keep them from having to testify before the grand jury."

"Whatever," I said.

"A man was killed in that fire, Mr. Quinn, a night watchman I believe. I don't think 'whatever' is quite the right response."

"Well, whatever Teal may have been involved in as a kid, she's in a good groove now. She's in a sorority at her college, engaged to the captain of the tennis team, and making straight A's in pre-med. On Sundays she co-hosts a cable channel religious show. All that other stuff is history. Limitations has run."

"There's no statute of limitations on homicide, my friend."

Now it was my turn to shrug. The sheriff leaned forward so far I could smell a night's worth of coffee and cigarettes on his breath. He locked his eyes on mine.

"I've seen her on that TV show," he said. "She's a mighty pretty young woman. You spend any time with her?"

"Some. I've taken her scuba diving a time or two, maybe fishing once or twice," I said. "She likes the outdoors."

"You wouldn't have the hots for her, would you?"

"No."

"Wouldn't blame you if you did."

"Look, Sheriff, as a man grows older he should learn to prefer older women, that is, if he knows what's good for him. I like to think I know what's good for me."

"A stiff prick doesn't give a hoot in hell about what's good for anybody."

"The answer is still no, Sheriff."

He exhaled heavily and leaned back in his chair. He took the paper sack out of his lap and placed it on the table. His gaze turned inward; he ran his tongue around the inside of his mouth; he squirmed slightly and changed his position at least twice. I suspected he was getting tired and was wrapping things up so he could go home. I was wrong.

"Let me ask you a couple of more questions," he said.

I tried to hide any disappointment in my face. "Go ahead."

"How come them A-rabs grabbed those girls anyway? What'd they want?" he asked.

"The usual," I said, "close down Guantanamo, make Israel withdraw to its 1967 borders, stop sending carrier groups into the Persian Gulf, and accept the Quran as the basis for a new world order."

"And they thought holding two little Texas girls would give them leverage to get all that?"

"I don't know what they thought they'd get. What they got was a midnight visit from my SEAL team."

"How'd you know where to find them?"

"The embassy in Cairo got an anonymous tip. For once, it panned out. We re-conned the place for weeks. The two girls were in that old fort, all right."

He nodded and scratched the stubble on his chin with a yellow thumbnail. "One more question."

"Sure."

"How come a team of limeys went in with you?"

"SEALS usually don't take on partners," I said, "But this raid was a little different. Back in colonial days the Brits governed Sudan. They had maps and charts and hard-to-find information that made the planning process much easier. They even had the original architectural plans for the old fort where the girls were held. The price they wanted for sharing the info was an opportunity to go along. They wanted some headlines, I guess. It's been a while for them."

"That's a damn foolish reason to get shot at."

"Show me a good reason."

"They get in the way?"

"No. As a matter of fact, I liked working with them. I got to be good buds with the SAS team leader, a big sergeant-major. We're still in touch."

"SAS?" He raised an eyebrow.

"Special Air Service. That's what they call their special ops guys."

There was a long silence as the sheriff fidgeted around in his chair some more, sucked his lips in and out, patted the little paper sack on the table some more. I felt my eyes getting heavier and fatigue setting into my muscles like quick drying cement.

"Look, Sheriff," I said finally, "is there anything else? It's late. I'm tired, you're tired. I appreciate your bringing me the news about Robin, but let's call it a night if you're finished."

"I'm not quite finished," he said, stopping his fidgeting and locking his eyes on mine.

"Oh?"

"I have to make a decision."

"About what?"

"About you."

"You mean whether to arrest me for coming down a little too hard on that white trash asylum attendant?"

"No, Mr. Quinn," he said, opening the paper sack he had been pawing all night, "whether to give you this." He reached into the sack and pulled out a girl's diary with Minnie Mouse in sailor's costume on the cover. He placed it on the table half-way between us. "Recognize this?" he asked.

"Of course, I gave it to Robin. Where'd you get it?"

"It was at the death scene. I think maybe the poor girl wanted us to be sure not to miss it."

"Why bring it to me?"

"Because, son, this is Sunday morning. Come tomorrow morning the county attorney, the coroner's office, and every newspaper and TV station in Texas is going to start grand-standing this story, on account of the girl being who she was, the daughter of a United States Senator and all. It'll probably go down as just another suicide by an asylum patient . . . unless someone gets a-holt of this little book."

"Why? What's in it?"

"Things that could embarrass lots of folks, maybe stir things up that are best left unstirred."

"Why not just burn it?"

"Because there's some things in there what bother me, bother me greatly. I want someone to look into them, someone who will take care of business and keep his mouth shut. I'm thinking that would be you."

"Why not look into them yourself?"

"Well, for one thing, you know more than I do about what this girl might be talking about in here."

"And the other thing?"

"I'll be honest, Mr. Quinn," he said, lowering his voice as he spoke, as though sharing a secret, "Albert DeLong is the biggest bull-of-the-woods in Texas politics since Lyndon Baines Johnson. If you're in politics in this state Albert can make you or break you, and to him it don't matter which. I plan to stand for one more re-election and then retire. I don't need Albert DeLong holding a grudge against me for embarrassing his family by releasing this little book."

"That bad, huh?"

"Could be."

"Sheriff," I said, "you better think twice before getting me involved in this. Did you know I've been in Huntsville?"

He nodded. "I heard that. Want to tell me about it?"

Now it was my turn to rub my temples. I hated remembering the episode, much less talking about it. I stopped rubbing, took a deep breath and recounted what had happened.

"It was about six months after my wife was killed in California. I was on extended leave back here in Texas. This is where I was born and grew up. I was at a self-serve gas station in Houston filling up when a farm boy in a pick-up drove up, followed by a police cruiser with its flashers on. I found out later the cop was pulling him over for some minor traffic violation, 35 in a 30 zone, something like that." I paused.

"Go on, son."

"Well, the farm boy had a big dog in the bed of his truck, a Golden Retriever. When the cop got out of his cruiser and approached the truck, the dog started barking. Without batting an eyelash the cop took out his weapon and shot the dog dead, right there in the back of the truck. This sent the farm boy into a rage. He jumped out and went after the cop. The cop was about to shoot him, too, when I stepped in."

"What do you mean, 'you stepped in'?"

"I disarmed the cop and took him down. I guess I took him down a little too hard. He spent some time in sick bay."

"I ain't never heard of no unarmed man taking down an armed police officer by his-self."

"I know things they don't teach at the police academy."

"Oh? Then what happened, son?"

"The cop was taken to the hospital; I was taken to jail. Later I was indicted for interfering with police business and for assaulting a police officer. It turned out the cop had a long history of complaints for brutality and the use of excessive force. He skated on every one, so it didn't make any difference. He got ten days in the hospital, I got ten years to do. That's about it."

"You ever regret what you done?"

"What was I supposed to do, let that cop waste that kid like he did the dog?"

He nodded. "I see what you mean."

He sat silent for another minute, his eyes focused on an invisible spot on the table, his face sober with thought. Eventually he looked up, his decision apparently made. He reached out and nudged the diary across the table until it was right before me. "You're it," he said.

I picked up the diary; it felt as heavy as a corpse in my hand. I sat it back down.

"What do you expect me to do?" I asked.

"You say you're the trouble-shooter for Albert DeLong, so trouble-shoot."

I thought about it. Were those warning bells in the back of my brain, or just the dull ringing of my ears from interrupted sleep?

"Okay," I said, "I'll look into it. Anybody else know about this?"

"Nope, just you and me, son."

"What about Robocop out in the cruiser?"

"He thinks I'm here just asking you questions about that poor dead girl."

With that he rose from his chair with a wheeze, slapped his hat on his head, and shook my hand. He labored across the room to the door, but before he went out he turned and pointed a gnarled index finger in my direction. "Do what you gotta do," he said, "just keep your mouth shut." He stepped out into the night, closing the door softly behind him.

After the sheriff left I took my coffee and the diary and went out to my back gallery. The old ranch house I had bought and restored was built in the 1870's by a German immigrant on 200 acres of prime pasture land in Washington County, about a hundred miles northwest of Houston. The house had a screened-in back gallery on the south side, where I liked to sit in the mornings and read and imagine I was part of a big German family.

It was about an hour before sunup when I plopped down in a big wicker lounge chair I had bought at an estate sale. I sat very still in the dark, trying to clear my mind before opening Robin's little diary. I dreaded the task, but after a blood-red morning sun topped the tree line at the rear of my property and there was light enough to read, I turned to the grim chore.

The first few pages were nothing but transcriptions of newspaper advertisements, clothing labels, and the backs of seed packages. The writing was hesitant and squiggly at first, but it gradually improved from one page to the next. Robin clearly had been teaching herself to write with her left hand. After about twenty pages her writing leveled out and she began her story.

It was a rambling series of dark and bitter memories of her ordeal in Africa: the desert rats as big as rabbits, the beatings on the back of the legs with cane poles, the endless recitals from the Quran. But when I had finished reading I understood why the sheriff had been so hesitant to just burn the little book and chalk its contents up to things best forgotten. The last entry summed it up:

I couldn't believe it when I saw them last week, Teal and that dirty sponge-faced Malaku, standing there on the other side of the fence when I was working in my garden, looking at me like I was some weird creature in a zoo. I surprised him, didn't I? After he raped me I slapped him good and hard right across his ugly ass face. He chopped off my hand for that. I spit in his face. That made him really mad. So he told me everything that was going to happen and left me to die in that stinky cell. He said the greatest torture is knowing the future without being able to do anything about it. I would die in torment. But I didn't die, HA, HA! I know what he has come here to do. I know the hold he has over Teal and that she will have to help him or go to jail. He has that video where she spills her guts about setting that fire. She will be his Perry Abella or whatever, like he told me. Only she won't know it. He said he would even let the Great Satan know where to find her. Then she will breathe out the fire of hell and the children of the Great Satan will wither and die. Malaku knows I know all this. He probably wants to kill me to keep me quiet. BUT HE WON'T!!!!!! I swear to God he'll never touch me again.

What did it mean? Was it true? Was Malaku actually alive and here in Texas? And with Teal? Or was it the fevered imaginings of a troubled and suicidal young woman? It all seemed so fantastic. I was going to need a second set of eyes on this one, a doctor's eyes. I knew just the doctor.

Chapter Three

Mikail "Mickey" Simski was raised in the Crown Heights section of Brooklyn, in a neighborhood so tough he would often lament that "in my neighborhood if you didn't grow up tough, you didn't grow up at all." But unlike many of his childhood buds, he channeled his toughness in the right direction. When he was seventeen he won the welterweight Golden Gloves title for the City of New York, a feat not accomplished by a Jewish kid in living memory. This, together with a 4.0 high school average and perfect SAT's, made him an easy pick for his local congressman to recommend for the United States Naval Academy. He was accepted on the first pass. At the academy he continued to box and to ace out his coursework. He also more or less adopted me as his special ward, rolling his eyes and referring to me as his "football jock Texas roommate." He tutored me in math and counseled me on my various situations with girls. And he stuck up for me when it counted.

My sophomore year I caught a blue-blooded upper-classman cheating in a clandestine poker game and called him out on it. I showed the other open-mouth middies present exactly how the jerk did it, duplicating his last four deals card for card. His humiliation was total and he never forgave me. A month later he falsely accused me of cheating on an exam he was proctoring, claiming I was cribbing. All I could do was deny it. It was my word against his, and his was the odds-on-favorite. I couldn't even claim retaliation for my catching him in a poker game because gambling at the academy is strictly forbidden. Admitting having participated in a poker game could have been the end of my naval career in and of itself. I was in a terrible jam until Mickey caught my accuser one night behind Bancroft Hall, punched out his lights, and swore that next time he would gouge out his eyes with a screw driver and cut off his tongue with a pair of tin snips if he didn't come clean about me with the honor council. Mick must have been very convincing because the next day the upperclassman recanted his charge and the following week bilged out of the academy altogether.

After graduation the Navy sent Mickey to medical school at nearby Johns Hopkins, while I went into the SEALS. But we continued to be friends. When a Marine helicopter crew evacuated me from Iraq, a phosphorous grenade wound in my side that I had self-treated in sloppy fashion with my sheath knife, it was my great good fortune that Mick was one of the attending surgeons on duty on the aircraft carrier where I was deposited. I was in cardiovascular free-fall from shock and loss of blood. I had probably passed over the great dark river, but Mick wouldn't give up on me. He cracked open my chest and massaged my heart back to life by hand, even as the other attending surgeon was filling out my toe tag.

Then two years later he volunteered for the Sudan rescue mission. This earned him the gratitude of Senator DeLong, who secured an appointment for him as head of trauma surgery in the leading Houston hospital at five times his Navy salary. Mick was never one to let money get in the way of friendship, though. When I was doing my time in the Eastham Unit up the road in Huntsville, he came to visit me every single week. He was that kind of friend.

Now we were seated together at the memorial service held for Robin later that week at a Houston mega-church, where

Teal often appeared on the Sunday morning telecast. Teal gave the eulogy, a moving statement of sisterly love and admiration sprinkled with heart-warming anecdotes from their childhood. No mention was made of their joint ordeal in Sudan, or of Robin's mode of death. I sat through the entire service with my head down, studying the backs of my hands as though I had never seen them before.

"Let's go, *jefé,* the service is over," Mickey whispered from beside me. "I don't think they're going to have a floor show."

"It wouldn't surprise me if they did," I whispered back, to the annoyance of a stern-looking woman in the pew in front of us who whipped her head around and raised her index finger to her lips.

Indeed it had been a spectacular service. In addition to the family, seated discreetly in a side vestibule shrouded by a black gauze curtain, at least a thousand mourners were in attendance. The lead tenor during the hymns had once toured with an east coast opera company. He was accompanied by a twenty piece orchestra and an array of vocalists only slightly fewer in number than the Mormon Tabernacle Choir. Church deacons lined both sides of the sanctuary like cardinals at a papal investiture. All of this had been presided over by a silver-haired, hominy-and-grits voiced pastor.

I stood up. "I need to talk to you, Mick. Let's see if they're serving refreshments."

"Copy that. Singing makes me thirsty."

"Everything makes you thirsty. Let's go."

Mickey and I made our way out. We found the punch bowl in what was called the Abundance Room, an elegantly appointed room that reminded me of the main ballroom at the Waldorf Astoria. A waiter with the professionally sympathetic demeanor of a funeral director served up two crystal cups of pink punch. We stood in a corner, trying to avoid being trampled by the incoming crowd.

"This New York Jew is a little confused, Jeff," Mickey said.

"How so?"

"I know this church isn't Catholic, and I'm damn sure it

isn't Jewish. I can't figure it out. Is it Baptist? Methodist? Presbyterian?"

"Monetarian," I answered.

He nodded. "Gotcha. Too bad about Robin."

"Yeah, tough break."

He took a sip of punch and scratched the side of his nose.

"What's on your mind, *jefé*?" he asked. "You said you wanted to talk to me."

"I've got something I want to show you, get your opinion."

"Got it with you?"

"Nope. In the truck."

"Why don't we go to the house? You can show me there."

"I'd like to pay my respects to the family first."

"You won't have long to wait. Here they come now."

I looked up to see the Delong family making their entrance at the far end of the hall: the silver-haired senator, followed by his wife, his son Travis, and the senator's personal bodyguard, a Texas Ranger named Conway Crowley. Crowley and I had a history, and it wasn't a good one.

Last in line was Teal—blonde, athletic, radiant with self-confident beauty. More than anything it was her eyes that caught your attention: deep water blue, sparkling with energy and intelligence, reflective of knowledge and experience beyond her years. She was lovely to look at, all right; I tried not to look too much. Instead, I ran my eyes around the hall. It was an old military habit: always check the faces inside your perimeter. You may find one that doesn't belong.

I saw at least three congressmen, the mayor of Houston, the owner of our NFL team, a bevy of local television personalities, and the predictable assortment of real estate developers, bankers, lawyers, lobbyists, and political fixers, together with their tanning bed wives. In one way or another they were all part of the ruling class. Their faces all belonged there.

Then I saw the face that didn't belong.

A woman was standing alone by a side exit, apparently doing what I was doing, surveying the room. Her dark eyes seemed to click from one person to another, pause to register something, and in the next instant click away. She was dressed simply but appropriately in a black pants suit and low black heels, although the oversized and frayed wood-bead purse she had slung over her shoulder told me she didn't shop at Neiman-Marcus like the other women present. When her eyes settled on me for a brief moment I noticed that she was easily as attractive as any woman in the room. But that didn't matter. The black headscarf she was wearing marked her as a Muslim. What was she doing here? I had just started over to find out when Mickey grabbed my arm.

"Hold on, Jeff" he said, "Teal's headed your way."

I looked up to see Teal making her way through the throng, shaking hands with some, demurely hugging others, even lightly kissing others on the cheek. She had her old man's knack for working a crowd.

"Jeff," was all she said when she got to me.

She rested her head on my shoulder and wrapped her arms around my midsection, pulling me so close I could feel the softness of her breasts through my sport coat and feel her warmth radiate through my body, to the point that my personal first responder began stirring to action. Out of the corner of my eye I saw the Muslim woman staring at us. I slid out of Teal's embrace.

"I knew you'd be here, Jeff. You've always been there for Robin and me," she said, "like a big angel."

"Better not let a real angel hear you say that," I said, "and don't forget Angel Simski here."

She touched cheeks with Mickey, thanked him for coming to the service, and turned back to me. "Can we get together tomorrow, Jeff, lunch or something? I want to get away from all this for a while."

"I wish we could, but I have to go out on the *Persephone* with Travis tomorrow. He's booked a big dive party out of Austin."

"But they say a nasty storm is moving into the gulf from Yucatan tomorrow."

"I'll keep an eye on it."

"Well, how about we meet for dinner at Gaido's after you get back. You think around seven?"

"Okay, partner. Say seven."

"Good. There's something I want to ask you."

"I have a question or two for you, too," I said, Robin's diary entry very much on my mind.

"Seven then." She traced her hand across the side of my face. She started to turn back to the crowd but stopped as though seized by an afterthought. "Don't turn your back on Trav," she said, "he'd use you for fish chum if he could." She walked away before I could answer.

Mickey watched her melt into the crowd, his mouth open, his face full of thought. "What was that all about?" he said.

"Beats me."

"You been playing hide-the-weenie with the boss's daughter without cluing in your old podjo?"

"No, sir," I said.

"I thought for a moment there I thought she was going to put you in a half-Nelson."

"For a moment there I would have let her."

"Who wouldn't? She was hitting on you, *jefé.*"

"No way. Family funerals make some people a little over-emotional. That's all."

"She was hitting on you."

"Ridiculous," I said.

"I'm telling you."

"She already has a boyfriend."

"Who?"

"A nice frat boy over at her college, captain of the tennis team, too. A real good boy."

"Sometimes a girl will wake up one morning and decide she likes bad boys better."

"I'll try to go to church more often. Meanwhile, cut Teal some slack, will you?"

"Okay, Okay. Just remember that some women can turn boys into men, and some men back into boys. That would be Teal."

I laughed. "I'll be cautious. Let's get out of here."

I walked with Mickey to his car and then went back inside. I wanted to find the Muslim woman I had seen and find out what she wanted. But she was nowhere to be seen.

An hour later I was at Mickey's house. He kept shaking his head. "No, no," he said for the fiftieth time, "this can't be right."

"Right or wrong, there it is," I said.

We were in Mickey's study, a quiet, oak-paneled enclave off the entryway to his house. The house was a big Tudor mini-mansion in a Houston neighborhood populated by a great many doctors, lawyers, and oil company executives, and very few ex-Navy SEALS, none in fact. In his lighter moments he kidded me that this was a SEAL-free zone. He was not in a lighter moment. Neither was I.

"I don't believe it," he said. "Do you?"

"I know I don't want to believe it."

"That schmuck, Malaku, here in Texas? With Teal? No friggin' way! You going to run with this?"

He slammed Robin's diary shut, plopped it on his desk, and leaned back in his swivel chair. He squinted at me from over a tent he made with his fingers. I slouched down in a big armchair and rubbed the palms of my hands over my face. I could hear Mickey's pregnant second wife Beth puttering around in the kitchen. Outside, I could hear birds singing. I tried to recognize their warble; I didn't want to think about the business at hand.

"Well, *jefé?"*

"I told the sheriff I'd look into it. That's all."

"Okay, you've looked into it. Now, as your friend, I'm telling you to toss this book in the fireplace behind you and burn it. I have some matches right here."

"You don't think I should pursue it?"

"I think you should run like hell from it."

"How come?"

Mick took off his thick horn-rimmed glasses, which he had started wearing a few years back, and pinched the bridge of his nose. He looked tired.

"Look, Jeff, as much as we both cared for Robin, let's admit that she was *non compos mentis* ever since Sudan. That's a legal term, and I use it deliberately."

"I went to college, Mick."

"Then you know that nothing she's written here could ever be used to justify any kind of case against Teal. The sheriff knew that; he couldn't even make Teal go stand in the corner. That's why he flipped this over to you."

"I don't want to dime Teal. If this Malaku guy is running around loose in Texas, I want to find him and finish the job."

He shook his head. "Whoa, now, *jefé,* don't even think about breaking the kind of rules that'll get you permanent residence in the graybar hotel."

"When you deal with thugs like that you throw away the rulebook. You can be sure they do."

"I like to think that playing by the rules is what separates us from them."

"You think too much," I said, and in an instant regretted saying it. I saw the hurt flash across his face before he reached down and picked up the diary again.

"Jeff, as one of her treating physicians I got to see Robin's medical file out at the home. It reads like the Diagnostic and Statistical Manual. At one time or another she was diagnosed with post-traumatic stress disorder, paranoid-schizophrenia, not to mention morbid depression. They even charted a diagnosis of General Personality Disorder."

"What's that?"

"Anything they can't pin another label on. The point is that patients like Robin live in their own world. I've personally known them to speak in tongues that bear no resemblance to any known language, and to invent stories starring themselves that are as long and complex as *Gone With the Wind.*"

"You think she made all this up?"

"More than likely."

"What about her hand? We always wondered why they cut it off. She says here that Malaku chopped it off as punishment for slapping him across the face."

"She may have written this to self-dramatize what may have been a very quotidian incident. Maybe her hand got infected from a rat bite or something and they had to remove the hand to keep her alive as a hostage."

"Why would they do that, and next thing toss her in a catacomb?"

"That's a good question."

"And what she says about Malaku letting us know where they were being held jives with our receiving a one-in-a-million accurate anonymous tip."

"I'm just pointing out the possibilities."

I stood up and went to the window. "What about this 'Perry Abella' person she talks about," I said while looking out the window at nothing in particular, "think she was speaking in tongues there?"

"Could be," he said, rising from his chair and walking over to my side. "I've never heard that name anywhere." He placed his hand on my shoulder and spoke in the fatherly tone he used when trying to pull me back from my latest cliff. "You take this on and you'll be waltzing yourself right back into the slam. Better tuck and roll on this one, *jefé*."

"I know, Mick, I know."

I left Mickey's around four o'clock and drove down to Galveston to prepare the *Persephone* for the scuba diving party arriving from Austin the next day. The *Persephone* was a ninety-foot, ocean-going yacht built in Scotland in the 1950's for a British newspaper tycoon. It was by far the largest yacht in harbor, requiring a railed and creaky wooden gangway to board her. Experts might disagree as to whether she was a boat or a ship. To me, having spent much of my life on aircraft carriers, she was just a boat.

But she was a hell of a boat. She was of classic trawler design, with a raked bow and a fantail stern and a raised pilot house in lieu of a bridge. There were even two masts, one forward and one astern, although they were rarely used. Originally powered with traditional dual diesel engines, she had been re-fitted with high performance diesel-electric engines manufactured in Germany. She was as fast, or faster, than any Coast Guard cutter. If she had a weakness, it was in her electronics. While she had an up-to-date GPS navigation system, her on-board weather radar was woefully inadequate. This made us all too dependent on third-party weather reports. Nevertheless, the interior accommodations were plush: mahogany trim, polished brass fittings, marble in the heads and showers. She had a history, too. The story was that Richard Burton and Elizabeth Taylor had free use of the boat and used to sunbathe naked on the afterdeck when cruising in the Mediterranean.

Senator DeLong had bought the boat at an estate auction several years earlier, primarily to give his son Travis something to do. That usually meant taking local scuba diving parties from Galveston a few miles off shore into the Gulf of Mexico, although sometimes it meant open water excursions as far south as the Panama Canal. When I was released from prison the senator put me on the crew at a generous salary. Nominally, given my SEAL background, I was the yacht's dive master. In reality, I was the adult supervision.

That evening as the sun sank low into the sky I ran through my seaworthiness checklist. I made sure the bilge pump was working and the bilge vents free of obstruction. I tested the sump pumps in the showers and heads and topped off the fresh water tanks for those venues. I checked the engine oil, the electrical system, and the steering gear. I inventoried our life preservers, first aid kits, flashlights, and fire extinguishers. The divers would be bringing their own masks, fins, and regulators, but I made sure we had spares for all of these, just in case. We had an on-board air compressor, so I filled the dozen or so air tanks we would need to regulation pressure. Lastly, I opened the combination lock on the gun cabinet in the galley and checked the action on the iron-sighted, bolt-action, stainless steel 30.06 we kept on board to shoot sharks that swam too close to our surfaced divers. The action was working smoothly, but I squeezed a tiny drop of gun oil onto a rag anyway and worked it over the bolt several times. Next, I removed the magazine, loaded it with the 180 grain cartridges that I found to be most effective on sharks, and slid it back into place beneath the bolt. I placed the weapon back where I found it and locked the cabinet. All set for a day of diving, if the weather held.

It was after nine o'clock when I finished my checklist, but it was too early for bed. So I opened the utility drawer in the galley where we kept the flashlights, took out a deck of well-worn playing cards, and began a game of solitaire at the crew's mess table. Whenever I did this my thoughts turned to my father.

My father, Stuart Quinn, had been born into a prominent banking family in Roanoke, Virginia. After attending VMI on a football scholarship and serving in the army during the Viet Nam war, he settled in Houston to go into the banking business. He proved to be a natural in that line of work, eventually working his way up to vice-president in charge of petroleum lending at Houston's largest bank. He was a tall, handsome guy, who could charm a snake into a lawnmower. My mother adored him, as did any number of other women. Busy as he was, he always made it home for my birthdays, little league games, and high school football games. By all accounts he was a successful, if somewhat obscure, businessman and a good family man. But he led a double life, and it was in this second life that he achieved a measure of quiet fame. He was widely regarded in gambling circles as the best poker player in Texas.

He knew the rules, odds, and strategies of virtually every variation of poker: Five-Card Draw, Seven-Card Stud, Texas Hold-'Em, Omaha High-Low, and many others. Always the southern gentleman, he took a decidedly aristocratic view of the game. He declined to play in the come-one-come-all casinos in Louisiana, Oklahoma, and even Las Vegas. "I do not play cards," he would say, "with men in blue jeans or women in Spandex pants." He confined his gaming to the quiet backrooms of the Downtown Athletic Club and the Petroleum Club, where he took on some of the wealthiest and most powerful men in the country, if not the world. He once took down a Saudi oil prince for a cool million in a marathon game right out of the movies.

He rarely lost. That could have been because he was just lucky, or it could have been because he worked on his poker game the way other men worked on their golf swings or their tennis backhands. He spent hours in his study at a green-felt card table, practicing shuffles, riffles, cuts, shifts, skins, and all the other fine points of the art. He usually practiced before a small table mirror so he could see his hands and fingers at work. I used to watch him practice with quiet fascination. Often he would show me how to do this shuffle or that, and how to tell if another player was cheating. Eventually, however, all this brought the inevitable question to mind. One day, when I was about twelve, I burst into his study and blurted it out. "Dad, do you cheat at cards?"

He looked up startled, but soon he regained his composure and ruffled my hair with his hand. "Jeff, a gentleman does not cheat at cards or anything else." He then added solemnly, "But in the event he finds himself in a crooked game, he needs to know how to fight fire with fire."

It was a lesson I never forgot.

He drowned during a violent Gulf Coast thunderstorm the year after I graduated from Annapolis, trying to help extricate a woman and her child from a car that was caught in a flash flood not far from our home. He was just fifty-six.

At ten o'clock I stowed away the playing cards, but before I retired to my Spartan cabin I turned on the galley radio and tuned in to the local marine station. I didn't like what I heard.

Chapter Four

The morning sky had broken brassy and red over the Gulf. The surface of the water was as listless as a man in a morphine stupor. Gulls and other seabirds that normally feed far out to sea during early daylight were beating landward. Experienced sailors seeing these signs don't need a cute chick on the Weather Channel to give them a weather forecast. I was an experienced sailor.

"Bad day to go out on the salt, Travis," I said.

I was speaking to Travis DeLong on the pier where the *Persephone* was tied up. He was dressed in khaki cargo shorts, an orange tank top, and an Astros' baseball cap worn reversed on his head. He already had a longneck beer in his hand.

"There's not one fucking cloud in the sky, Quinn."

"There will be."

"The babe on the Weather Channel says that the crap moving in from Yucatan won't be here until tonight."

"She's wrong. It's on its way now."

"Oh, watch out, the big expert," he said, rolling his eyes and shaking his free hand in front of his body as though he were afflicted with palsy. "What do you think, Soos?"

Soos was the man standing next to him. Soos was a tough Mexican, whose full name was Jesus Raza. He served as the mate on the *Persephone* by day and Travis' bodyguard and drinking companion by night. No one ever forgot Soos. His oddly shaped, reddish-brown body looked angular and metallic, as though it had been welded together from junkyard scrap then baked in a high-intensity oven. A jagged scar, the kind a broken beer bottle makes, ran across the left side of his face. His black eyes projected thoughts on which you didn't want to dwell.

"I think the *puta* is afraid of a little rain," Soos said.

"It's not a matter of being afraid or not," I said, "it's a matter of using good judgment. We don't want to lose any of these kids out there."

Travis shook his head in disgust. "You're the last person on God's good earth to be talking about good judgment, Quinn. If you don't want to go out with us, take the day off. I can take the kids down on their dives myself. No prob."

I knew better.

Two hours later I was eighty feet below the surface of the Gulf of Mexico, herding a group of young divers around an oil tanker that had been torpedoed in 1942 by a German U-boat in plain view of sunbathers on the beach. The divers all worked for the same tech company in Austin. Techies may be nerds on dry land, but they make good divers. They keep sharp eyes on their gauges and timers and they don't stick their valuable little fingers into underwater crevices and holes, where who-knows-what might be waiting to snap off a good lunch. It wasn't them I was worried about; it was Captain America above us on the *Persephone.*

When our air tanks timed out I brought the four divers up in rulebook decompression stages. As soon as we broke surface I tore off my mask and had a look around. There was a chop in the water that had not been there before, and the southern horizon was black and veined with lightning. I swam the techies over to the boat, helped them aboard, and then climbed aboard myself. I hit the deck running.

"All right, Travis," I said as I burst into the pilot house, "let's up anchor and make port. We've got a serious situation here."

"Oh, fuck off, Quinn. You're worse than an old lady with

hemorrhoids."

"I'm through jacking around with you, boy. Do it."

Instead of answering, he leaned back in his elevated captain's chair and took a long swallow out of an aluminum coffee thermos, his eyes peering over the edge of the thermos like two marbles that had rolled to a stop. But the two eyes weren't focused on me. They were riveted on one of our divers on the foredeck, an attractive young Asian woman in a hot pink bikini.

"We've got time for one more dive," he said, lowering the thermos and placing it in the cup-holder of his chair. "I'll take them down myself. I bet that wahini down there would appreciate an upgrade in her guide service."

"We're out of time," I said. "Not a second to spare."

Travis pointed over to Soos, who was sitting on a metal Budweiser cooler. "What do you think, Soos?"

"*Mucho tiempo,* boss," Soos said. "Plenty time."

"Look, you two," I said, "put about before I call the Coast Guard."

Travis made a motion with his hand as though he were brushing away an irritating insect. "What are you going to tell them, Quinn? That nobody gives a shit what you say anymore? That you were a big swinging dick in the Navy once, but that you blew it, and now nobody listens to you? So what are you going to tell them?"

"I'm going to tell them that Beavis and Butthead fell overboard during a squall and should be considered lost at sea."

Travis and Soos snickered together. While they were chuckling away I reached over and grabbed the thermos out of the cup-holder and held it to my nose. "Since when does coffee smell like Wild Turkey, Travis?"

"Give me that."

"You know your father's rule about hard liquor on the *Persephone.*"

"You going to snitch me out to my old man?"

"That's what I'm paid to do, junior."

"You're a piece of work, Quinn."

"You don't know the half of it. Now, get these kids on dry land and maybe I'll have a lapse of memory about the funky coffee."

There were a few tense moments, then Travis signaled Soos to up anchor. I stayed in the pilot house to make sure we got underway as soon as possible. I had learned to keep Travis on a short leash. In spite of his thirty years, he was a playground bully in an adult world, his narrow face twisted by a permanent jeer. His close-set eyes invariably radiated an undisguised contempt for the world in general, and for me in particular. Years earlier he had dropped out of the University of Texas to pursue a career in Hollywood. He landed some bit parts that convinced everyone that he should open a car wash. Eventually the casting directors stopped returning even the senator's phone calls. But he was ever the actor, at least in his own mind. As I was lowering myself down the short ladder leading to the afterdeck deck, he raised his right arm and leveled his index finger at me. "A pox on you, sir," he said, as though auditioning for a part in a Shakespearean play, "a pox on you."

We docked just as the sky turned green-black and dirty looking waves began crashing against the seawall that runs the southern shore of Galveston Island. The seawall is an engineering relic constructed a hundred years ago to prevent a repeat of the catastrophe of 1900, when a fifteen foot storm surge drowned the island and killed ten thousand men, women, and children. There were so many casualties that their corpses had to be stacked like cordwood on the beach and burned. Since, old-timers on the island, who probably first heard about the storm from their parents or grandparents, have treated all incoming storms with due respect. I wasn't an old-timer, but I knew the story and I wanted our divers across the causeway and onto the mainland as soon as possible.

I was helping the divers load their gear into their SUV when Soos strolled up, a merry light in his eye. A yellow rubber chicken, the kind they sell in novelty shops, dangled from his right hand.

"Hey, *puta,*" he said, "I got something for you."

"Mail it to me, bud, I'm busy here."

"You dissing me, man?"

"Take it however you want."

"Hey, man, look at me when I'm talking to you."

He grabbed me by the shoulder and spun me around. Before I could react he had shoved the rubber chicken in my hands.

"Here, man, this belongs with you," he said. "I think it must be your sister or something, same color and everything. What you think about that?"

"You're getting up on the wrong porch, bud."

"You got a house? You got a porch at your house? How about some night I come out and sit on your porch a little bit, maybe piss in your window a little bit? What you think about that?"

"Sure, come on out. I love company. I'll be happy to exsanguinate you."

"Ex . . . What you mean?"

I smiled, reached down, and slid my dive knife out of the scabbard I still had buckled around my right calf. I kept smiling as I sliced the chicken's head off and held the rubber carcass upside down by its legs.

"That's what I mean," I said.

Throughout this episode the techies from Austin had stood open-mouthed, their eyes wide, their Nike-clad feet seemingly glued to the asphalt. Finally, the Asian girl in the hot pink bikini stepped forward.

"Sir, would it help you if I called the police?"

I guided her behind me while still smiling at Soos. "No, we're just having a little fun. Aren't we Soos?"

Soos ground his fist into his palm, his eyes narrowing into slits. "Sure, just a little fun. Maybe we have a little more fun later. What you think?"

"Anytime, anytime at all."

He turned and strolled away, the muscles in his back and shoulders working like a team of oxen under his flimsy T-shirt. He walked over to where Travis was waiting in Travis' other prize toy: a fully restored, bright yellow, 1973 Corvette Stingray. Soos got in and the two drove off, Travis peeling rubber on the parking lot to prove whatever it was he needed to prove.

I had talked tough to Soos but I was happy to see him go. Two years earlier a pair of hardhats from a Texas City oil refinery had stomped into a paint-peeled clapboard bar on the Houston ship channel. I knew the place; I'd gone on a bender there not long after my wife's death. It had a white chalk parking lot littered with flattened beer cans, cigarette butts, and used rubbers. Dust from the lot caked the undersides of the surrounding trees like so much white fungi. Cracks in the windows were repaired with strips of duct tape and the bottom half of the door was weathered into curling strips of wood. The dank interior smelled of cheap whiskey, refrigerated body odor, and bathroom disinfectant. It was a place where you could get down as far as you wanted and nobody would care, or even notice.

The two hardhats made it loudly known that they didn't drink with "white trash, coloreds, or wets" so the other patrons were free to go. Everyone in the house—a black couple, some Hispanic fruit pickers and several blue collar white men—took one look at the two toughs, gathered up their meager belongings, and hustled out the door. Everyone boogied, that is, except the oddly shaped, reddish-brown man drinking alone at the bar. Ten minutes later the oddly shaped man walked out the door, casually wiping blood off his sling blade knife with a bar napkin. The two hardhats died on the way to the hospital. The DA couldn't find anyone to testify about what happened, so the manslaughter charges against the killer were dropped.

I didn't know if I could take Soos by myself. I didn't know if anyone could.

The storm hit the island just after noon, blowing garbage cans and debris through the streets, shredding the fronds on the palm trees, and sending frantic motorists under the awnings of self-service gas stations and motel entrances. Rain hammered down with tropical ferocity. Then, just as suddenly as it arrived, it blew northward. No one died in this storm.

I rode out the gale in my cabin on the *Persephone.* It was a bumpy ride, the boat alternately straining at its moorings and banging into the padded pilings of the dock. But she was a big, tough boat, and I never really worried. Instead, I focused on the questions I intended to ask Teal that night. Why was Robin's hand chopped off? Was Malaku here in the U.S.? Had she seen him? Who was Perry Abella? I had a hundred questions and I intended to get answers. I was prepared to be as menacing and unforgiving as the Grand Inquisitor himself. I was resolved to get at the truth.

Gaido's is an upscale seafood restaurant on Seawall Boulevard. It's a holdover from Galveston's glory days in the 1940's, when the Maceo brothers ran all the action on the island from the second floor of the Galvez Hotel. Newly-minted oil millionaires would drive down from Houston with their wives or girlfriends for dinner at Gaido's and a night of dancing and gambling at the Maceo's Balinese Ballroom, a nightclub built on piers out over the Gulf. I got to Gaido's early and had an iced tea at the bar.

Teal glided through the door a few minutes past seven. She was wearing a gray terry cloth sheath dress and outrageously high cork platform shoes. I didn't know if her outfit was intended to impress me; it certainly impressed every male in the restaurant over the age of twelve.

"How do you like my puddle-jumpers?" she asked.

"Great," I said. "Where can I get a pair? I've been feeling short lately."

She punched me playfully on the arm. "You're tall enough, handsome."

The waiter led us to a reserved window table that over looked the water. The sky had mellowed to a washed-out blue, highlighted only by some strips of pink cloud toward sunset. It was a fine setting for a dinner of redfish and rice. I let Teal lead the conversation while we ate.

At first she roamed over the weather, sports, and the latest local scandals. Then she got serious.

"Thanks for being such a good friend to Robin, Jeff."

"Maybe I could have been a better one."

"You shouldn't blame yourself for what happened. You did all you could."

"I tried."

"You did more than that."

"What do you mean?"

"The sheriff up there told us what you did to that trashy attendant. Did you really grab his ear and threaten to kill him if he molested Robin."

"Yes."

"And would you have, kill him I mean?"

"If that was the only way to protect her."

"If you had done that, wouldn't you have gone back to prison, for a long time, maybe?"

"Probably."

"Then why?"

I shrugged. "I don't know, princess, sometimes I think I was born in the wrong century. There was a time when people took care of their own business."

"Maybe you should ride a horse and carry a six-shooter."

"I've thought about it."

She laughed. "Walk me to my hotel, big guy."

We left Gaido's, jaywalked across Seawall Boulevard, and joined the throng of joggers, skateboarders, women pushing baby carriages, and couples just holding hands moving along the seawall at sunset. Teal took my hand in hers.

"I've always wanted to do this, Jeff, ever since we got back from Africa."

"What's that, partner?"

"Walk hand-in-hand with you along the seawall."

"What would your boyfriend say?"

"He'd probably want to hold your other hand."

"He's like that, is he?"

"You never know about frat boys."

She pulled me closer so that I could feel her hips sway as

we walked and smell the perfume on her neck. A night breeze came in off the water, lifting her hair off her shoulders and blowing it into swirls.

"I love it after a storm, Jeff. Everything's so fresh and clean. It's like nature cleansing itself, washing away its past. That's what I'd like to do, wash away the past. Wouldn't you?"

"Palmolive doesn't work on the past, Teal. It's always with you, no matter how hard you scrub. Sooner or later the stain always returns."

"That's a very negative attitude, Jeff."

"I've earned the right to be negative."

"Well, I think you can wash away the past, if you try hard enough."

She took her hand out of mine and swatted me on the forearm. We walked a little further without talking. It was completely dark now. The stars were out, newly polished diamonds strewn across a black velvet sky.

"Teal, I have to ask you, does any of this have to do with what happened to you and Robin in Sudan?"

"You're prying, Jeff."

I let it pass for the time being. We walked on in silence for a while. She took my hand again and led me to a concrete and iron pergola attached to the seawall. She sat me down on a concrete bench, still holding my hand. We were alone. I was keenly aware of the warm Gulf breeze, the sound of waves lapping the shore, the smell of wet sand, and the feel of soft blonde hair that was now blowing against the side of my face. She spoke without looking directly at me.

"Would you do it for *me*, Jeff?"

"Do what?"

"Kill someone who was threatening me, like you would have for Robin?"

"Is someone threatening you?"

"I'm just saying suppose someone was?"

Sitting there on the bench alone with her, her body feeling like a sensuous magnetic field, I embraced the moment.

"I'd do whatever was necessary. You know that. Why do

you even ask?"

"A girl wants to know there's someone she can rely on in a worst case scenario."

"You can rely on me."

She reached her arms around me and hugged me tightly, resting her head on my shoulder. Any thoughts I may have had of grilling her on the contents of Robin's little diary wafted away on the breeze. I felt her raise her chin slightly. Then she reached up and pulled my face to hers. I didn't resist.

Much later that evening I lay in my bunk on the *Persephone,* lights out, listening to classical music floating across the ether from an all-night station in Monterrey, Mexico. I was born long after the golden age of border radio, when a powerful pirate station just across the Rio Grande from Del Rio flooded the night-time air waves with live performances by the likes of The Lonesome Cowboy, Nevada Slim, and Lydia Mendoza aka the Mexican Nightingale. Even so, there was a certain golden glow in hearing Rodrigo's *Concerto de Aranjuez* broadcast in the darkness from south of the border, especially after the evening I had just had. It was relaxing, too. In minutes I was asleep.

I was dreaming of a playful barracuda forging through the tangled undergrowth of a tropical lagoon, twisting and thrashing before disappearing into a dark crevice in a pink coral reef, when my cell phone went off.

"Mick here. I've been trying to reach you and invite you to lunch at the hospital tomorrow."

"I had my phone off."

"How come?"

"I was out late."

"With Teal?"

"With Teal."

I could almost see him close his eyes and slowly shake his head. "I thought you had more judgment than that."

"I thought I had, too."

"So what made you throw caution to the wind?"

"I don't know, my love of butterflies I guess."

"Butterflies?"

"She has a tattoo of a butterfly on the inside of her left thigh."

"Oh, *jefé*!"

Chapter Five

I rose early the next morning. The sky was blue as porcelain, the breeze soft and cool out of the south. I tugged on my shorts and running shoes, ran five miles along the beach, did a set of push-ups and sit-ups on the now empty seawall, and finished off my workout with a swim out to the third sand-bar and back. I was back in the *Persephone* by eight, intending to clean up the boat from the previous day's outing, shower and shave, and drive into Houston for lunch with Mickey. I was interrupted by a shout from the dock.

"Ahoy, the ship!"

I went on deck to find Senator Albert Delong trudging up the gangway, a Styrofoam cooler swinging at his side. "Ahoy, Quinn," he said, "how about a cool one?"

"Why not?

"Bring some chairs up to the foredeck, will you?"

A few minutes later the senator and I were sitting across from one another on the foredeck. He was stripped to the waist, chugging a long neck beer bottoms up, his throat working the liquid down non-stop, foam dripping from his chin onto the gray hairs on his chest. I figured he was just a cell phone camera shot away from a first-class publicity scandal. He read my thoughts.

"Don't worry," he said, lowering the bottle, "even in today's world a man has a right to have a beer on his own boat, especially two days after burying his child. Anybody doesn't like it can kiss my royal Irish ass."

"I like your attitude, cap," I said

I sipped from my own beer and waited. He wasn't talking much yet, but he would. This is where he liked to do his talking, and I was the one he liked to talk with. I didn't know why. They say in Washington that if you want a friend, get a dog, or maybe just an over-the-hill, recently imprisoned, down-on-his-luck ex-Navy SEAL. They make great pets.

"How was Travis out on the salt yesterday?" he asked.

"A perfect gentleman."

"I bet. I don't know where I went wrong with that boy."

"He went wrong all on his own, cap."

"No, No, you're wrong there. When a kid doesn't turn out right, it's always the parents' fault."

"I wouldn't know."

"Oh, sorry Quinn, your wife was pregnant when she was killed, wasn't she?"

"Yes, our first."

"Well, no offense, but being a parent, especially a father, isn't always what it's cranked-up to be. There's always a lot of stress. There've been times I've wanted to strangle Travis."

"Me, too."

He reached out and punched me playfully on the knee. "Did I ever tell you my father tried to strangle me?"

"Tell me again, cap."

I had heard the story of the senator's hard-scrabble childhood many times before: the abusive and neglectful truck driver father who squandered the rent money on vodka and truck stop prostitutes, the mother who had left in the middle of the night and had never been heard from again, the brothers and sisters little Albert had assumed responsibility for at age fourteen. But it was the strangulation part he liked to tell best.

"One night I caught the old man whipping my little brother with a razor strop," he began.

"What did you do?"

"I tore the goddamn strop out of his hands and cut him across the face with it."

"Then what happened?"

"The old son-of-a-bitch tried to strangle me. If he hadn't been so drunk at the time, he might have killed me."

"I guess your dad didn't like kids."

"Oh, hell no, he loved kids. Every time he couldn't feed the ones he had, he went and got himself another one."

"So now you make up for what happened by being the world's best father to your kids?"

He shrugged, as if to say 'what could I do'? "Yeah, I guess I spoiled the hell out of them. Travis turned out bad, of course. Robin was a good girl, but she was weak, couldn't handle her situation."

Who could? I thought. But I let it pass and sat silently. I wanted to talk about Teal, but I didn't want to give away the fact I had spent half the night with her. I watched the senator chug another beer. That made four by my count.

"So how do you think Teal stacks up?" I asked, keeping my face flat and my eyes trained on the horizon.

He lowered the bottle and belched loudly. His eyes seemed slightly glazed. "Oh, hell, Quinn, she's daddy's girl. She's just like her old man: tough, strong, handle anything."

"She can certainly work a crowd. I've see her do it."

"She damn sure can. I think it's in her eyes. Ever take a close look at her eyes? Those eyes could hypnotize a whole room full of bishops."

"Roger that."

"She knows people, too. She's knows how to get the best out of anybody."

Boy howdy, I thought. "She been doing okay?"

"Sure. How come you to ask?"

"With all that's been going on, you know, with Robin's death, I thought maybe she might be a little depressed. Anybody would be."

"Teal depressed? No way. She's an absolute trooper."

I phrased my next question carefully. "She ever mention anyone from her past causing her trouble?"

"Hell, no. Teal's all through with the past. She had a rough patch there when she was seventeen or eighteen—you know about the situation in Africa—but that's all behind her now. Never says a word about it."

"I see."

He sat down his now empty bottle and reached into the cooler for another. He popped it open and took another long draw. His eyes were definitely glazed now.

"Something else about Teal, Quinn, is that she has a heart of gold. She really cares about others."

"Oh?"

"Damn sure does. See that cruise ship over there?" He pointed to the commercial side of the harbor where a fifteen story Caribbean cruise ship was docked, looming over city like a giant beast.

"Yes, sir."

"Well, Teal raised money to take hundreds of disadvantaged kids on a cruise over the Fourth of July holidays. Kids from all over the country, their parents and chaperones, too. Been raising the money herself ever since the first of the year on that gospel show she co-hosts on Sundays. You know about that?"

"I didn't. I don't want much TV, especially on Sunday mornings."

"Well, that's what she's done. What do you think about that?"

"Pretty impressive."

"Damn sure is."

"When do they ship out?"

"Let's see, July third. That's a Friday. Want to go along? I'm sure Teal would comp you a ticket."

I had a sudden vision of being on the high seas for a week with Teal and her butterfly. "Sure, why not?"

"I'll say something to her. Pack your bags."

We sat some more, drank some more. The senator was on

his sixth bottle now. He kept blinking his eyes to keep them open, but he was fighting a losing battle. There were longer and longer intervals of shut-eye between each blink. When he next spoke his words were slurred and mispronounced.

"Yes, sir, I lub my lil gurl, my lil angel. Sometin' happen to her and I'd just point this ol' tub out to sea and neber be herd from agin."

With that, his eyes shut for good and his head sank onto his chest. I got up and walked over to the railing around the deck. I saw the senator's chauffeur, a tall black man who had once played point guard for the Knicks before drugs and alcohol fouled him out, leaning back against the hood of the senator's limousine. He was another of the senator's reclamation projects. I motioned to him. He hustled up the gangway. Together we schlepped the senator, whose over-heated skin now smelled of beer and sunburn, onto the bed in the master stateroom. Then I showered and dressed and took off for Houston to meet Mickey for lunch.

The hospital where Mickey is chief of trauma surgery is the main receiving hospital for Harris County. This means it gets the vast majority of the gun, knife, rape, and assault victims for the fourth largest metropolitan area in the United States. It always has plenty of customers. That morning was no different; the emergency room waiting area was packed. I stood in the hallway by the Coke machine waiting for Mickey to come out of surgery.

I didn't have long to wait. After about half an hour he exploded out of some double doors into the hallway like a man shot out of a cannon. He was still dressed in green surgical scrubs and a white gauze surgical cap. A white surgical mask dangled from his neck.

"Goddam it," he said, "if the cops don't nail this guy, I'm going to find him and shoot his worthless ass myself!"

"Slow your roll, partner," I said, "shoot who?"

He grabbed my arm. "C'mon, *jefé,* I'll tell you on the way."

He led me down the hallway to a bank of elevators, fuming all the way. His grip on my arm felt like a tourniquet.

"Okay, Mick," I said while we were about to step into an elevator, "who are you going to gun down?" Two nurses who were about to get on the elevator with us looked at Mickey, then me, then backed back into the hallway as the door was closing.

"Get this," Mickey said. "This bimbo has a fourteen year old boy by her husband. Along comes Mr. Love-of-Her-Life, so she takes off with the kid and moves in with the boyfriend. Only the boyfriend doesn't want to share mama with the little boy, so he whips the kid with a bicycle chain and kicks him out into the street. A neighbor finds the kid, sees the lacerations that look like a lion mauling, and calls the cops. Now, here's the part you won't believe. The bimbo leans on her kid to say his injuries were the result of a bicycle accident, not as a result of anything the boyfriend did. She doesn't want the boyfriend to go to the slam. Why? 'He's a better fuck than your father ever was,' she tells him. Can you believe that?"

"Might as well shoot the woman while you're at it," I said as we got off the elevator.

"Damn right. The only person who's worse than a person who hits a child is a person who betrays a child. That wound never heals."

Mickey and I ate lunch in the hospital cafeteria, a dingy, cheerless place that smelled of prune juice, baby formula, and boiled cabbage. I didn't eat much.

"Not hungry?" Mickey asked.

"This is the kind of food they serve in POW camps, Mick."

"Look at some of our customers in here and you'll think that's where you're at. Tell me what happened last night."

I filled Mick in on my evening with Teal. He listened closely, occasionally grunting or nodding his head. When I finished, he leaned back in his chair and ran his fingers through his frizzy hair.

"You mean to tell me," he said, "that Teal wined and dined you, casually asked you to cap somebody for her, then took you up to the house?"

"That's about it."

"You got the full treatment, my man."

"And then some."

"What did you tell her?"

"I forget."

"Well, let me remember for you. You told her that her wish was your command, or something like that."

"She's a lot of woman, Mick."

He shook his head and rubbed his face with the palms of his hands. I sat perfectly still.

"So what are you going to do now?"

"I don't know. She's scared of something—or somebody. I think it's just possible that Robin actually saw Malaku at the fence with Teal, just as she wrote."

"If that's what you think, my advice is to turn this over to the FBI and let them sort it out."

"I don't want to involve Teal."

"You don't have to. Just go down and tell them that you've received information that a terrorist is in the vicinity. That way you're on record of having made a report if this guy actually turns up and makes trouble. You can be sure they'll sit on the information anyway. They're just bureaucrats with badges."

"I'll give it some thought," I said, "but whatever I do, I'm going to leave Teal out of it. It would crush her old man if she got sucked back into yesterday's trouble."

"Okay, okay. By the way, I Googled that name Perry Abella mentioned in Robin's diary."

"What'd you come up with?"

"About a thousand entries from coast-to-coast. It's a pretty common name, for both men and women."

"Women?"

"Some cute ones, too. I checked out the really promising ones on Facebook."

"I admire your thoroughness."

"Well, what I thoroughly came up with was a lot of nothing. Like I told you, Robin may have picked that name up from anywhere and plugged it into her little story."

"Thanks for trying."

Mickey continued to eat, all the while studying my face as

if preparing me for emergency surgery. "Is your determination to keep Teal invisible in all this out of concern for her old man, or because you like playing in her squeeze box?"

I thought for a while before giving a completely honest answer. "I don't know."

After lunch I went to a branch of my bank not far from Mickey's house and rented a safe deposit box. I put Robin's little diary inside and left to find a barbecue shack and have a real lunch.

I ran some errands, went to a movie, and had dinner, all the while trying to decide whether to follow Mickey's advice and check in with the FBI. I didn't arrive back at my ranch until the sun was melting into a sliver of red on the western horizon. I expected no one to be there, but to my surprise I found Derwood Smith in the barn making up a cot to sleep in the stall next to Sergeant Pepper's. Derwood was my hired man.

"*Que pasa,* partner?" I asked a little tentatively, as though I were a trespasser in my own barn.

"Sergeant Pepper needs a little company tonight," he said. "Horses get that way, especially pregnant horses."

"I see."

"Gets down right lonely out here, no other animals being around, except them coyotes living in that cedar break over yonder."

"She tell you that?"

"In her way, yes sir, in her way. She shore did."

"You don't mind sleeping outside?"

"No, sir. In fact, I like sleeping outside. Hell, I had a job in Africa once where I could sleep outside under the Southern Cross. That's something to see, if you ain't never seen it."

I had hired Derwood not long after I had been released from Huntsville and bought the ranch. My wife had been the horse person. She'd been raised on a ranch in Montana, where horses are still a way of life. She started her competitive career doing barrel races in local rodeos, and then took up more traditional equestrian events when she was in college. When she was just twenty-two she represented the United States in the Olympics in jumping. After her death I couldn't part with her Olympic mount, an Arabian mare she had named Sergeant Pepper as a wry tease of her father. He had been a bird colonel in the Army and was outspoken in his disdain for female soldiers. I brought Sergeant Pepper to the ranch soon after I bought it. She was why I had bought the ranch in the first place; I had promised Lori Ann that if anything ever happened to her, I'd take care of her horse. The next step was to breed her. A few months earlier I had had her bred with a local Arabian stallion named Texas Thunder. That's where Derwood came in.

He was of indeterminate age, but I'd place him around sixty. He was no Hollywood cowboy. He was tall, bony, balding, and had fair skin so red-splotched that he always looked as if he had just emerged from a hot shower. He wore nothing but long khaki work pants and long-sleeved khaki work shirts buttoned all the way to the top. Rain or shine, freezing or frying, he wore Red Wing work boots and a sweat-stained western hat that as far as I knew he never took off, even when eating in a restaurant. He didn't smoke, but he chewed tobacco incessantly, always carrying a coffee can around to catch his spittle. But I didn't hire him for his looks or his personal hygiene. I hired him because he knew horses better than any man I'd ever met. He had wrangled horses on ranches all across Texas and Oklahoma, including some of the big-name outfits such as the Four Sixes Ranch in West Texas and the King Ranch in South Texas. But Africa? This was a new one on me.

"What took you to Africa, Derwood?"

He straightened out a bed roll on the cot as he talked with his high-pitched West Texas accent. "Oh, I guess it was about ten, fifteen years ago. An oilman out in Amarillo took a notion to start a safari company over there. These oilmen are always taking notions of one kind or another, you know. I reckon all that money kind of rots out their brains. Anyway, at the time I was working on Mr. Big Belt Buckle's ranch, and he just kind of sent me over there to help out with the chores."

"How'd you like it?"

"Real well, at first. There's a lot of weird and wonderful things to see over there."

"Such as?"

"Well, such as, did you know that when you shine a light on a crocodile at night, its eyes glow red? Hell, I thought only my ex's eyes did that." He spit a wad of tobacco into his coffee can.

I laughed. "How long were you over there?" I asked.

"Just half a season."

"Why did you come back early?"

"I saw something that broke my heart, and I couldn't stand it no more."

"What happened?"

He stepped away from his cot and walked over to the adjoining stall, where Sergeant Pepper was standing quietly. He stood by her rump, gently running his bony hands along her withers as he talked.

"Our hunting concession was in Zambia, along the Mahpamudzi River. There was a herd of elephants used to come across the river from the national park on the other side of the river. I got to be real fond of them elephants. It was real-heartwarming to see how gentle the adult elephants was with the young'uns, always helping the babies up and down the banks and across the river. They reminded me of horses, how gentle they was."

"What happened?"

"Well, we didn't see them elephants for a good long while, figured they'd moved on somewheres else."

"Had they?"

"Nope. We found them about ten miles up-river. They'd been massacred by poachers using machine guns, the whole lot of 'em. All we found was the bones. But the adult elephants had made a good show of it. Their bones were all in a circle around the young'uns' bones. You could see where they had died trying to protect their babies."

I shook my head. "It makes you ashamed to be human," I said.

"It shore does, Quinnie. Every time I see a grown man or grown woman whipping up on a child, I think about them elephants. I think that if even the beasts of the jungle know to be gentle with the young, there's something terribly wrong with men with the God-given gift of reason who don't know the same thing."

"Amen, brother."

He stepped back around to the stall where he intended to sleep, sat down on his cot, and began taking off his boots.

"Know anybody that drives a navy blue Crown Vic?" he said.

"No. Why do you ask?"

"There was one parked out on the right-of-way this afternoon for almost thirty minutes."

"See who was in it?"

"Yep, a woman."

"It's a good quarter mile down to the highway. How could you tell?"

"I ain't that old."

"Blow it off," I said. "It was probably just some chick trying to check me out."

He stood up in his stocking feet to his full height. His khaki shirt was stained with tobacco juice, his khaki pants speckled with pee spots. His face suddenly flushed with anger and his ears turned red as signal flares. "What makes you think she weren't checking me out?" he said.

I slept fitfully that night, drifting in and out of sleep like an opium addict in withdrawal. I dreamt of chain-whipped children. I dreamt of ponderous and stately elephants driven to hysteria by an evil they could scarcely comprehend, sacrificing themselves like Spartans to protect their young. It was a restless and exhausting night. Nevertheless, by morning I knew what I had to do.

Chapter Six

I was up before dawn, the eastern horizon just beginning to turn from dark to gray. I wanted to fortify myself with a stiff workout before getting down to the business for the day. I did a four mile run, two out, two back, along the shoulder of the county road that fronts my ranch. It was light when I reached the turn-around point, so on the return leg I kept in the shade of the semi-canopy of oak and cottonwood trees that lines the eastern side of the roadway. The day promised to be hot and humid; already at this early hour insects were boiling in the drainage ditches next to the shoulder.

After I got back to the ranch I chopped out a quarter-cord of cedar firewood with a four pound wood-axe I kept in the barn. An oak stump near the horse lot served as my chop-block. I was in the process of doing this when a Texas Ranger cruiser turned into my drive. I saw no reason to stop what I was doing. I knew who it was.

Texas Ranger Conway Crowley and I were not on good terms. A year earlier, his wife, a pretty Cajun woman from Lafayette, Louisiana, showed up on my doorstep at one in the morning. Her dress was torn and she was wearing only one shoe. She said she lost the other one on the twelve mile walk to my ranch. Rivulets of dried blood ran from both nostrils down to her upper lip. Another rivulet ran out of her left ear. The left side of her face was swollen as hard and black as an eggplant. A gash of the kind a baton or a gun barrel might make stretched above her right temple. I heard her story. Crowley had beaten her senseless then pistol whipped her for having lunch at McDonald's with two black men, teachers at the public school where she worked as an occupational therapist. She said she had nowhere to turn, so I let her spend the night on the couch. At first light I drove her to the bus station in Houston. She was never heard from again. I reported the incident to Ranger headquarters in Austin, but nothing ever came of it. Crowley blamed me for the entire episode.

He pulled his cruiser to about ten feet from where I was working, unwound his six-foot-four frame from behind the wheel, and stepped out into the sunlight. He pulled his hat down on his forehead like a B-movie cowboy.

"What's happening, Quinn?" he said.

"I'm splitting firewood, that's what's happening."

"That's a mighty good stroke you have with that axe, little brother. You ever chop anybody's head off with it?"

"No, but if you want to stretch your neck across this stump here, I'll be glad to give it a try."

"Is that anyway to talk to a friend?"

"No, but it's a good way to talk to you."

He cocked his hands on his hips and turned his head toward the soft dirt exercise lot next to the barn. Derwood was just leading Sergeant Pepper out for a morning stroll. "Where'd you get the wino, some day-labor outfit?"

"I got him from the King Ranch, and he's not a wino. What do you want Crowley?" I split a final log of wood, leaving the head of the axe buried in the stump.

"A couple of things."

"Like what?"

"Travis' friend Soos says you threatened to cut his head off if he came out here."

"I said no such thing."

"He says you made some kind of threatening gesture with a knife."

"I confess, Crowley, I cut the head off a rubber chicken."

"Oh, is that what it was? Who gave you the chicken?"

"Soos did."

"How come he was to do that?"

"Ask him."

"Why'd you cut its head off?"

"To demonstrate what the word exsanguinate means."

"How come?"

"Soos said he's applying for graduate school and he's trying to improve his vocabulary."

Crowley sucked in his cheeks as though he had just bit into a persimmon. "Well, I guess there's no law against decapitating a rubber chicken, but if I were you I wouldn't mess with that boy Soos. You hear what he done to those two refinery workers down in Texas City?"

"I heard. What else do you want?"

"Don't be so touchy. The other thing is I want to give you some big ol' Texas-size congratulations. I hear you were out with Teal the other night."

"That's right. Who told you?"

"An off-duty on security duty at the hotel where she was staying. He's a fishing buddy of mine."

"I didn't know you had any buddies."

He clucked his tongue and stepped over from his car to where I was standing and placed his arm around my shoulders. "You're cutting yourself some kind of fat hog, aren't you, little brother? Teal's young, beautiful, rich, and about as well connected as you can get."

I felt his fingers bite into my skin. I tried to shrug him lose without crossing the line into another assaulting a police officer beef. "Shove off, Crowley," I said.

"Just being friendly, little brother. Say, I bet she's some kind of piece of ass. She as good as that pepper belly social worker from San Antonio you was humping last year?"

Now I didn't give a damn about an assault charge. I reached

up and twisted his fingers and hand off my shoulder. "Crowley, what kind of fungus did you spawn from?"

"Watch it, boy. You do that again, and I'm going to cuff you on the spot. If you weren't the senator's fair-haired boy, I'd cuff you now."

"Then shove off. And don't bad mouth Teal. She's way out of your league."

"Oh, is she?"

He sauntered back to his car, whistling under his breath. He got in, fired up the motor, and made a wide sweeping circle through my back yard so that his rolled down window ended up two feet from where I was standing.

"Say, little brother," he said out the window, "she show you her butterfly?"

He winked at me. Then he drove off with a sophomoric grin on his face, as though he had just shared a dirty little secret in the shower of the boy's gym.

After I had showered, dressed, and had a breakfast of oatmeal and toast, I left for Houston.

Professional photographers call what I was about to do "cropping": slicing out the part of a picture you don't want the viewer to see. I would give the FBI as full a picture as I could of the situation, but I would crop Teal entirely out of it. Of course, a prosecutor might call what I was about to do withholding evidence. But evidence had to be true, didn't it? I didn't know if what was written in the diary about Teal was true or not. At best it had only a slim chance of being true. I had a doctor's opinion on that. So why injure a probably innocent person with a slim chance of the truth? This, in any event, was what I told myself.

I didn't have an appointment, so I had to sit in the FBI's office in Houston for two full hours before a receptionist ushered me into the office of the Assistant Agent-in-Charge. A man was sitting behind a desk doing some paperwork. The nameplate on the desk said Alan Biderman.

He was about thirty-five, with the kind of eternally boyish look that seems to never get five o'clock shadow. His eyes were a soft blue, his thick blonde hair brushed straight back and lightly oiled. He had on a starched white button down shirt, a bright yellow tie, and red suspenders with real brass fittings. He glanced up when I came in, let his eyes roll over me in leisurely fashion, and lowered them back to the papers in the desk. He didn't stand up when I came in nor did he extend his hand.

"Sit down, cowboy," he said.

I sat down in one of the two wooden chairs in front of his desk. I took off my hat and placed it in my lap.

"I understand you have some information on a possible terrorist threat," he said, his eyes still on the papers on his desk, which he now shuffled ostentatiously.

"That's right," I said.

He nodded slightly, let out a deep breath, and let the papers in his hand drop to the desk. He leaned back in his chair, locked his hands behind his head, and put his feet up on his desk.

"Okay, cowboy, what you got?"

I gave him my sweet smile and began. "I have information that a man of Middle Eastern descent may be in the country planning a terrorist event."

Before I could go any further he held his hand up, palm outward, like a tired traffic cop.

"Have you personally seen this man?" he asked.

"No."

"Do you know his name?"

"He calls himself Malaku."

"Is that his real name?"

"I don't know, but I doubt it."

"Do you know his real name?"

"No."

"Can you describe him?"

"I've heard him described as having skin like a dirty sponge."

Biderman leaned forward and took a stick of gum out of the desk drawer. He popped the gum in his mouth and talked, all the while examining the gum wrapper as though it might have a secret message encoded on it.

"Look, cowboy," he said, "that's not a lot to go on. We can't very well put out a BOLO for Sponge Bob. What's your source for this hot tip."

"A friend."

"Where's your friend now?"

"She's dead."

"Oh, great, maybe we should have a séance, maybe pick a few more details—like who and where this guy is. You'd be surprised how much that helps."

I didn't respond.

He arched his back and stifled a yawn. "You're good to go," he said.

"I drove almost a hundred miles to make this report. I'd appreciate a little attention to this."

"Go on. You're wasting my time."

"I'm a taxpayer. I'm paying for your time."

His face darkened and his eyes narrowed into slits. He chewed his gum so hard I could count the muscles in his jaw.

"Okay, cowboy," he said, "you want to make a report, I'll let you make a report, but you'll have to talk to somebody else."

"Like who, somebody else?"

"A specialist in these kinds of things. I think you'll be pleased." He picked up his desk phone and punched in a short number. "Send Agent Sassani in here," he barked.

He hung up, leaned back in his chair and glared at me. I glared back. We spent a silent minute this way. Then I heard a soft knock and the door open behind me. When I twisted around and turned my head I got a shock that would stun a rhinoceros. The Muslim woman whom I'd seen at Robin's funeral was standing in the doorway.

"This is Special Agent Parvin Sassani," Biderman said.

He motioned her to the chair next to me. As she sat down I noticed that today she was dressed in a navy pants, a beige sweater, and a gold-embroidered navy headscarf. Very chic, in a Muslim sort of way, I supposed. So far she didn't seem to recognize me, nor did she look at me when she was introduced.

Biderman took an expansive tone. "Agent Sassani, this is Mr. Quinn. He says he has some information on a possible terrorist threat."

The woman nodded in my direction but still didn't look at me. I noticed she was gripping the edge of her chair so tightly that the ridges oh her knuckles were straining white against the skin.

"Agent Sassani here is head of our URS Division," Biderman went on, looking directly at me and smiling now.

"URS Division?" I asked.

His smile morphed into a big pumpkin grin. "Unconfirmed Raghead Sightings," he said.

I put on my hat, stood up, and stepped over to the door.

"What's wrong, cowboy?" I heard Biderman ask over my shoulder. "Can't take a little joke?"

I turned around. "Bud, if you ask me, you're in the wrong line of work." I closed the door softly behind me.

I was halfway back to the front office, cursing myself for having gone on a fool's errand, when I heard a woman's voice call out behind me.

"Mr. Quinn."

I looked over my shoulder and saw Agent Sassani, or whatever her name was, double-timing down the hall. I kept on walking.

"Mr. Quinn," she said again.

I didn't stop. A few seconds later a surprisingly strong hand gripped my right arm. I turned around and she let me go.

"Am I under arrest?" I asked.

"Of course not."

"Then I'm outa here."

"But I would like to talk with you."

"Look, lady," I said, "I don't know who you are or what your game is, but I've had enough fun with the FBI today. I'm outa here."

"But it is important I talk with you, Mr. Quinn."

"Yeah? About what?"

She clicked her eyes from side to side, as though to insure we were alone, then locked them on to mine. She spoke in a soft voice, almost a whisper. "About Teal DeLong," she said.

I felt a knot form in my stomach. "What about her?"

"She may be in trouble. Perhaps I can help her."

"Not likely," I said.

"You will not speak with me about her?"

"No."

"You do not trust me?"

"I'm not in the trust business."

She stepped around and stood between me and the exit to the outer office. "Is it because I am a woman you do not trust me, or . . . because I am a Muslim?"

"Lady, I don't care what you are. Please get out of the way."

But she didn't move. She studied my face carefully, her eyes lingering on mine for a long time. Then she spoke softly.

"It is because I am a Muslim."

"What makes you thing that?"

"Because I know how your wife died."

"Go to hell," I said. I started to shove past her, but she stood firm. She reached into her pants pocket and took out a ballpoint pen and some business cards. She flipped over one of the cards and wrote something on the back.

"This is my card," she said. "I've written my private cell phone number on the back. I urge you to call me. Think it over, my friend, there may be more at stake here than your personal feelings."

She slid the card into the breast pocket of my sport coat and stepped aside. I shoved past her but as I walked away I heard her mutter to herself, "It is a pity that such a man should be a bigot."

I walked stiff-necked to my truck. The afternoon sun was so harsh that the reflections of light off the windows of the parked cars I passed on the way were like shards of splintered glass in my eye. But that was nothing compared to the harshness in my mind.

I was not a bigot, I told myself. A bigot is a person who dislikes another because the other is different: Catholic, Jewish, black-skinned or copper-skinned or yellow skinned, or simply from a part of the world where not all the buildings are air-conditioned. A bigot burns crosses in front yards, lynches blameless men, and blows up churches filled with children. A bigot wears goofy uniforms and comic book masks and attends secret meetings late at night to hear other bigots spout conspiracy fantasies or just tell snide and nasty little jokes. A bigot takes a bath once a week in a galvanized tub and brushes his teeth with his forefinger. A bigot is a classless jerk who hates for no reason. Well, that wasn't me. I wasn't a bigot. I just wasn't going to have anything to do with the woman, that's all.

I drove northwest from downtown Houston directly to my ranch. Far away to the west thunderheads were building, beautiful to behold but trembling with lightning. I tried to get my mind around the day's events. Biderman had seemed as uninterested in what I had to say as a man could seem uninterested in anything. That Agent Sassani, however, she had tuned right in. She knew who Teal DeLong was, and she knew there was a connection between Teal and me. She knew how Lori Ann had died. What else did she know? And why did she know? I figured that if I cooperated with this woman I could very well find out the answers to these questions. But it wasn't going to happen. I wasn't going to cooperate with her one bit. I wasn't going to give the damn woman the time of day. If Teal was in trouble, I'd handle it myself.

Chapter Seven

The storms I had seen on my way home passed through during the night. I was glad; I sleep well during thunderstorms. It wasn't until eight in the morning that the sounds of screaming children woke me out of a deep sleep. I stumbled out of bed and looked out my bedroom window. A van with a horse trailer attached to its rear bumper had just unloaded half a dozen kids next to my horse lot. A white haired gentleman in a Roman collar and black slacks was getting out of the driver's side. Oh boy! I had forgotten that Father Blanton from the Brenham parish had told me some two weeks earlier that he might be coming over with some kids to stable a rescue horse at my ranch. I had said, "Sure, why not?"

I slipped on a khaki shirt, some jeans, and a pair of slip-on boots and went outside to help them unload the horse. Derwood was already with them, looking as befuddled as I had ever seen him. He had a way with horses; he knew zip about kids. That's about what I knew.

"Yo, padre," I said as I approached the old priest, now standing next to the trailer. The kids were already straddling the white railings of the horse lot fence.

"Oh, hello, Jeffrey," he said. "We wake you up?"

"Like a mortar attack. Better keep the kids on this side of the fence."

He turned and spoke in a kindly tone to the kids whooping it up on the fence. "You children climb down from there and stay next to me." To my amazement, the kids did exactly as they were told. I counted four boys and two girls, all about ten or eleven, all Mexican in appearance. They circled around him as though he were giving out free ice cream. He turned back to me.

"Thanks, Jeffrey, for helping us with our project. It means a lot to these children. You're a good man."

"It may mean a lot to the horse, too. A stallion or mare?"

"A mare."

"Where'd you pick her up?"

"A sheriff's deputy found her wandering along the side of the Austin Highway. No fences were down anywhere near. Nobody had reported a missing animal. He figured she'd been abandoned by somebody on their way to a new life who didn't want the responsibility of a horse anymore. Sort of a castaway, you might say."

"A castaway, huh? Well, she's come to the right place."

He gave me a quizzical look. He was an old-timer, almost eighty, with white hair and bristly white eyebrows that reminded me of toothbrushes. He was thinner than a jailhouse sandwich, but he was still sharp. Not much got by Father Blanton.

"Let's give her the once-over," I said.

Derwood and I were about to climb into the trailer to ease the horse out when Derwood punched me in the arm. "Remember that blue Ford I said was parked out on the right-of-way the other day?"

"Uh-huh."

"Well, here it comes now."

I looked up to see a navy blue Crown Vic bouncing through the ruts of my gravel drive. A woman was driving, all right. It was Agent Sassani. She crunched the car to a stop about ten feet from where we were standing and practically leapt out of the car with a wood bead purse over her shoulder and a leather briefcase in her hand. She was wearing dark pants, a white blouse, a denim jacket with sequins sewn in, and of course the black headscarf. She was also wearing medium high-heels, which promptly sank into the turf that was still soft and damp from the night's storm. She stumbled and fell to one knee. I stood my station. Father Blanton stepped over and held out his hand.

"May I help you?" he asked.

She looked up and grasped his hand. "Thank you," she said while struggling to her feet.

"Is there something we can do for you, young lady?" he asked. His toothbrush eyebrows arched into a question mark.

"I'm here to talk to Mr. Quinn."

"You have a warrant?" I asked.

"No, of course not."

"Then you're trespassing. Shove off."

"I will not."

We glared at each other. I could see in his face that Father Blanton was trying to get a grasp on the situation.

"Are you with law enforcement?" he asked her.

"Yes. Special Agent Parvin Sassani, FBI office, Houston." She took a small leather folder out of her shoulder bag and opened it for Father Blanton to see. "Here are my credentials."

Now the priest's face registered a level of understanding acquired from years of ministering to convicts, parolees, and juvenile delinquents. He had once been the Catholic chaplain at the state prison in Huntsville. When I was doing my one year stretch in the Eastham Unit, he stopped in to visit me at least every other week.

He spoke respectfully to the woman. "Is this man a target of an investigation? If he is, you should give him an opportunity to consult with a lawyer."

"No," she said. "I merely want to talk to him. He can aid an investigation, if he can grow-up long enough to do it."

He nodded his head and turned back to me. "Jeffrey, we all have an obligation to assist law enforcement. I think you should talk with this woman. What will it hurt?"

Father Blanton was my friend, and I owed him. I cut my eyes to the woman. "Come inside," I said.

We sat across from one another at my dining room table. I sat with my back to the wall. I leaned my chair back against the wall, crossed my arms, and studied the woman's face as she unlatched her briefcase. The features were regular, the cheekbones high, the skin smooth without any sign of aging. The eyes were as I remembered them from the funeral service: dark, intelligent, and intense. I noticed there were flecks of green in them.

"How come you didn't tell Biderman you'd seen me before?" I asked.

She answered without looking up. "I chose not to tell him."

"Why?"

"That is not any of your business, Mr. Quinn." She pulled a document from the briefcase and slid it across the table. It was an 8x11 color photo of a powerfully built Middle Eastern man in a gray suit and dark tie. He appeared to be leaving a low class joint on the Gulf Freeway called the Blue Parrot. He had a thick, close-cropped black beard that concealed the lower part of his face, but I could see that the skin above the beard was badly pitted and scarred: sponge-like.

"Is this the man you reported being in the country planning a terrorist attack?" she asked.

"I don't know."

"You don't know?"

"No. I never saw the man myself. I was only reporting what I had heard."

"You agree the description you gave matches this man?"

"I suppose so," I said. "Who is he?"

"We believe he is a member of the Quds Force."

"You mean the overseas branch of the Iranian Revolutionary Guards?"

"Yes. You know about them?"

"I was a SEAL. I knew about most of the terrorist organizations. My job was to kill them on the spot. I thought this group operated exclusively in the Middle East."

"Many people think that," she said, "but they are a very active intelligence and terrorist organization worldwide. Their role is to export the Iranian Islamic revolution whenever and wherever and however possible. They provided arms and bomb-making technology to the insurgents in Iraq and dissident suppression assistance to Assad in Syria. Beheading captives is their signature suppression method. We believe this man works for Major-General Qasem Soleimani, chief of the Quds since 1997."

"These guys don't operate here."

"Oh no? In 2011 Soleimani was indicted by the Justice Department for his role in plotting to assassinate the Saudi ambassador in Washington. This man was almost certainly involved."

"Was he indicted?"

"No."

"Why not?"

"We had no actual proof of his involvement. He simply turned up in a number of surveillance photos like this one. "

I leaned forward so that all four legs of my chair were now on the floor. "So what's his name?"

"He probably uses many names. Currently, he is using the name Victor Vecciano."

"Never heard of that one."

"He may also be using an alias."

"Oh? What would that be?"

"Malaku."

I kept my face as expressionless as possible, smiling as I spoke. "Never heard of that one either."

"Oh, really, sir? Did you not once lead a rescue mission in Sudan to rescue the two daughters of Senator DeLong being held hostage by a man named Malaku?"

"What makes you think that?"

"I read your military file, and . . ." Her voice trailed off.

"And what?" I asked, although I already knew.

"And your prison file."

"Okay, I've been a bad boy. So what? How did this guy in the photograph get into the country?"

"He came through customs at Miami International on a stolen Venezuelan passport in the name I just told you."

"How do you know that?"

"I took down the license number of the car he got into when he left the restaurant shown here. Of course, it was a rental. I got their records, found out the name he had rented the car under, and traced it back through the TSA records of international arrivals. Not difficult."

"What's he doing here?"

"That's what I would like to know, Mr. Quinn."

"How would I know?"

"Take another good look, Mr. Quinn."

I picked up the photo and studied it again. It was taken with high resolution digital camera, digitally dated and time stamped the several weeks earlier. It was a surveillance photo. I had seen many over the years.

"How did you come to make this shot?" I asked.

"I was part of a surveillance team at The Blue Parrot. It caters to South Americans, especially ones here on drug business. We were interested in two Panamanian bankers suspected of using their bank to launder cartel money from the United States, an unrelated matter. Just by chance this individual emerged from the restaurant."

"And you just happened to take his picture."

"We take photographs of everyone seen at a surveillance venue, Mr. Quinn."

"And you just happened to jot down his vehicle license number."

"Standard procedure, Mr. Quinn."

"Are you sure he's who you say he is, a member of some Iranian spook unit calling himself Malaku? Maybe he really is a South American. You think of that?"

"I am positive in my identification, Mr. Quinn."

"How can you be?"

"I have a source with firsthand knowledge of this man."

"So, again, why show this to me?"

She shook her head. "Please do not insult me, Mr. Quinn. The description you gave Agent Biderman exactly matches this man: a Middle Eastern man with a bad complexion. A sponge-faced man, I believe you said."

"I've never seen him before."

"Then how did you know his description?"

"I heard a rumor, that's all."

"From Teal DeLong?"

"No, from her sister Robin. Robin told me just before she killed herself that she had seen a man meeting this description watching her from over the fence. I was skeptical, given her mental health history. But I reported it anyway. I try to be a good citizen."

"And Teal DeLong has told you nothing?"

"Not a word. Why would she? Why do you think she knows this guy?"

"Fair enough, sir." She reached into her briefcase, extracted another 8x11, and slid it across the table. It was a picture of Teal coming out of the Blue Parrot a few minutes after Sponge-Face, according to the time stamp. I tried to keep my eyes veiled.

"You're getting way out over your skis, ma'am, with all due respect," I said. "Teal's brother Travis hangs out in the Blue Parrot with a dude named Jesus Raza, whom everybody calls Soos. Teal was probably just there to meet them."

"What are their names again?"

I told her. She wrote down the names in a little leather notebook, then reached in her briefcase. She pulled out what appeared to be a typed list of names and compared them to the names she had just written down. "No, Mr. Quinn. They were not there that day."

"Maybe you overlooked someone."

"I doubt it, but I will check it out."

"Good. Let's leave Teal out of this. She wouldn't know anything about this."

"Would you be protecting Ms. DeLong, Mr. Quinn?"

"Why would I do that?"

"Because you are involved with this young woman, are you not?"

"Why do you say that?"

"I do my homework, Mr. Quinn. I know a great deal about you. I told you I know you were the leader of the SEAL team that rescued Teal and her sister from their imprisonment in the Sudan."

"So what?"

She ignored my comment. "I know you now work for Senator DeLong." She stopped momentarily, and then added, "I know you are on intimate terms with his daughter."

"How do you know that?"

"I saw her embrace you at the funeral of her unfortunate sister. That was not the embrace of casual friends."

"She was just emotional that day. I could have been anybody."

"Yes, you could have been. That's why I noted the license number of your truck when you left the service."

"You did what?"

"You heard me."

"And you traced the registration to me?"

"Exactly."

I gave her my sweet smile. "You must be a trained detective."

"Trained enough," she said, "to become very interested in who you were and the nature of your relationship to Teal DeLong."

"There is no relationship."

She shook her head again. She reached into her briefcase and pulled out two more surveillance photos and passed them to me. The first was of my ranch, apparently taken from the right-of-way. I could just make out Derwood leading Sergeant Pepper around the horse lot with her pink rope bridle. The second was of Teal and I walking hand-in-hand along the seawall in Galveston at sunset.

"We're just friends. Besides, she has a boyfriend."

"Who?"

"A kid named Todd Meyer. He's a student over at her college."

She wrote his name down in her little leather notebook, and then looked back up at me. "Does Mr. Meyer know you are sleeping with his girlfriend?"

"I am not."

"Oh?" She pulled out another photo. This one showed Teal and I on the balcony of her hotel room engaged in an unmistakable sex act.

"Okay, so what if we're involved," I asked, "what has that got to do with the dude coming out of the Blue Parrot?"

"That is what I am trying to find out. Why is this foreign agent in the United States? Why is Ms. DeLong associating with him?" She paused, adding, "And what information do you have about this situation?"

"I gave you and Mr. Biderman all the information I have: a sponge-faced Middle Eastern type is in the country and up to no good."

"Mr. Quinn, that is ridiculous. No one of your background and training would expect the agency to believe that is all you know. I think you have other information, something you're holding back. You were just trying to . . ." Her voice trailed off.

"Cover my ass?" I said.

"That is one way to put it, sir."

As every schoolboy knows, when backed into a corner, go on the offensive. "This really chaps me off, lady," I said. "You've got a lot of gall to waltz in here and accuse Teal and me of knowing things we absolutely know nothing about. I come into your office like a good citizen to report a rumor I had heard and get laughed out of the room by your boss. Then the next thing I know I find Teal and I are under FBI surveillance, like we're the reincarnation of Bonnie and Clyde. Gather up your crap and get out."

She said nothing. She didn't even look at me. She calmly placed the photographs back in her briefcase, snapped it shut, stood up and walked to the door. But before she went out she turned and faced me, her eyes burning with the intensity of a welder's arc. "You're a fool, Mr. Quinn," she said. She turned and walked out, slamming the kitchen door behind her.

I watched from the kitchen window as she strode toward her car. I thought she would simply get in her car and leave.

But I was wrong. Instead, she walked through the gate leading to the soft dirt lot where Derwood had taken the rescue horse, Father Blanton, and the kids. She appeared to start a conversation with Derwood and Father Blanton, occasionally patting the heads of the kids that circled around her as though she were a visitor from another planet. She stepped over to the rescue horse, bent down, and felt around the tops of her hooves as Derwood disappeared into the barn. Momentarily, Derwood returned, leading Sergeant Pepper by a rope bridle. Now the woman stepped over to my wife's horse. Again she bent down and felt around the tops of her hooves as she had with those of the rescue horse. There was some more conversation with Derwood and Father Blanton. Then she shook hands with both of them, got in her car, and left, driving more slowly this time so that no gravel sprayed in the direction of the horse lot or the kids.

After she had cleared my property, I went back outside. Derwood must have seen the question mark on my face.

"She sure knows her horses, Quinnie," he said.

"How so?"

"I told her we had a horse in the barn, but we couldn't figure out the horse's breed, sort of testing her, just for fun you know."

"Okay."

"Well, right away she knew Sergeant Pepper was an Arabian."

"Oh?"

"She said she had one just like it when she was a girl."

"Did she say where?"

"Just that it was long ago and far away."

"I see," I said, pondering whether to scold Derwood for letting this irritating FBI agent touch my wife's prize possession. I decided to let it go. "Let's get to work," I said.

"There's one more thing, Quinnie."

"What's that?"

"She said we should have this stray here checked out for laminitis."

"For what?"

"Laminitis."

"What's that?"

"It's a misalignment of the bones inside the hoof, kind of like fallen arches for us."

"How would she know that?"

"Somebody with a lot of horse savvy can tell by feeling the tops of the horse's hooves. When the bones are misaligned, the hoof gets sort of inflamed and gives off extra heat."

"Someone can tell that just by feel?"

"A pro can, yes, sir. Who is that woman anyway?"

But before I could answer I felt a feather-light hand on my shoulder. I turned around to find Father Blanton looking me in the eye, his jaw raised slightly. He spoke sternly but softly, the way my own father used to do when I misbehaved. "May I speak with you, Jeffrey? Privately, I mean."

"Sure." I led him over to a couple of garage-sale lawn chairs under an oak tree in my back yard. We sat down across from one another. A slight breeze ruffled the leaves overhead.

"I'm disappointed in you, Jeffrey," he began.

"How so?"

"You were very rude to that woman who was just here."

"I have a hard time making nice with Muslims, Father. You know how my troubles started."

"Not all Muslims are bad, Jeffrey."

"Oh? I've yet to meet a good one."

"It's wrong to judge someone out of hate."

"Tell that to the guy who killed my wife."

"This woman didn't kill your wife."

"Maybe not, but in my view she and her kind just don't belong here."

"Her kind? Jeffrey, we should judge everyone as individuals, not as part of a kind, as you put it."

"I'm not judging her. I'm just not rolling out the welcome mat."

"Jeffrey, St. Paul says we should be hospitable to the foreigners among us. They may be angels sent to test our charity. And the Church teaches that angels are sometimes sent to help us when we need help most."

"This woman is no angel, Father, she's a cop."

"You shouldn't judge too quickly."

"I didn't see any wings."

"Not all angels have wings. They can be hard to recognize, even to themselves. Some scholars think even Christ wasn't fully aware of his own divinity until the night in the Garden."

"I recognize a cop when I see one."

"Yes, but can you recognize an angel?"

"I suppose you're telling me demons are lurking around, too."

"In my many years I have seen many things that are hard to explain otherwise."

I shook my head. "I think you're twisting my tail, Father. Angels don't walk among us, neither do demons."

"Don't be so sure."

I always considered Father Blanton's face to be kindly, even whimsical. Now his face seemed suffused with a dark and ancient knowledge that made me want to look away. I averted my eyes. When I looked back, his face had returned to normal. I considered whether to chide him for rolling out the old angels and demons thing from the Middle Ages, but I knew better than to get in a theological debate with a priest who had once studied in Rome.

"The point is, Jeffrey," he went on, "you were rude to that woman, whether she's an angel or not. That's not how you were brought up, I'm sure."

"I've crossed a lot of rivers since then." I slapped the old priest lightly on the knee. "Work to do, padre," I said.

I spent the rest of the morning helping Derwood, Father Blanton, and the kids get the rescue horse fed and scrubbed down. Around noon I grilled up a mess of hamburgers and fried potatoes on a grill I had fashioned out of a junked metal horse feeder. I served the burgers with sweet tea, baked beans, and dessert of vanilla ice cream. By two o'clock, however, I was showered and shaved and on my way to Houston. If I was going to keep Teal out of whatever investigation this FBI agent was conducting, I was going to have find out the facts first and formulate a strategy to fit them. This Agent What's-Her-Name was hot on the trail. I was going to have to move fast.

The Gulf Freeway stretches fifty miles southward from Houston to Galveston. It would never make anyone's list of America's Most Scenic Highways. It's fifty miles of car dealerships, strip malls, fast-food joints, funeral homes and semi-industrial sweat-shops. In this environment the Blue Parrot was inconspicuous to the point of being invisible. No one would wander in there by accident looking for a cheeseburger.

It was four o'clock the same blistering day. I parked my truck on the super-heated asphalt parking lot near a Big Lots store. I took an old photograph I had of Teal out of the cab console and slipped it into the inside pocket of my sport coat. I combed my hair and put on my best Stetson hat. Sometimes people take me for a county cop when I dress this way. Take whatever edge you can get.

The asphalt was soft and sticky under my boots as I walked across the lot to the Blue Parrot. I pushed open the bright blue entrance door and went inside. It was about what I expected: a beer joint disguised as a South American style sports bar. Fake leather booths with knife-scarred tables lined the walls. A few empty cocktail tables were scattered about, with chairs plopped upside down on their tops as if someone was actually going to mop the place. Some glass doors leading to a back room hung in middle of the rear wall, their panes blacked out. A pool table and a shuffle board competed for breathing space in a dim alcove to the left. A big U-shaped bar extended from the right. Three giant HD television screens hung from the ceiling along the rim of the U. The air smelled of refrigerated cigarette smoke, re-breathed alcohol, and cheap bathroom disinfectant. The place was empty except for a barman polishing some shot glasses with a white towel. He was a large swarthy man, pony-tailed, completely bare-chested but for a black leather vest trendily unbuttoned. He had enough body hair to frighten a Bigfoot.

I took Teal's photograph out of my jacket pocket. "Say, partner," I said, "has this woman been in lately?"

"Who wants to know?" he said. His expression was as flat as an iron skillet. So was his accent. The closest he ever came to South America would have been a weekend in Miami.

"I do."

"You a cop?"

"I look like a cop?"

"You look like a redneck who pees off the back porch and eats goober peas with a knife."

So much for Plan A; I wasn't going to pass as a cop. I studied the barman more closely. I noticed he had tattoos running up and down both arms. Not just any tattoos, however, but the kind you see in prison: coiled snakes, fire-breathing dragons, naked women with their legs spread. One tattoo caught my attention. It was a tat of a three leaf-clover with the letters AB overlaid in gothic script. This identified him as a member of the Aryan Brotherhood. I pointed to his arm.

"I see you're tight with the Brand," I said.

"What makes you an expert, redneck?"

"I spent a year in the Eastham Unit."

"Oh yeah, what for? Diddling sheep?"

"For busting up a cop."

Those were the magic words. If they aren't born with it, cons acquire a visceral dislike of all authority, but especially cops. They daydream about trashing out a cop the way other men daydream about making the cut at Augusta or catching the checkered flag at Daytona. Anyone who's actually bruised up a cop gets a certain level of street cred from the jump. He put down the shot glass and towel and reached across the bar.

"Okay, chief, show me the picture again."

I handed Teal's photograph to him and watched as he looked it over, squinting now and again, turning it this way and that, shaking his head. He handed it back to me.

"I don't know, chief," he said, "maybe. Broads come and go. When we're busy they buzz around in here like hummingbirds."

"This would have been a couple of weeks ago. She might have been here with a guy who looks like he was dipped in battery acid."

He shrugged. "Like I said, chief, I don't know. I'll tell you the same thing I told the FBI broad: maybe."

I felt my jaw drop. "What FBI broad?"

He nodded in the direction of the glass doors at the rear of the room. "The one in there with a hard guy named Soos, one of my regulars. I bet she ain't met one like him before."

I shoved the glass doors open and entered a room decorated, if want to call it that, with some threadbare sofas, a couple of floor lamps, and a poker table under a hanging green lampshade in the middle of the room. A closet sized door led off from this room to some more rooms back further. Special Agent Parvin Sassani, wood bead purse slung over her shoulder, was seated at the poker table across from Soos and a couple of hookers of indeterminate race in shorts and tank tops. The hookers looked old, tired, and bored. Soos looked high, tight, and glassy eyed. Perfectly sober, Soos was dangerous. Drunk, he was dangerous and unpredictable. A nearly empty Tequila bottle was on the table next to three smudgy glasses.

Agent Sassani had spread her photo array out on the table and was pointing to them, as if to draw them to Soos' attention. Soos' eyes flicked in my direction when I walked in but flicked away almost immediately. Something was working behind those eyes, like a busy insect trapped in an upside-down glass jar.

"You're wasting your time, lady," I said.

Agent Sassani looked up with a start. She rose out of her chair. "What are you doing here?" she asked.

"Came by to visit my old buddy Soos," I said. "Hey, Soos,

que pasa?"

He didn't respond, but the woman sure did. "Get out."

"Why?"

"You're interfering with a federal investigation."

"I thought you wanted my help."

"I don't need your help to interrogate a witness."

"You never know," I said. "Let's give it a try. Hey, Soos, has Teal ever been by here to see you, maybe when Travis was with you?"

There was silence in the room except for the muted sound of a radio playing some Mexican music somewhere in back. Soos didn't respond at first, but after a few seconds he rolled his eyes in my direction. He wet his thick lips with his tongue.

"Sure, *puta,"* he said. "Little Teal, she come by here every week, just about this time. We sit a little, we talk a little, bye and bye we go in back. She say,'Soos, what's that?' I tell her, 'that is my rope.' And she say, "Soos, what are those?' I tell her, 'those are my knots.' And she say, 'Oh, Soos, untie your knots and give me some more rope.' What you think about that, *puta?"*

I stood silent. Something dark and primeval was churning somewhere down deep inside me. For a moment I thought I felt Agent Sassani's hand on my arm. The moment passed quickly, however, because in the next instant Soos had reached up with his left hand and grabbed Agent Sassani in the crotch, the veins in his arm popping out as he squeezed. Shock and surprise spread across her face. In a nano-second she whipped a 40mm Glock automatic out of the wood bead purse. Quick as she was, she was too late. I had already swung the Tequila bottle across Soos' face in a powerful backhanded arc that exploded in a shower of glass shards and alcohol just above his right eye. He dropped to the floor, holding his face in his hands, blood oozing out between his fingers.

"Someday soon I come to kill you *puta*. I'll fucking kill you and burn ever fucking thing you got," he screamed. "You hear me, *puta*? You hear me?"

"Don't lose your head, amigo," I said. I kicked him in the

side of the head. He rolled over on the floor and passed out.

Ten minutes later the woman was stomping around in a little circle, holding her hands to the side of her black scarfed head. It might have been an amusing sight if she still didn't have the Glock in her right hand. She was saying something in a foreign language I didn't recognize. It wasn't complimentary, though, I knew that. We were outside in the parking lot of the Blue Parrot.

"Lady, you want to holster that weapon?" I said. "This is how accidents happen."

She paused as if to consider what I had said. It took her a long time to think it over. I had the feeling she was considering her options, one of which was to park a couple of rounds in my power zone. Finally she dropped the Glock into her wood bead bag. She stepped up to within a foot of where I was standing. If I had seen fire in her eyes before, what I saw now was something truly thermonuclear.

"You are an absolute disgrace, Mr. Quinn," she said.

"I get that a lot."

"What makes you think you can interfere with a federal investigation?"

"I didn't think I was interfering. I thought I was helping."

"You deliberately provoked that witness."

"He wasn't a witness. You could have flashed your little surveillance photos all day and he wouldn't have told you jack."

"So you know everything?"

"I know Soos."

"And what do you know about him?"

"I know he intends to kill me the first time he has the chance. He wasn't joking in there."

She shook her head ever so slightly. "By God," she said, "I hope he does."

I looked at my watch. "Say, ma'am, its four o'clock. Shouldn't you be getting out your prayer rug and facing Mecca or something?"

She slapped me so hard it popped a temporary crown off a

molar. I turned and walked away.

I called Derwood on my cell phone as I trucked down to Galveston to spend the night on the *Persephone*.

"Say, partner, I want you to load up the horses and carry them over to that cute little Aggie vet in Bellville. Tell her I want to board them there until further notice."

"What's going on, Quinnie?"

"Trouble's coming."

"What kind of trouble?"

"The worst kind."

"Cop?"

"Nope, a stone killer. And he's got a hard-on for your old podjo."

"I ain't never met no kind of trouble I couldn't handle with my twelve gauge."

"You never met trouble like this. Trust me. Do it today, as in right now. And don't be hanging around the ranch. This guy will do you just for fun if he can't find me."

"Whatever you say, Quinnie. What are you going to do?"

"Take care of some business then get back as soon I can to guard the fort."

I drove on, trying to wrap my mind around the day's events. Just before I got to the causeway over to the island my cell phone rang. I expected it was Derwood reporting on the relocation of the horses. I was wrong.

"Mr. Quinn, this is Agent Sassani."

"How did you get my number?"

"It is not hard for the bureau to obtain information like that."

"I bet. What do you want?"

"I want to apologize for striking you."

"No apology necessary," I said. "I can take a punch."

"Yes, I believe one is necessary," she said. "I also want to advise you that you have a right to file a complaint against me."

"I take care of my own business. I don't file complaints against people. That's a form of whining, and I don't like whiners."

There were a few seconds of silence before she spoke again.

"Mr. Quinn, are you ready to help me, tell me all you know?"

"No."

I could almost see her squeeze her phone until the connection was broken.

I spent the night on *The Persephone*. I may have spent the night but I didn't sleep. Images of blood, broken glass, and jailhouse tats kept me awake. Besides, my jaw hurt.

Chapter Eight

The next morning I had an early breakfast of toast and eggs, the only food my sore jaw would tolerate. After breakfast I headed up to Teal's college. Maybe Teal's boyfriend Todd Meyer would know if Teal had been keeping company with the foreign man depicted in Agent Sassani's surveillance photo. I had met Todd on any number of occasions. I liked him, but that hadn't stopped me from bedding his girlfriend. Guilt nagged me all the way up the Gulf Freeway.

I made it to Todd's frat house by nine o'clock. It was located on a street over-arched with ancient oak trees, whose roots had long ago churned the sidewalks into a jumble of upended concrete. The house itself was a full-scale version of Mount Vernon. George Washington would not have been pleased. The paint on the Greek columns in front was so peeled that they looked as if they were covered with tiny bird feathers. After generations of fraternity lawn parties and flag football games, the grass in the front was just algae clinging to dirt. If as they say college kids like their digs seedy, this place would rate five stars in the college Michelin.

My knock at the front door was answered by a chubby blonde kid in khaki cargo shorts and a faded "Girls Gone

Wild" T-shirt. His ruddy cheeks had a two-day stubble, his breath was stale, and his eyes were bright as asteroids with alcoholic shine. A longneck beer bottle swung at his side as leaned against the door frame. "Yeah?"

"I'm looking for Todd Meyer," I said.

"Gud for you, dude."

"Is he here?"

The kid swung the bottle up to his mouth. Beer dribbled out the corners of his mouth as he swallowed, spotting the front of his T-shirt, much to the dismay of his mother had she been there. He finished, lowered the bottle, and belched.

"I'll schtell him you came by," he said.

"I'd like to see him if he's here."

"Visitin' hours are uver, pop. Beshides, he dun't want to see nobody right now, specially geezers."

"This is important, son."

He started to raise the bottle again but I grabbed his wrist. "I'd like to see him now."

"Hey, okay." He wrenched his wrist free. "You'll have to gib me the pathwurd, though."

"The what?"

"The pathwurd. We don't let just anybuddy in here."

"This is serious business."

"No pathwurd? Then fug-off."

Password? This was ridiculous, but then I can be as ridiculous as the next guy.

"Okay, partner," I said. "I've got a password for you."

"Yeah? Like whut?"

I reached out, grabbed the end of his nose between by thumb and index finger, and squeezed it hard enough to draw blood.

"How does 'nose-nose-anything-goes' sound?" I said.

"Hey, that hurts," he whined, dropping the beer bottle with a clunk.

"That's the idea, junior."

"I'm gonna start bleeding."

"You should've thought of that before you put me in a bad

mood. How's my password sounding now?"

He wiggled and squirmed and tried to bat my hand away, but he was flabby as he was drunk. "Sounds good to me," he finally said in a tinny nasal voice.

I let go of his nose. He stepped back, knotting up his T-shirt to hold it up to his nose. I pushed through the doorway.

"Where is he?" I said.

The kid pointed to an expansive back yard visible through a row of French doors at the rear of the house. "He's out there," he said, then, remembering some long ago lesson in politeness, added: "sir."

I walked through the house, stepping over and around empty beer bottles and fast food containers, and out the French doors.

A group of frat boys in cutoffs and tennis shoes were playing basketball on an asphalt half-court, their white skin glistening with perspiration. There was a screened-in tennis court, too, but no one was using it. I finally saw Todd Meyer sitting by himself on the top of redwood picnic table at the rear of the yard, his elbows on his knees, his chin propped in his hands. His face was as long as a football field. His khaki shorts and red T-shirt were streaked with dirt and sweat stains. He barely looked up when I walked over.

"What's the haps, Todd?" I asked when I was about five feet away. He rolled his eyes in my direction and shrugged. I tried again. "Got a minute?"

He straightened up and gave me a weak smile. "Sure, Mr. Quinn. I got minutes out the wazoo. What's on your mind?"

"Teal."

"You've come to the right place. I'm the world's leading expert on that little bitch."

"Let's talk about it over a beer."

"Sure. Why not?"

There was a red plastic barrel by the basketball court full of ice and beer. I fished out a couple of longnecks and went back and sat down on the picnic table next to Todd. I tried to keep my face blank while he told me his tale of woe.

It happened about two months earlier. After class one day Todd had gone over to Teal's apartment near the university. He saw her white BMW parked out front, so he knew she was home. But there was no answer when he rang the bell. He tried to reach her on her cell phone, still no answer. Worried, he walked around to the back of the apartments. Teal's unit was on the first floor and it had rear entry into the kitchen. He tried knocking there. No luck.

"I guess I sound like a weirdo, Mr. Quinn," he said, "but I thought maybe Teal had slipped in the shower or something, so I went over to her bedroom window, squeezed through the bushes and tried to look inside."

"See anything?" I asked.

"Nope, the blinds were closed. But I heard stuff."

"Stuff? What kind of stuff?"

"You know, stuff."

"No, I don't know. What kind of stuff?"

"Noises."

"Noises?"

"Yeah, you know, bedroom noises, like when you're lying on your bed in your room and you hear your mom and dad in the next room giggling and carrying on."

"I see. What did you do then?"

He paused, took in his breath, and set his jaw. I could see that just telling the story was a challenge for him.

"I was pissed, I mean really pissed," he went on, "so I went over to the back door, the one that goes into the kitchen, and started banging on it."

"Any answer?"

"No, so I started kicking it. I was going to kick that fucking door in and punch out everybody inside."

"Is that what you did?"

"I didn't get the chance. All of a sudden this big dude opened the door and stepped outside."

"What did this dude look like?"

"He was big, Mr. Quinn. I mean really big, bigger than you maybe. And he had scars all over his body, like when he was a kid he had a world-record case of acne or something."

"How do you know they were all over his body?"

"All he had on were a pair of pants with the fucking zipper down."

"Okay. What happened?"

"Well, I said 'I want to see Teal.'"

"And?"

"He said, 'She is busy.'"

"'Oh, yeah ?"I said, 'doin' what?'"

He suddenly clinched his eyes shut and sobbed. This went on for a full minute.

"What'd he say, Todd?"

He pulled himself together and went on with his story. "He didn't say anything, Mr. Quinn. He just grabbed me by the shoulder. Then he stuck his index finger inside of his mouth, pulled it out with a big wad of spit on the end, and twisted it around in my ear. And you know what I did? I didn't do nothin', I mean not fuckin' nothin'."

I let that sink in for a while, trying to keep any expression out of my face. Todd took his face into his hands, pressing his fingers into the skin as though to squeeze the memory of his humiliation out of his head. But there are memories that never fade away, no matter how hard we try to forget them, drown them in alcohol or drugs, or take them out on others. This memory, I knew, had worked itself into Todd's very bones and would stay there till the end of his days.

"Have you seen Teal since?" I said finally.

"Haven't laid eyes on the bitch."

I patted him on the knee and eased off the table. "Okay, partner," I said. "It'll pass." I started to walk away, but decided to ask one final question. "You tell any of this to anyone else?"

He shook his head. "Nope, nobody, except . . ."

"Except?"

"Except that FBI lady."

"Oh?"

"She was kind of weird. She had on this black scarf. I

thought she was some kind of Mexican cleaning lady or something until she showed me her ID."

"When was this?"

"This morning. Why do you ask?"

I left Todd to his miseries and drove over to Teal's former apartment house. I didn't know what to expect to find; she had moved out at the end of May. In fact, I had helped her move. I held out hope, however, that I might find some little detail that would disprove Todd's account. After all, he was a jilted lover. Maybe he had made it all up to cause her some trouble or just to embarrass her. These are the kinds of things you tell yourself when your stomach is turning upside down.

I parked my truck on the street in front of the apartment house, a fine old colonial style structure of red brick and white trim not far from the art museum. I cut across the spongy St. Augustine grass lawn directly to her former first floor apartment. I rang the bell. No answer. I peered through a window by the door. The place still looked vacant. I went around back.

The back was just as Todd described it: a window partially concealed by some wax-leaf holly bushes and a rear door that led into the kitchen. Even though it had rained once or twice since Todd's encounter with his nemesis, I got on my knees and checked under the bushes for his footprints by the window. All washed away, if they had ever been there at all. I breathed a sigh of relief. The relief was short lived. There was no mistaking what I found on the back door leading into the kitchen: multiple imprints of the sole of a man's athletic shoe on the white paint next to the lock.

I was standing there hands on my hips, letting the significance of this find sink into my brain, when I felt a strong pair of hands twist my own hands behind my back. Next I felt the cold hard bite of handcuffs being snapped on my wrists. "You are under arrest, my friend," I heard a female voice say. I whipped around to see Special Agent Parvin Sassani's eyes boring into my face.

"All right, lady," I said, "what the hell is going on?"

"I said you were under arrest. You heard me."

"For what? And don't use any big out-of-town words that I might not understand."

"For interfering with a federal investigation."

"How? Just by standing here?"

"You're here trying to check out Todd Meyer's story. Don't tell me you're not."

"How do you know I've talked to Todd Meyer?"

"I saw you go into the young man's fraternity house and I saw you come out. And I saw you come directly here."

"You mean you've been tailing me?"

"We call it surveillance, Mr. Quinn."

"Why, lady? Why?"

"Because I believe you are withholding information vital to this investigation."

"You better cut me loose or so help me I'll sic the meanest lawyer in Houston on you and your stupid agency."

"I eat lawyers for breakfast, Mr. Quinn."

That I believed. She might have thrown in she ate Navy SEALS for lunch. We glared at each other for a full minute. Strands of coarse black hair had worked out from under her headscarf and hung across her face.

"I'll tell you what I'll do, Mr. Quinn," she said after our minute of pure hostility was up, "you agree to come with me and I'll release you this time."

"Come with you where?"

"That I cannot tell you."

"Then shove off."

"If that's the way you want to play it, I'll be happy to bring you downtown. You'll like our new holding cell. Much nicer than the Texas prison cells you're used to."

I gave it some more thought. "Okay, lady, you win," I said. "I don't like cells no matter how new they are."

She pushed me around to the front of the apartments and out to a dark blue Crown Victoria parked behind my truck. The car must have been a hand-me down from a rural county sheriff's department. The paint was sun-faded, the front window spidered from road chips, the warped front bumper hanging like a broken tooth below the grill. She opened the rear passenger door, snatched the hat off my head, and all but shoved me inside. She tossed the hat onto the seat beside me.

"Careful, that's a four hundred dollar hat there, ma'am," I said."

"Fine. Now it's riding in a four hundred dollar car."

"I thought you were going to un-cuff me," I said.

"I lied."

She whipped a black scarf out of her wood-bead purse and tied it around my head, as a blindfold I supposed. She skipped the seat-belt part of the routine. I heard her slam my door then get in and fire up the Vic. It sounded like an old man with a cough. She peeled away from the curb like we were at a drag strip. I bounced from side to side in the back seat.

"You want to tell me where we're going?" I asked.

"I cannot," she said over her shoulder.

"How come?"

"It is a forbidden place."

"Forbidden?"

"Yes. Forbidden to men."

"So why are you taking me there?"

"There is someone I want you to meet. That is the only place you can meet her at this time."

"Why is it important for me to meet her?"

"You will see. Now please be quiet and let me drive."

I sat closed-mouth in the back seat, leaning forward like a dog begging for a treat so as to keep my weight from bearing down on my handcuffed wrists behind me. I tried to figure out by dead-reckoning were we were going. I gave it up after three turns. The air conditioner in the old Ford barely breathed out a wisp of cold air. I could feel a line of sweat forming on my lip and I could smell my own odor. I heard my captor flip a CD into the dashboard CD player. To my surprise, the soothing sounds of classical piano filled the car. I tried to make conversation again. Maybe I could talk her into taking off the cuffs.

"That's a piece by Eric Satie, isn't it?" I asked.

"Yes," Agent Sassani replied.

"I like classical piano. My wife turned me on to it before she was killed. She was quite a pianist herself. I've kind of kept up with it since. Makes me think of her, like she was playing for me still."

"That is nice."

"Satie used to play in a Paris nightclub call *Le Chat Noir*. That means 'The Black Cat' in French, if you didn't know."

"I speak perfect French, Mr. Quinn."

"Oh? Where did you learn to speak it?"

"In Brussels."

"Is that where you're from?"

"No. I am from Iran."

"What took you to Belgium?"

"It is none of your business, Mr. Quinn."

"I get the feeling we're not going to be friends."

"I do not become friends with individuals who withhold information from me."

"You want to slack these cuffs, ma'am? I can feel my hands turning blue."

"No." As if for emphasis, she made a sharp turn that threw me sideways and backwards. The cuffs bit into my wrists like vise-grips. I clinched my jaw to keep from moaning in pain.

We came to a screeching stop about five minutes later. I heard her get out, walk around to side of the car, and open the rear passenger door. She half-guided and half-pulled me out of the back seat. She held me up as I stumbled over a curb. I felt my feet sink into thick grass. A few moments later she walked me up some steps and onto a concrete flat area. I took this to be a porch. I heard a doorbell ring somewhere inside the building or house, whichever it was. I heard the click of bolts being slid back and the creak of a door being opened. Agent Sassani engaged in a brief conversation with another woman in a language I did not understand or even recognize. After a minute or two of this parlay she gripped my arm and led me inside. I heard the door being closed behind me and the bolts being slid back into place. At last she removed the blindfold and the cuffs.

We were alone in the front room of a ranch-style house, probably somewhere in the Bellaire section of Houston, where these types of houses are common. This was no imitation ranch house. Instead of the usual couch and wingback chairs plunked down around a coffee table, there was a scattering of ottomans around a thick red Persian rug. Soft indirect lighting radiated from sconces on the walls. The walls themselves were a soft white. The hardwood floor under the rug was polished to a shine. A single closed door led to the other parts of the house. A security key-pad was on the wall next to the door. As I ran my eyes around the room, I noticed through the blinds that there were bars on the inside of the windows. I wondered if they were put there to keep someone out or to keep someone in.

"Tell me again what kind of place this is, ma'am," I said to Agent Sassani. She was standing to my side, clutching the big wood-bead purse slung over her shoulder. She didn't look at me when she spoke.

"It is a safe house."

"A what?"

"A shelter for women." She paused then added, "a shelter for Muslim women."

"Sheltered from what?"

"From the evil that men do. What do you think? Now please be quiet."

So we stood there waiting, not speaking. For the first time I noticed an exotic aroma in the air, as though someone was cooking with the kinds herbs and spices that once might have been transported on camel back along the Silk Road. An eternity passed before the single door at the back of the room opened. A woman in a beige robe and black headscarf emerged and walked, or better yet trudged, to where we were standing. The woman kept her head and eyes down the whole time. She stopped when she was about four feet away from us. Only then did she raise her eyes briefly to Agent Sassani and nod. She made no eye contact with me. She lowered her head again.

"Mr. Quinn," Agent Sassani said, "this is Najwa. Najwa is very shy."

"Yes, I can see that," I said.

"I would like for you to hear her story."

"Okay."

"We must be patient with her. She is like a wounded bird."

I nodded as my thoughts flashed back to Robin's lonely, wounded existence at the asylum. I snapped back to the present when Agent Sassani motioned for us to sit down. I sat down gingerly on one of the ottomans. Agent Sassani sat on the ottoman next to mine. The woman named Najwa simply kneeled on the rug.

"Najwa," Agent Sassani began, "tell Mr. Quinn where you are from."

"From Kuwait," the woman said in a soft, almost toneless voice.

"And how long have you lived in this country?"

"About five years. Yes, five years."

"Are you married?"

"Yes."

"What is your husband's name?"

"Fasil."

"What does he do?"

A question formed on Najwa's face. She sat back slightly on her heels.

"I mean," Agent Sassani said, "what does he do for a living?"

"He works at the cancer hospital. He is a laboratory technician."

"What does he do in that job?"

Najwa shrugged. "I do not know ma'am, but I think it has to do with producement ."

"You mean 'procurement'?" Agent Sassani said.

"Yes, yes, that is what I mean, procurement."

Agent Sassani paused in her questioning, as if to let these last words sink in. Then she went on.

"Tell Mr. Quinn what happened a few weeks ago."

"I do not know if I can," Najwa said, bowing her head almost to her chest, "it is so embarrassing for me."

"You musn't feel embarrassed, Najwa. You must be strong. I will help you. Tell Mr. Quinn what you were doing when this all started."

The woman nodded, sat up off her heels, and took a deep breath. "I am preparing dinner for us when I hear the bell ring. Fasil is in the shower, so I go to the door. I am wearing just a short American dress and no scarf. This is because it is very hot and humid here and I am pregnant."

"Who was at the door?" Agent Sassani asked.

"A big man, a Middle Eastern man who I never see before. And a woman, an American woman."

"How do you know the man was Middle Eastern?" I asked, butting in.

"Because he speak Arabic to me."

"Was there anything special about the way he looked, Najwa?" Agent Sassani asked.

Najwa nodded. "Yes, he has terrible scars all over his face. He is very ugly."

"What did they want?"

"They want to see Fasil. I tell him that this is a bad time because Fasil is in the shower and we are about to eat our dinner. Perhaps he can come back later."

"What did the man say to that?"

"He said they would come in and wait. Then he just open the screened door and let himself and the woman in. He squeeze my shoulder as they go by. It hurt because he is very strong. They go and sit on the divan in the front room and tell me to first go tell Fasil his visitors are here and then make them some tea."

"And what did you do?"

"I do what he tell me. I am very afraid."

"Then what happened, Najwa?"

"I stay in the kitchen making the tea while Fasil go into the front room and talk with this man and woman."

"Could you hear what Fasil and the visitors were talking about?"

"No. I close the door from the kitchen to the front part of the house. I am afraid, afraid of this man. I do not want to hear. I do not want to see."

"How long were you in the kitchen making the tea?"

Najwa shrugged. "I do not know, ten, maybe fifteen minutes. When the tea is ready, I place the pot and three porcelain demitasses on a silver tray and take them into the front room and place them on the little coffee table in front of the divan. I keep my eyes down. I do not want to look at this man or the woman."

"Did you hear what they were talking about then?"

"This man keep saying to Fasil in Arabic 'do you understand, do you understand?'"

"And what did Fasil say?"

"Fasil say nothing. He just nod that he understands. I think Fasil is very afraid. Yes, great fear is in his eyes. I never see such fear in his eyes."

"Then what happened."

"I go back into the kitchen while the men and woman drink their tea. But after a few minutes, Fasil come and get me. He say, 'Najwa, come quick. Our visitor wants to speak with you.'

I say, "No, I do not want to go in there,' but Fasil grab me by the arm and lead me into the front room. He make me stand before the terrible man."

"Did the man say anything?"

"Yes, but not to me. He look at Fasil and say, 'Fasil, when I come to your door this woman present herself dressed like a whore. She does not welcome me. She tries to turn me away like I am some kind of beggar stinking up her doorway. I ask you, is this the way a woman of faith dresses and acts?' Fasil, he just say, 'No, Malaku.'"

"Are you sure, Najwa?" Agent Kofuri asked. "Fasil addressed this man as Malaku?"

"Yes, Parvin. I am sure. Malaku is a sacred name. I would never mistake that."

"What happened next, Najwa? Tell Mr. Quinn."

"This man say, 'Fasil, this woman must be taught a lesson. Hold her across the table.' Fasil say, 'please no, Malaku.' But the man motions with his hands and Fasil grab me from behind and force me down across the coffee table."

"And then, Najwa?"

Najwa took another deep breath. "The man take his belt from his pants and whip me across the back. He whip me so hard that my water break and I lose the baby. I feel the baby dying inside me. Then I pass out from the pain."

"How long were you unconscious, Najwa?"

"I do not know. A long time, I think. When I wake up Fasil is gone. The man and woman gone. That is when I call you."

I interrupted again. "Why did you call Agent Sassani and not the police?"

"Because, sir, every Muslim woman in Houston know to call Parvin when she have trouble. The police just talk, they don't want to get involved in a Muslim woman's troubles. Parvin, she do something."

"I see," I said. I cut my eyes in a sideways glance at Agent Sassani.

"And Parvin come and bring me first to the hospital then here," Najwa added.

Najwa sat back on her heals again and ran her fingers across her brow. I let out my breath, my mouth forming into a small 0 that squeezed the breath into a barely audible whistle. While I was doing this, Agent Sassani was reaching into her big purse. She brought out two eight-by-eleven photographs. "Here, Najwa," she said, "let me show you a picture of a man. Is this the man who came to your house, the man who beat you?"

Najwa looked at the photograph, and averted her eyes quickly, as though the man in the photo still had the power to hurt her. "Yes, that is the man. I told you before."

Agent Sassani slid the second photo to the top and held it up for Najwa to see. "Is this the woman that was with him?"

Najwa glanced at the photo and nodded. "Yes," was all she said.

Agent Sassani held the photos up side by side for me to see. They were the two surveillance shots she had shown me before: the alleged member of the Iranian Quds force and Teal DeLong.

I turned to Najwa. "While you were being beaten, what did the American woman do?"

"She do nothing?"

"Nothing at all?"

"No, sir, nothing at all."

"Did she say anything?"

"No, sir, she say nothing."

"Did she try to stop the man from beating you?"

"No, sir."

"I can't believe it," I said. "I won't believe it."

"You are a stubborn man," Agent Sassani said. "In your Bible, your Christian Bible, there is a story about a stubborn man. I see the look on your face. You do not think I have read your Christian Bible? You may trust that I have. The stubborn man's name was Thomas. He was one of the followers of the Christ, one of the apostles, a true believer, yes. But even he would not believe the Christ had risen. Too fantastic a story, perhaps, even for him, as for many after him. 'Show me the wounds in his hands and the wound in his side' he said, 'let me place my hands on them and then I will believe.'"

She nodded and Najwa stood up and turned around. Slowly, gingerly, Agent Sassani unfastened the back of Najwa's robe and removed a large square of cotton fastened to Najwa's back with medical tape. I gagged at what I saw. Najwa's back was a snakes' nest of lacerations, contusions, torn skin, and dried blood. It was as though she had been lashed to a mainmast and worked over with a cat-o'-nine tails by Captain Bligh.

"Here, Mr. Quinn," Agent Sassani said, "would you like to place your hands on these wounds? Would you believe then?"

I remained silent.

On the ride back to my truck Agent Sassani left me uncuffed, but she had replaced the blindfold around my eyes.

I ran the situation over in my mind. I had no answer for the problem of evil. I had only seen evil in its pure form twice: when we found Robin with her amputated arm in the underground cell in Sudan, and now this woman with the brutally beaten back. In both cases a man calling himself Malaku was the central actor.

"Najwa said 'Malaku' is a sacred name," I said to Agent Sassani from the back seat. "Isn't that the name for the Angel of Death in the Quran?"

"That is correct," she answered from over her shoulder, "Malaku is the Angel of Death."

"Islam has angels?"

"Yes, of course."

"Do you believe in angels?" I asked, Father Blanton's little lecture on angels coming to mind.

She didn't answer right away, and when she did it was in a surprisingly soft tone of voice. "It is not important what I believe."

We drove on in silence. Again I marveled at the credulity of people in the modern world buying into the angels and demons thing from the Middle Ages.

"Are you ready to help me now, Mr. Quinn?" Agent Sassani said as she removed my blindfold and the cuffs. We were standing next to my truck.

"I have to do something first," I replied.

"And what is that, sir?"

"I have to talk to Teal. Give her a chance to explain."

She shook her head in disbelief. "You are a foolish man, Mr. Quinn."

"It's never foolish to look out for a friend."

"It is when the friend is using you."

"What makes you think Teal is using me?"

"Ask yourself, sir, why would a young woman like her wish to involve herself with a man with your history of trouble? A man who's been in prison? A hero fallen from grace at best?"

"That's pretty cold."

"Yes, it is cold. But it is the truth. This woman is using you.

For what I don't know, but she is using you."

"I'm getting tired of this."

"Yes, and I am getting tired of your stubbornness. Something very evil is about to happen here, and very soon perhaps. I need your help to stop it."

"I'll give it some thought," I said.

With that, she threw up her hands, climbed into her junked-out cruiser, and peeled out of the apartment parking lot in a whirl of burning rubber and spraying gravel.

As soon as I was in my truck I called Teal. She told me we couldn't get together until the following evening. I drove back to the ranch, mentally calculating the box score for the day. I had struck out on my every turn at the plate.

Chapter Nine

The sky the following morning was pink as a bunny's ear. I took that as a good omen, at least a temporary one. I decided to get some work done around the ranch and try to think through the trouble I found myself in. I was in the process of mowing my little patch of front lawn, enjoying the smell of freshly cut grass, when I saw the mail truck stop at my mailbox out by the highway. The mailman put something in my box then drove away. I clicked off the mower engine, took off my shirt to get some rays from a friendly feeling sun, and walked the quarter mile down to the box. There was a single envelope waiting for me. It was post-marked London. I opened it.

The letter was on the letterhead of a British "security" firm. It sounded like an insurance company, or maybe a stock brokerage, but it was neither of those things. In the trade these days they call themselves security contractors, or maybe security consultants, or even just security experts, as though they might be hired to send a man out in a little truck to repair your residential burglar alarm or your smoke detector. But in reality "security contractor", "security consultant", and "security expert" are just euphemisms for that notorious military reprobate: the mercenary.

The letter was written by Derek Brown, the Special Air Service sergeant-major who had led the British team in the Sudan hostage rescue mission. Now he was the chief recruiter and field director for this British mercenary outfit. He was still calling me "Yank."

"Hey, Yank," the letter began, "still thinking about our offer? Chap with your background has a golden future in our line of work, I keep telling you. Why don't you pop over to London and we'll discuss the details over an American steak and a bottle of French wine. I know a lady or two who would like to meet you. One of them is a bona fide Ethiopian princess, the other an acrobat with a Czech circus. Never know, might bring you a little change in luck. Derek."

I walked into the house smiling, went into my study, and placed the letter in my desk drawer next to the several others I had received from Derek along the same lines. It was an outrageous idea, of course. No United States Naval Academy graduate would ever dirty his hands in the dark waters of the mercenary underworld. But then my hands were already dirty.

And I was starting to need money. Modern horse ranching is an expensive undertaking. Expenses for me included Derwood's salary, winter feed, dietary supplements, veterinary care, shoes and hoof-trimming, and tooth floating (the periodic filing down of Sergeant Pepper's occasionally overgrown teeth). Now I was caring for two horses and boarding them with a top rate equine vet. True, I had my job with the Senator DeLong, but that and the proceeds from the life insurance policy on my wife would only last so long and go so far. I took Derek's letter out of the desk drawer and read it again. I thought about it for a few minutes then put it back. For now, I thought, I had better go call on the vet and see what I could work out on the boarding charges. First, however, I would stop and order some more hay for the winter. I had two horses to feed now, and one on the way. I showered, shaved, and drove into town.

Coffee Jack's Feed and Tack store was on the outskirts of Brenham along the main highway to Houston. The gravel parking lot was half-occupied by a large inventory of tractors, hay balers, cattle guards, giant galvanized livestock watering tubs, and even a few windmills. Inside, it was a throwback to the era of the country hardware store, where a rancher could buy the kind of merchandise he would never find today at the local Home Depot: saddles, horse blankets, bits, bridles, post-hole diggers, fence-stretchers, barbed wire, electric cattle prods, hay forks, feed shovels, double-bit axes, rabbit pellets, deer feed, pump shotguns, lever action rifles, faux leather gun cases, ammunition, chewing tobacco, and rough canvas work clothes that fit you like a stall fits a horse. It was also the place I ordered hay for the winter. Few small ranchers have the time or money to grow their own hay. My hay came from Kansas, where the farmers make comfortable livings growing the brome and blue-stem grasses that make up the premium hay bales shipped to supposedly rich Texans like me. Coffee Jack was the broker.

Coffee Jack was a tall, spare, dour man. He was almost always dressed in black slacks, a short sleeve white dress shirt, and a black tie. The somber dress was in case he was called away to his other local enterprise, a mortuary and funeral home. All his businesses were no-credit operations. He once kept a dearly departed on ice for over a month until the bereaved relatives made the final payment on the burial costs. He claimed to be a descendant of Coffee Jack Hays, one of the great Texas Rangers of the nineteenth century. Hence his name: Coffee Jack.

"Hey, Jack," I said as I walked through the door, "*que pasa*?"

He was seated on a high stool behind the counter, paging through an open Bible on the countertop. He barely looked up when I spoke.

"Hello, Quinn. What can I do for you?" His voice was as flat and cold as a tombstone.

"I need to double my order for hay this winter."

"How come?"

"Father Blanton brought a rescue horse out to the ranch.

So now I've got two horses to feed, not counting the foal due in the fall."

"That old pirate expects you to pay?"

"He says the kids the parish is sheltering are going to throw a car wash or something."

"There aren't that many cars in the whole county."

"What can I say? How much deposit do you need?"

He shrugged and looked back down. "Skip the deposit. I know you're good for it."

Now this was something new. Never once in all our dealings had I skated out of Coffee Jack's without putting down hard money on an order. I looked at him more closely. His face was always long and sad, fitting for a funeral director I always thought, but today it looked long enough to wrap around his neck a couple of times.

"What's the matter, Jack?" I asked.

He shrugged.

"There's gotta be something, podna. Bad health news?"

He spoke without looking at me. "I can't understand it, Quinn. I've been burying folks around here for thirty years and I ain't never seen nothing like it."

"Like what?"

"Haven't you seen the news?"

"I've been tied up lately. What news?"

He shook his head as if to shake away unwanted images from his memory. "Last week a young gal over on the north side took a notion and drowned her twin boys in the bathtub. Those kids were just two years old. I buried them this morning."

"Why'd she do that?"

"She claims she was depressed."

"You buy that?"

"I don't buy nothin' that ain't mentioned in this book here, and I don't see nothin' about depression." He nodded in the direction of the Bible on the counter.

"That's pretty old school, Jack."

"You didn't have to prepare those two little angels for burial."

Maybe he had a point. As for me, I had no answer for why a woman would kill her children, or why a live-in boyfriend would whip a child with a bicycle chain, or why a brutal foreign man would beat a pregnant woman until her water broke. I decided to leave Coffee Jack to his thoughts. He'd be thinking on this dark problem for a long, long time. The best minds had done so for millennia and had never worked out a definitive answer. Nevertheless, I considered it a mark of decency that a man would try. I silently wished him well as I turned to leave. Just as I reached the door he called out to me

"Hey, Quinn."

"Sir?"

"When Blanton throws that car wash, have him let me know. I'll send over the hearse and the limo."

"You're a good man, Jack."

I meant it, too.

From Coffee Jack's I drove on to check on Sergeant Pepper. The veterinary clinic was on the outskirts of Bellville, about twenty miles south of my ranch. It was a picture-book layout: a hundred acres of prime pasture separated by white pipe fencing into maybe twenty sub-pastures, each with its own horse shed, feed bin, and water tank. The coastal Bermuda grass in the pastures was as green as a pool table, the result I was sure of a state-of-the-art irrigation system. I calculated that the modern steel building combination office and barn covered at least an acre in itself. The black asphalt drive up to it was lined with palm trees and carefully tended flower beds. This wasn't a horse clinic, it was a horse resort. I steeled myself to the sticker shock on the boarding fees I knew was coming.

"Hi, Jeff," the blonde woman in a white lab coat said as I walked into the barn. She was holding a horse-sized syringe in her hand at eye level, apparently measuring the dosage of whatever was in it.

"Yo, Sally, that for me?"

"If you want it."

"What will it do?"

"It'll kill you or cure you."

"Make mine a double."

"What's up, big guy?"

"I came to discuss the boarding charges for Sergeant Pepper and the rescue horse Derwood brought over the other day."

"Just a minute."

She went over to a nearby horse stall, leaned over, and injected whatever it was into the rump of a big Appaloosa stallion. Afterwards, she put the syringe into a red plastic bucket of used syringes and went to wash her hands in a nearby stainless steel sink. She was about thirty-five, with a shock of blonde hair that made you forget about the thick glasses she always wore. I had known her forever; we had gone to high school together. She and her husband, both Texas A&M veterinary school graduates, had built this place from scratch. Sadly, the gossip was that he had run off the previous year with a rodeo trick rider. Maybe her husband had taken an injection of that whatever it was that was in the giant syringe. She finished washing up and walked over to me. She gave me a friendly hug.

"It's good to talk to you in person, Jeff, and not through that tobacco spitting yahoo who works for you."

"Derwood is the one who knows about horses, Sally."

"He should. He smells like one."

"He gets very involved in his work."

"So do I, but I don't roll in it. Come take a walk with me."

She took me by the arm and led me down a soft dirt walkway between two rows of horse stalls holding every conceivable breed of horse. The air had an old-fashioned livery stable smell of horses, hay, and saddle leather. Sergeant Pepper and the rescue horse were in adjoining stalls at the end of the walkway.

"Here's our girls," she said.

The two horses looked contented, relaxed. I wondered if they knew they were in the Club Med of horse clinics.

"Okay, Sally, I'll get to the point. What's all this going to cost?"

She didn't respond immediately. She leaned back against Sergeant Pepper's stall and locked her eyes on mine. "This was your wife's horse, wasn't it?"

"That's right."

"Terrible what happened to her."

"I try not to think about it."

"I bet you live with it every day. Is breeding her horse your way of dealing with it?"

"Not exactly. I promised my wife that if anything ever happened to her, I'd take care of her horse. She loved this animal. She rode it in the Olympics, you know. Won a medal, too."

"So you're keeping your promise to your wife, even though she's no longer with us?"

"Something like that."

She shook her head. "My, God, some men keep their promises to their wives to the grave and beyond, and others forget everything they promised the minute a cutie with a nice boob job slinks into view."

I lowered my eyes and tried not to look embarrassed for her. I must not have done a very good job.

"Okay, Jeff, I didn't mean to cry in my beer in front of you. Let's talk about the boarding charges, but first I want to know why you brought Sergeant Pepper over here. She's a perfectly healthy pregnant mare." Her eyes looked quizzical now.

"When your enemies can't get at you, they'll try for your family or property."

"You have those kinds of enemies?"

"I seem to have a talent for collecting them."

"So you're hiding her out until the heat's off."

"That's about it."

"How long will this situation go on?"

"I think it'll be coming to a head pretty soon."

She reached up and patted me on the cheek. "Okay, you big softie, tell you what I'm gonna do. It's a privilege to have a true Olympian boarding with us, so I'll throw in a month a free board and feed, medicine and treatment, too, if necessary. And just to be nice, I'll do the same for this sick one here."

"Sick one?"

She nodded to the rescue horse in the adjoining stall.

"This one."

"Sick?"

"Sure. Didn't anyone tell you?"

"Sick with what?"

"Laminitis. I confirmed it this morning with some x-rays. Derwood said some foreign woman made the original diagnosis by touch out at your ranch. She must be some kind of wizard."

"Actually, she's an FBI agent."

Sally knitted her eyebrows together and bit on her lower lip. She looked down in the dirt, then back up at me. "FBI agent? Jeff, are you in trouble again?

I got back to my ranch in time to shower and change and get mentally prepared for my appointment with Teal. I set my mind to it this time. It wasn't hard to do. The image of Najwa's savaged back was never far from my thoughts.

I arrived at the DeLong family home just before nine that evening, decked out in khaki pants, an old SEAL polo shirt, and lace-up desert boots. Teal had said to come casual and be prepared to do a lot of walking. The Spanish style house was modest enough by River Oaks standards, just six-thousand square feet and only an acre of carefully tended lawn. The sun had just dipped behind the tree line, leaving the house in romantic shadow. But I was in no mood for romance this night. I was determined to get some answers. My task was to get them without ripping my relationship with Teal and her father. I had bills to pay. I still needed my job. I decided on the soft approach. I parked my truck in the circular driveway, walked up to the double entry doors and punched the doorbell. The black housemaid let me in.

A few moments later Teal came down the stairs in a white linen dress that tied around the neck but left her shoulders bare. Sun freckles dotted her tan skin. When we embraced I could detect the faint aroma of coconut oil on the back of her neck.

"Been out in the sun, partner?" I asked.

She squeezed me tightly around the waist, pressing her stomach into my loins. "I wanted to look good for you."

"You're making it hard for me to be a gentleman."

"That's the idea, sweetie."

She took me by the hand and guided me out to my truck. "C'mon, Jeff," she said, "there's a carnival over at the church. Let's go be kids for a while."

There was indeed a carnival, an old fashioned neon and canvas extravaganza straight from Bradenton, Florida, where the carnies migrate for the winter like Canadian geese. The rides were right out of my childhood memories: a tilt-a-whirl, an octopus, a merry-go-round with traditional wooden steeds. A large circular tank, its sides painted with white-capping waves, held kiddie motor boats guided by underwater steel spokes. Seedy food vendors hawked corny dogs, cotton candy, and every other kind of junk food your mother warned you never to eat. There was even a sideshow with garish canvas murals outside the entrance promising glimpses of the bearded lady, the tiger man, the seal boy, and a busty lady named "LoLeeTa."

"I thought sideshows went out with black-and-white movies," I said to Teal as we strolled-arm-in-arm through this neon fantasy land.

"This is the last of the Mohicans," she said, "the only carnival left that has all the traditional attractions."

"The bearded lady an attraction?"

She punched me in the side playfully. "You know what I mean. Weird stuff people will pay to see."

"On a church playground?"

"It's all in a good cause."

"Who put all this together?"

"I did," she said, squeezing my arm. "I've been working on it all year. Proud of me?"

"Always", I said, keeping my face as empty as I could.

"I hope so, Jeff, I hope you always will be," she said, then added enigmatically, "no matter what happens."

So we wandered through the neon night, arm-in-arm, weaving through excited swarms of children and around stands of drooping adults, their faces turned a sickly yellow in the chemical lighting. We rode the merry-go-round and ate corny dogs and saw the bearded lady in all her hirsute glory. Finally, I steered Teal through a grove of pin-oaks at the far end of the midway to the half-lit church softball and soccer field. I sat her down in the bleachers behind the backstop and sat down beside her. "We need to talk," I said.

"Talk? I thought you wanted to make out." She giggled. "What's this all about?" She laced her hands around one knee and threw back her head, catching a breeze that gently lifted her hair from her shoulders. Her eyes met mine momentarily but drifted away to gaze at the few stars dimly visible through the haze from the city lights.

"It's about you, partner," I said.

Now her head turned and her eyes riveted on mine. "What about me?"

"Things I've been hearing."

"What kind of things?"

"Things I can hardly believe."

"Well, don't just sit there like some kind of mysterious swami. Tell me."

I took a deep breath and started in. I told her about Special Agent Sassani. I told her about my conversation with Todd Meyer. I told her about the unfortunate Najwa. Lastly, I told her about Robin's little diary and the reference in it to someone named Perry Abella. I met her stare the whole time, trying to note even the most fleeting of emotions in her eyes or face. But there were none. She was totally expressionless. When I finished, she simply turned her head away and sat silently. I gave her a minute, but only a minute.

"Well?" I said at last.

"Well what?" Her voice was as flat and cold as a marble slab. She still refused to look at me.

"Well, do you admit or deny this stuff?"

"You sound like a goddamn lawyer. Admit or deny? Who

do you think you are to cross examine me like this?"

"I'm your friend. If you're in trouble, I want to know what it is. Maybe I can help."

"You can help, all right. Get the hell out of my life."

"It's not that simple."

"It sounds simple to me. Just get in your truck and boogie out of here. I'll walk home. I need the exercise."

"It's not that simple because there may be others involved."

"Like who?"

"This FBI agent believes the man you've been seen with is planning some kind of terror attack."

"Now you sound like a jealous lover. *The Man You've Been Seen With,* didn't Jerry Lee Lewis do that one?"

"Cut it out, Teal. I can't help you unless I know the truth."

"The truth is you're a shit."

I stood up. She sat there silently. Lights from the carnival flickered across her face in unnatural combinations of yellow, orange, and red, making her look other-worldly. She closed her eyes and bit her lip and squeezed her hands between her knees. I thought we were finished talking. I was wrong. After a good ten minutes of icy poise and determined silence she burst into tears, holding her hands to her face, heaving her shoulders spasmodically. This went on seemingly forever. I let her cry it out.

"It's true, Jeff, all of it," she said finally, rubbing her eyes with her fists. "I've tried everything to put that stupid stuff I did as a kid behind me. I study hard, I work in the church. But that part of my past just won't go away. It's like it's stalking me."

"I was hoping it wouldn't be true. What happened?"

"A few months ago that horrible man showed up at my apartment. After five years the nightmare was starting over again. I nearly passed out."

"Why didn't you call the police then and there?"

"He told me if I did, he'd give them a copy of a video he made when Robin and I were held in that terrible place. I said a lot of things in it that might put me in prison. You know how he got me to say them? He and his pals water boarded me, as if I was some kind of terrorist. Can you believe it? "

"You talked about the guy killed in the refinery fire?"

"Yes."

"That video would never have been used in court against you. Talk about something being acquired under duress."

"Maybe not, but it would have ruined my father. No way to keep something like that out of the news. That shit would have sent a copy to every news outlet in the country. At least that's what he said."

"Why would it have ruined your old man?"

"Because I say in it that he shipped me and Robin overseas so he could fix the prosecution. Duress or not, that was true. His political enemies would have had a heyday with it. I can see the attack ads now: Senator DeLong Cheats Law. My father's career would be fucked all to hell. Mine, too."

"So what does this guy want from you?"

"I don't know exactly. Mostly, he wants sex all the time. Sometimes he likes to take me places, like over to that woman's house, or out to look at Robin through the fence. But, you're right, he's planning something. I just don't know what it is."

"How does he contact you?"

"He calls me on a cell phone at least five times a day, always from a different number. He's probably going to call again in about twenty minutes. I think it's a control thing for him."

"Where does he stay?"

"I don't know. He just shows up, like a ghost or something. I even moved out of my apartment and moved home. That stopped him for a while, but then he found the gym where I go, the grocery store where I shop, even where I get my nails done. He just carts me off to the nearest motel and does what he's going to do. It's like rape. Sometimes while he's doing me he gives off this animal smell, like a dead rat or something. I'm not even sure he's entirely human. I hate it but what can I do?"

"Talk to this FBI woman. She's a pain in the ass, but I think she understands things like this. She even runs a shelter for abused women."

"No way, Jeff. No way."

"So what are you going to do?"

"Wait it out. I keep hoping he'll just get tired of screwing around with me and move on."

"This guy won't go away, Teal. He's here for a purpose."

"We'll see."

I left it like that for a few moments, trying to figure another way to reach her.

"Has he ever mentioned the name Perry Abella to you?" I finally continued.

"No. Why do you keep mentioning that?"

"Like I said, Robin writes in her diary that you will be Malaku's Perry Abella. You will breathe out the fire of hell and the children of the Great Satan will wither and die. You know anything about that?"

"No, Jeff. Not a thing."

"Didn't you pick up anything when you were with him at Najwa's place, when he and her husband were talking?"

"No. They were speaking in some sort of foreign language, Arabic I think."

"Teal, I have to ask you this. Why didn't you try to stop him from beating Najwa?"

"What could I do?"

"You could have grabbed his arm."

"What? And have him chop off my hand like he did Robin's?"

I had no answer to that one. I took another deep breath.

"I think you need to come clean with all this, Teal. Talk to the feds. I'll set a meeting with this woman from the FBI."

"No, Jeff."

"You've got to. If this jerk is planning to kill a bunch of people, including kids, you've got to help stop him."

"I've got too much at risk here, Jeff. My father does, too. No, I can't go to the feds, kids or no kids."

"So you won't do anything?"

"No."

"You can't turn a blind eye to what this guy is up to, Teal. Guys like this don't bet it all in one hand. You're probably one sleeper cell among many. If you don't work out, he'll go on to the next one."

"Can't you see, Jeff? I'm trapped."

"You're the blind one, Teal, willfully blind. You just won't look at this situation in a mature way."

"I can see perfectly well that I can't do a damn thing about the situation, Jeff." She paused then added, "But you can do something."

"Do what?"

She turned her head and fixed her eyes on mine. Just then a spray of lights from the carnival splashed across her face and her eyes seemed to turn red, and I was reminded of Derwood's story about the red eyes of African crocodiles.

"You can kill him, Jeff, just like you said you would when we were in Galveston. That will solve everything."

"Is that what Galveston was about, Teal. I don't like being set up."

"Didn't you enjoy our time together? We can have a lot more like that."

"I don't like being used."

"But you said that you would kill anyone who was threatening me, just like you said you would kill that asylum attendant who was threatening Robin."

"Robin was defenseless, you're not. You have a choice in this matter. You can choose to cooperate with this FBI agent and have this guy cooled out the right way."

There was a long lull in the conversation. I flattered myself with the belief I had convinced Teal to talk to Agent Sassani and that she was gathering the psychological strength to say "yes" and get it over with. I couldn't have been more wrong.

"Well, Jeff?" she said.

"Well, what?"

"Well, are you going to kill him or not?"

I felt something hard and cold in my stomach. "You know perfectly well that will put me back in the joint if I kill him without good legal reason."

"Do you still have Robin's diary?"

"Yes."

"You haven't given it to that FBI woman?"

"Not yet."

"Then I can fix it up so it looks like self-defense."

"Are you kidding me?"

"I'm dead serious." With that she rose from the bleachers, walked up and put her arms around me, pressing her body into mine. "Look into my eyes, Jeff." She squeezed me tighter. "Let's go somewhere where we can be alone."

I didn't go anywhere with Teal. I left her at the carnival with some of her friends, telling her I needed to check some equipment on the *Persephone* and that I would just spend the night there. I arrived round eleven and went straight to my bunk. I crashed there with my clothes still on, trying to wrap my mind around what Teal had just said: *I can fix it up to look like self-defense.*

I never went to sleep, and that probably saved my life. It was just after midnight when I heard the first footstep, soft and muted, like the paw of a big cat stalking its prey in the African bush. I sat up to listen more closely. Was I just hearing things?

I wasn't. There was another soft paw-step, then another. I slid out of bed and went into the galley. I entered the three number combination to the lock on the gun cabinet, doing so by Braille in the dark, and slowly opened the cabinet door. I took out the stainless steel .30-06, chambered a round, grabbed a flashlight from the drawer where we kept the playing cards, and went up the short flight of stairs to the main deck. Fog was swirling off the harbor surface and there was an unusual chill in the air. There was no sound except the lapping of the water against the hull of the *Persephone.*

I caught him with a flashlight beam just as he was coming off the gangway and onto the deck. He was a big man, as powerfully built as an NFL linebacker. He was wearing khakis, a linen sport shirt, and oxblood loafers. He was quite sporty looking until you saw his face. Even in the limited light from the flashlight I could see his face was disfigured with scars that his dark beard did little to conceal. He was carrying a large duffle bag, the kind golfer's use to transport their golf bags and clubs. He raised a hand, palm outward, to shield his eyes from the flashlight's beam.

"You may put down your weapon," he said, "I am not here to hurt you."

"If I do that, how do I know you will still be friendly?"

"I would hope for more hospitality since you do not yet know why I am here."

"Well, if you're here to sell me insurance, I don't need any."

He lowered his hand, blinking several times to adjust his eyes to the flashlight beam. I half-expected his eyes to shine red in the light, but they didn't. They were as black and dead as buckshot.

"Do you know who I am?" he asked.

"I believe so."

"Tell me."

"Five years ago you abducted two young American women and held them hostage in Sudan in conditions that made Auschwitz look like a country club. Now you're here for God-knows-what."

"Perhaps God does know, but he turns away his eyes."

"Well, I haven't turned away mine. You take one more step and I'll take you off at the neck."

He remained motionless. "Do you know my name?"

"You're in this country on a stolen passport in the name of some Venezuelan. I know you like to call yourself Malaku, especially when you're whipping the crap out of some defenseless girl. But I don't know your real name."

"Yes, I am Malaku," he said. "That is my real name."

He tilted his head back and exhaled deeply. I was too far away from him to smell his breath, but the wind carried something to me that smelled like rotting flesh. Perhaps it was from the commercial fishing dock up the harbor. At least that is what I told myself. When he spoke again his voice seemed to have changed. Earlier it had been a resonant baritone; now it was hoarse and guttural, like a voice from a fire damaged throat.

"Do you know why I have come here tonight?"

"Teal told you I have something you want."

"Yes, a little diary. Do you have it?"

"Yes, but not here."

"Where, then?"

"I'm like anyone else, bud, I keep important documents like that in a shoe box in my closet at home."

"I believe you are lying."

"Well, if you don't believe me, you can believe this .30-06. It never lies. And I never miss."

He said nothing, nodding almost imperceptibly. "Then I will leave you for now, but perhaps someday I will come back."

"Don't lose your head."

He pointed a dirty looking finger at me. "Don't lose yours," he said. Then he turned and padded down the gangway as softly as he had come up.

I watched him disappear into the night. I locked up the *Persephone* and marched port-arms with the .30-06 to my truck, my head swiveling, my eyes and ears on high alert, as though I were point man on a jungle patrol. I jumped in the truck, placing the rifle close by on the seat beside me, and boogied right out of Galveston. I drove around for hours, trying to calm my nerves and sort out my thoughts. I had never come across anyone that damn spooky. Was he even human? I didn't know what to think. That damn Teal had set me up, that much was perfectly clear. I finally stopped at an all-night truck stop out on IH 10 near San Antonio. I pulled into a line of big rigs stopped for the night. I shut my eyes, intending just to rest them a bit.

Chapter Ten

I rested my eyes until ten in the morning. It was almost noon when I guided my truck through the curves and dips of the state road leading from the highway to my ranch. As I approached my ranch I could see emergency lights flashing like heliographs on the horizon. Accidents between cars, trucks, farm equipment, and even livestock are common on country roads. *Hope nobody got hurt,* I thought to myself. But when I reached the turn off to my ranch I was in for the kind of shock that every homeowner secretly dreads upon returning home.

Two sheriff's deputies, their faces as hard as ceramic, stopped me at the galvanized steel cattle guard that serves as my front gate. One of them spoke on a hand-held radio while the other stood a ways back from my truck door, his right hand resting on the butt of his holstered pistol. After a few minutes the guy on the hand-held waved me through.

At least a dozen vehicles were scattered in front of my house and near my horse barn: sheriff's cruisers, DPS road runners, EMS trucks, and the county coroner's white van. Prominent among them was a black and tan SUV marked "Texas Ranger" in large white letters. Everybody was present and everything was in order for a law enforcement jubilee that usually ends in some one going away for a very, very long time. One vehicle was out of order, though: a yellow Corvette convertible, top down, its blinkers tinkling as though it were trying to keep rhythm with the flashing lights of the police vehicles. The Vette was empty.

My little ranch was as busy as the flight deck of an aircraft carrier during operations. A police tape cordoned off my horse barn and horse lot. Behind it, white-uniformed crime scene techs were taking plaster impressions of this boot print and that, dusting the wooden lot rails and the barn doors for fingerprints, and generally scurrying around like so many worker ants. A pair of plainclothes opened the screen door on my back porch from the inside and came out shaking their heads and making notes in little spiral notebooks. I turned my gaze back toward the barn. A knot of deputies, DPS troopers and one civilian stood just outside the police tape. They all turned and stared at me when I got out of my truck. Derwood emerged from this group and practically ran up to me.

"What you doin' back here, Quinnie?" he asked, his face flushed and his ears a fire engine red.

"What the hell's going on?" I asked in return.

He didn't answer me directly. Rather, he looked away, took off his hat and slapped it against his thigh. "It's all my fault, Quinnie. I shouldn't have called the police. But when I found the goddamn thing I didn't know what else to do. I figured you'd be long gone by now."

"What 'goddamn thing'?"

"You know, in there." He tilted his head toward the dark interior of the barn.

"I don't know what the hell you're talking about. Crowley here?"

"Sure is. He's been looking for you."

"I bet. Where is he?"

He tilted his head toward the interior of the barn again. "In there . . . with it."

I grabbed the top rail of the horse lot fence and was about to vault over, police tape or no police tape, when Conway Crowley saved me the effort. He came striding out of the barn, a Hispanic DPS officer carrying a clipboard in his wake. Conway was all Texas Ranger today. He wore a starched open-necked white shirt, knife-creased jeans with a Lone Star belt buckle that must have weighed a full pound, a white Stetson, and spit-polished black ostrich boots. A pearl-handled .45 ACP in a hand-tooled leather gun belt completed the image. He took a cheroot out of his shirt pocket, un-wrapped it and stuck it between his teeth. He dropped the wrapper on the ground.

"I wish you'd stop littering my place, Crowley," I said. "What the hell is this all about?"

"You're a piece of work, Quinn," he said. "You turn your piss-ant little ranch into a butcher shop, and you worry about a cigar wrapper dropped in the dirt."

"I ask again: what's going on around here?"

He flicked a gold-plated lighter and held the flame to the end of his cigar. He inhaled deeply then blew out a cloud of smoke just to the left of my face. He lowered the cigar to his side between two stiffly extended fingers in a gesture of faux elegance.

"Come on inside, Quinn," he said. "Let's you and me see what's going on around here."

I climbed over the fence and followed him inside the horse barn. The young Hispanic DPS trooper carrying the clipboard followed us in. Inside, several crime scene techs were staring open-mouthed at an object hanging by a rope from the central rafter. The object was a simian-like creature, naked to the waist, hanging upside down, its arms outstretched toward the ground. Weird as that was, the object's most notable feature was that it had no head. A dark wetness, covered with flies, stained the dirt beneath the body. Crowley pointed at the wet spot. "This what you mean by 'exsanguinate', Quinn?"

"What are you talking about, Crowley?"

"I'll show you, sailor-boy."

He nodded toward the Hispanic DPS officer. The officer bent down to a horse blanket spread on the dirt over an object about the size of a basketball. His nose puckered as he drew the blanket slowly back and laid it to the side. A head lay upright in the dirt, its face staring at us. The eyes were bulged out, the mouth open in an eternal scream. A long line of fresh stitches ran from the lower right jaw all the way to the scalp line. Even in death it was a familiar face. It was Soos's face.

I turned away and took a deep breath and tried to beat down my nausea. Already there was the sickly-sweet odor in the air that combat veterans know too well, and that neither drink nor drugs ever fully expunge from the memory.

Crowley was yapping behind me. "Yep, now that's a fine piece of surgery there, Quinn," he said. "I didn't know you went to medical school, too. Hey, can you set me up with a nurse?"

I turned around, my stomach on full tilt-a-whirl now. "You think I did this?"

"Who else? Everybody knows you and Soos had words on the pier the last time ya'll was out on a dive job and that you threatened to exsanguinate him if he ever came out here. Soos told Travis and Travis told me. It took me half an hour to figure what word he was trying to repeat. Then I had to look it up in a dictionary just to make sure."

"Good for you. That all you got?"

"Well, that's your axe over there, isn't it?" He pointed to an axe marked with a numbered yellow evidence pylon laying a few feet further away. It was my axe, all right.

"What if it is? That doesn't mean I used it to do this."

"I guess not. Maybe ol' Soos used it to commit suicide."

I shook my head. "When did it happen?"

"The medical examiner says about two this morning."

"I wasn't here."

"Where were you?"

"Just driving around."

"You got any witnesses?"

I didn't answer.

I sat handcuffed to a fence post in the horse lot for the next hour. The midday sun was a flamethrower on my head. A war party of ants was exploring the inside of my right pants leg. I heard Crowley tell one of the news crews that had begun arriving from Houston that I wasn't a suspect, only a "person of interest." That's like calling a lobster on display in a tank in a fancy restaurant a "lobster of interest." Everybody knew why I was cuffed to the fence post.

I should have been getting used to being cuffed; it was the second time within a week. But you never quite get used to the stainless steel bite into your wrists, as though a dog with metallic dental implants is chewing on you. I shifted my weight to ease the pain. I must have grimaced because the Hispanic DPS trooper with the clipboard walked outside the fence and squatted down behind me.

"Cuff's a little too tight, boss?" he asked.

"I can feel my fingers turning into lead."

"Hold on. I'll slack 'em a bit. You'll be a good cowboy and not try to slip 'em off, eh boss?"

"You think I want to give Crowley a reason to drill me with that .45 he's lugging around?"

"I don't think you'd have to give him too much reason, no. He's got a *muy grande* hard-on for you, my friend."

"Tell me about it."

I thought that would be the end of our little conversation, but he stayed hunkered down. I took that as an invitation to talk.

"What's your name, Trooper?" I asked.

He answered in military format. "Gonzalez, Hector."

"Why don't they cut down the body?" I asked. The stench of death had wafted out of the barn and was now settling into the outside air. I noticed the news crews had moved back a few yards. As the day got hotter, they'd be moving back a lot further unless somebody cut the body down and hauled it to that nice refrigerated room with the white tile all around and the metal grate in the center of the floor.

The trooper answered softly. "The Ranger wants to be sure all the news crews get here and get their shots. Some big *cajones* from a national cable channel are supposed to be on their way."

Great, I was hitting the big time. There's nothing like making an appearance on national TV in handcuffs. Ask anyone who's had to do the perp walk for the benefit of the cameras. I kept talking to keep my mind off the prospect.

"You think I did that thing in there, Trooper?"

"It's what the Ranger thinks that counts, boss."

"I'm asking what you think."

There was a long silence behind me, then the soft voice again. "If you did it, why do you come back? Much likelier you put a lot of miles between you and that *chupacambra* in there. That's what I would do. Head south across the river, maybe."

"Me, too, if I did it. So what do you think did happen?"

"I don't know, boss. Your house is a mess, like someone was looking for something. Maybe Soos came here and surprised a burglar. You got something somebody wants real bad?"

"Can't think of a thing." But I was lying about that. I knew who the burglar had been, and I knew what he had been looking for. And I knew who sent him.

"You find any other bodies hanging around?"

"No. Why do you ask, boss?"

"That Vette is Travis DeLong's baby. He never let Soos drive it."

"Doesn't that big honcho Senator DeLong have a son named Travis? Is that who you mean?"

"That's who I mean."

He let out a low whistle. "You think Travis was out here, too?"

"I'd bet on it."

"So where is he now?"

"I don't know, partner. You're the policeman."

"I better tell the Ranger so we can start looking for him."

"If you tell Crowley, you'll never get credit for finding him."

Another pause, then the soft voice again. "I see what you mean. I'll check into this Travis situation, maybe tell the

Ranger later. Take it easy, boss. It'll work out."

He patted me on the shoulder. I heard him get back to his feet and out of the corner of my eye saw him scamper over the fence and into the barn. He had the build and quickness of a fast welterweight. I wondered if he would ever make Texas Ranger. *No,* I decided, *not mean enough.*

I sat another hour in the sun, my scalp constricting with sunburn, my shirt sopping with sweat. The ants were working their way up my leg to the power zone now. I was almost ready to confess if Crowley would just take me to a cool, clean jail, where I could shower and sack out. Even the TV crews were getting restless; one had even packed up and left. But the ones who stayed were about to get a camera full.

It must have been around three o'clock when Crowley and Trooper Gonzalez marched out of the barn and stood by the fence, shading their eyes with their hands and looking out in the direction of the highway. I assumed the national news crew Crowley had been waiting on was finally pulling in. I was wrong.

When I leaned forward as far as I could and craned my head around what remained of the crowd, I saw a navy blue Crown Vic stopped at the gate to my property. One of the deputies whom I had passed earlier was leaning down and talking to the driver while the other deputy was talking into his hand-held radio. I noticed Trooper Gonzalez had pulled a similar radio off his gun belt and was alternately talking into it, pausing as if to hear the other deputy, and then talking to Crowley. That done, he would talk back into the hand-held. I couldn't quite make out what was being said, but Crowley kept shaking his head as if to say "no" and Gonzalez kept nodding his head as if to say "yes". Finally, Crowley kicked a fence post with his boot and said loudly enough for me to hear, "Oh, what the hell, let her through."

Gonzalez said something into the hand-held. The two deputies at the gate stood back as the Crown Vic roared across the cattle guard and tore down my drive, trailing a plume of chalk dust and dirt. No sooner had it fishtailed to a stop next to a sheriff's department cruiser than a black-scarfed Special Agent Parvin Sassani jumped out wearing a dark blue jacket with FBI printed in large white block letters on the back. She had her wood bead bag over her shoulder and FBI credentials in her hand. She practically ran through the horse lot gate.

"Which of you is Texas Ranger Crowley?" she asked to the loose group of deputies and crime scene techs that had begun to assemble in the lot like a crowd making its way into a fight arena.

Crowley stepped forward, stretching himself to his full height and cocking his hands on his hips. "That would be me," he said.

"I am Special Agent Parvin Sassani. Would you please show me the crime scene. In the barn, no?" She turned in the direction of the barn door.

Crowley stepped in front of her, holding up both hands palms outward. "Hold on, darlin'," this is a state crime scene. I don't remember inviting you."

"I invite myself. And I am not your darling. Please step out of the way."

"What gives you the authority to blow in here like this and start telling people what to do?"

"The Patriot Act. You are familiar with it, of course."

"Why, sure, down here in Texas we talk of little else."

"Good, then show me the crime scene, please." She stepped to one side and started toward the barn door.

Crowley stepped across her path like a boxer cutting off the ring to his opponent. "Not so fast, darlin'. How do I know you are who you say you are?"

"I have already shown my credentials."

He gave her the kind of toothy grin a cop gives when he hands you a ticket. I noticed everyone else in the crowd, except for Trooper Gonzalez, gave out with the same grin in a kind of spontaneous outbreak of teeth. "Well, darlin'," he said, "how 'bout we check out those credentials anyway, just to be sure. Think of it as wearing both belt and suspenders. Of course, your kind don't wear belts, do they?"

Agent Sassani stopped and glared at him but said nothing. She handed him her little black leather credential folder. Crowley took it but didn't look at it. He just held it out to his side while keeping his eyes drilled into Agent Sassani. "Call it in, Hector," he said.

Trooper Gonzalez stepped forward and took the ID packet. As he trotted off to his cruiser to use the radio, I thought I saw him turn his head slightly in my direction and roll his eyes. There was a lull while he was on the radio. Finally, Agent Sassani spoke up. "This is taking too long. There is little time. I insist you let me through."

Crowley let out with the toothy smile again. "Hey, it's only three o'clock. We got all the time in the world. Why don't you go water your camel and relax."

Her response was simple and direct: she simply shoved past Crowley and headed into the barn. Crowley grabbed her by the arm and spun her around. "Come back here, you little sand nigger," he said.

The next few seconds defy chronological description because the events happened almost simultaneously. Trooper Gonzalez comes running back through the gate waving Agent Sassani's ID like a railroad yardman's lantern. He is shouting "She checks out, Ranger, she checks out." Agent Sassani is kneeing Crowley in the groin, so fast that there is as much surprise in his face as pain. Crowley hits the deck and begins squirming on his side, his hands cupped over his groin. Agent Sassani is on him like a panther. She slaps him repeatedly across the face. That, I knew from experience, had to hurt. "You touch me again, you hill-billy," she is screaming, "and I'll beat your brains into the center of the earth. Do you understand me?" Crowley isn't responding, so she slides her free hand up to his throat and shouts again, "Do you understand me? Do you understand me?" Crowley finally nods a weak "yes", his eyes now flooded with pain and humiliation.

When it was over Agent Sassani sprang up and marched into the barn. She motioned for Trooper Gonzalez to follow her. He did so without once looking back at Crowley. The crowd in the horse lot, which had been transfixed with amazement during the encounter, now watched open-mouthed as Crowley struggled up, still cupping his groin, and limped out of the horse lot to his vehicle, moving slowly and stiffly, like a dog passing glass. No one offered to help him.

This was not an episode that would go into the Texas Ranger Hall of Fame, but it was certainly going to go on the evening news. Reporters made a fresh round of on-the-scene reports and tried to get inside the barn to interview Agent Sassani. She wouldn't have it. She came out into the horse lot and instructed the sheriff's deputies to move the news crews out to the highway. Then she told the remaining law enforcement personnel to follow her back into the barn. I could hear her in there directing the techs and deputies with an air of authority that left no one in doubt who was in charge.

A few minutes later they brought out a lumpy body bag on a gurney and loaded it into an ambulance. As the ambulance was driving away, Trooper Gonzalez walked briskly out of the barn, vaulted over the fence, and squatted down behind me. He unlocked the handcuffs and lifted them off my wrists.

"The lady says to cut you loose," he said.

I stood up stiffly, rubbing my wrists, getting the feel of my legs again. I turned around. "How come?" I asked.

"She says you didn't do it."

"How does she know?"

We were both standing up know, looking at each other across the fence. Gonzalez's eyes were half-quizzical, half-amused. "The lady says you were with her all night."

I felt my jaw drop.

Gonzalez scampered back over the fence and patted me on the shoulder. "I told you it would work out, boss." He hustled back into the barn.

I stretched, dusted myself off, and headed for the barn, my mind spinning out questions. I never got a chance to ask them. I was half way across the lot when Agent Sassani marched out of the barn and stuck her face into mine. She poked an index finger into my chest so hard that I thought I had been shot.

"You," she said, pressing hard with the finger, "you I should leave chained to that fencepost forever. I ask you for help and you turn me away. I ask you to tell me what you know and you say you know nothing. I share with you a great secret and you disappear. Do you think I play a game here? Did that dead man in there look like a game to you? I tell you unless you help me there will be many more like him. One of them may be you. So I ask you again, are you ready to help me? Are you ready to tell me everything you know?"

There was enough fire in her voice to melt a slab of concrete, so I said the only sensible thing. "Lady, I was born ready."

By ten o'clock that evening Agent Sassani was sitting at Mickey's kitchen table, studying Robin's diary as though it were some ancient codex containing the secrets of the universe rather than the last reflections of a doomed girl. She read some, took notes on a yellow pad, read some more, drumming the fingers of her free hand on the table top as though it were a keyboard. She filled up half a yellow pad with scribbled notes, underlining some words and making little stars beside others. I sat silently across the table as she worked. Finally, she looked up.

"I must now make a telephone call," she said. "I am afraid it is very confidential."

We were at Mickey's house because the bank where I had stashed Robin's diary was only a few blocks from his house. The bank had let us in after closing hours because Agent Sassani had called them in advance and told them who she was and that they damn well better let her in when we got there. After we fetched the diary she wanted someplace in a hurry to review it, so I suggested Mickey's. I called Mickey and he said to bring her over. "This woman," he said, "I have to meet. We saw her take down Crowley on the six o'clock news." On the way I filled her in on my conversations with Teal and my late night encounter with Malaku.

While Agent Sassani made her call I went into Mickey's study and stretched out on a leather sofa. Mick mixed drinks in a bar he had had made in one of the oak bookcases. He handed me a scotch and soda and sat down behind his desk. His pregnant second wife Beth, a labor and delivery nurse whom he had met at the hospital, sat down in a wingback near the fireplace. She folded her hands in her lap and followed the conversation quietly as though she were a guest in someone else's home and not sitting in her own. I recounted all that had happened in the last two days.

"Teal really asked you straight-out to kill this guy?" Mickey asked.

"She said she could fix it so that it was self-defense," I answered.

"You think she sent Scarface out to the *Persephone*?"

"Who else knew where I was?"

"But why?"

"She figured that if he and I got into it, I might just take him out and her troubles would be over."

"And you could claim self-defense?"

"If anybody would believe me."

"Damn little bitch. I'd like to operate on her eyes."

I sat up, a sudden shiver running through me. "It was a miracle I heard him coming and got the drop on him, Mick. I don't know that I could win a fair fight with this guy. You should see his shoulders."

"I always bet on my old podjo."

"Don't bet the ranch on this one. I would have sworn this guy was supernatural. His eyes were dead-man's eyes and he had a stink on him that I bet never washes off. And he wanted me to be sure I knew his name was Malaku."

"The same guy mentioned in Robin's diary?"

"Has to be. She described him as a dirty sponge face. This guy must use battery acid as an after shave."

"You're being melodramatic, *jefé.*"

"I know, but you had to be there, Mick."

Mickey drank from his glass, ran his tongue around the inside of his mouth, and pursed his lips. He continued on, "So what do you think happened out at the ranch, *jefé*?"

I rolled my head against the armrest of the sofa. "I don't know, Mick, but I think after Malaku left the *Persephone* he went out to the ranch early this morning to look for the diary. My house was tossed pretty hard: drawers pulled out and dumped on the floor, cabinets opened, closets pawed through. It was hard to navigate through all the mess to shower and change clothes."

"He must want the diary pretty bad."

"Bad enough to kill for it. There's something in there he doesn't want anyone to see, especially the FBI."

"So what do you think happened next?" Mickey asked, leaning back in his chair now.

"I think Soos showed up while Malaku was ransacking my house. Soos had promised to come out to the ranch and kill me and burn everything I own. He sure picked the wrong time to make good on his threat. "

Mickey shook his head in disbelief. "I can't believe one guy took out Soos like that."

"I told you this guy is a monster."

"Must have been a bloody crime scene."

"It looked like the Somme battlefield. Not only that, Mick, Travis's Vette was out there, but Travis wasn't in it. He wasn't anywhere to be found."

"You're telling me this guy killed Soos then snatched Travis?"

"That's the way I read the signs."

Mickey let out a low whistle and leaned back in his chair, focusing his eyes somewhere on the ceiling. After a bit, he raised back up and tossed his head as if to shake unwanted images out of his mind.

"You heard from the boss about any of this yet?"

"Not yet."

"Worried?"

"I'd feel better if he'd call. DeLong's a guy who waits in the weeds for his enemies. I hope he doesn't think I'm one."

Mickey nodded in agreement. He went to the bar to top off his drink. I waved off a refill of mine.

"I would like to have been there in person to see our little friend pop her knee into Conway Crowley's power zone," he went on.

"It was a sight to behold."

"Crowley won't forget, you know. His kind never does. At some point he'll make trouble for that woman in there. And for you, too."

I nodded but said nothing. My wrists still pulsed with pain where the handcuffs had bit into them. I could hear the muffled voice of the woman talking on her cell phone out in the kitchen. I looked out the study window. It had turned dark and a halo of mist had formed around a street lamp. I closed my eyes.

"That little gal really stuck her neck out for you, *jefé*," I heard Mickey say. "She really say you were with her last night?"

"Yep."

"Any idea why?"

"She said this was no time for legal red tape."

"How did it happen she came out to the ranch in the first place?"

"She said she was coming out to the ranch to make a run at me to turn over the information I had. She heard a radio news flash that a headless body had been discovered at my ranch. She thought it might be me, so she stepped on it. When she got there she didn't see me cuffed to the fence post, at least not at first. That's why she was in such a hurry to get inside the barn. She didn't say it, but I think I'm the main lead in her case and she was afraid I had been snuffed."

"Maybe she was just concerned about you, Jeff," Beth said from across the room.

"Not likely. I think she sees me as a truant child."

"Well, if nothing else," Mickey said, "she's a good judge of character."

Beth spoke up again. "She's beautiful, Jeff."

I opened my eyes and turned my head in her direction. "Who?" I asked.

"That woman in there," Beth said, "that Muslim woman."

I turned my head back. "I try not to notice those kinds of things."

Mickey laughed. "Since when? Tell me about this woman."

"Something of a mystery woman, Mick. She says she's from Iran and once lived in Belgium. She speaks French like they do in Belgium. One thing's for sure, English is her second language: perfect grammar, perfect pronunciation, no slang. She sure didn't learn it here. By the time we're fifteen most of us sound as if we learned English reading graffiti on highway underpasses."

"How did she get to be an FBI agent."

"No idea."

Mickey laughed again. "She really slap you?"

"She damn near slapped the taste out of my mouth, Mick."

At that moment Special Agent Sassani walked into the study.

"I am finished, my friends. It is late and I must leave now. I have an early meeting tomorrow and it is a long drive to my house."

To my astonishment Beth stood up, went over to Agent Sassani, and took her gently by the arm. "Why don't you stay with us tonight? You can use the guest room that Jeff usually sleeps in. He can sleep in the alternate guest room on the lumpy bed we save for in-laws. Right, Jeff?" she asked, smiling in my direction.

I closed one eye and squinted at her with the other.

"No," Agent Sassani said. "I cannot impose on you."

"It's no imposition," Beth said, "I insist. I'll fix us all something to eat, too. I bet you're hungry. I know I am, and those two over there are hungry 24/7."

Agent Sassani furrowed her brow and bit lightly on her lower lip. "Yes, perhaps that might be best." Then she looked pointedly in my direction. "Yes, that might be best, especially since I must ask Mr. Quinn to accompany me to the meeting in the morning."

I sat up as though pulled aright by invisible wires.

"What?" I asked.

"You heard me, sir."

"Why me?"

"For one thing, I need you to identify the man you saw on your boat last night in the presence of the individual we are meeting."

"Why?"

"So there will be no mistake."

"And the other thing?"

"After you hear what this man has to say tomorrow morning I think you will agree to introduce me to Teal DeLong and persuade her to cooperate in the investigation."

"No way. I'm out."

"Yes, sir, you are in, at least for now."

"I produced the diary for you. That's what you said you wanted."

"I don't think you understand the gravity of the situation, Mr. Quinn."

I stood up and walked over to where she was standing. "Well, maybe it's about time I do. I want to know what this is all about. You've been on my case ever since I trooped into the FBI office downtown. Now I feel I'm being drafted into government service."

"Indeed, you are."

Her eyes held on mine, unblinking. I returned her stare. Her face became thoughtful.

"You're afraid that if you help me further you'll lose your job with Senator DeLong," she said finally.

"Right at the moment that's all that stands between me and the soup line."

She stood silent for a long moment, her eyes turned inward now, as though searching for a hidden thought. After a while she brought me back into focus.

"All right, Mr. Quinn. You have a lot at stake here on a personal basis, so perhaps you are owed a certain degree of explanation." She paused and took a deep breath before going on. "It has to do with that phrase the unfortunate Robin wrote in her little book: "Perry Abella. Remember? She wrote that Malaku wanted Teal to be his "Perry Abella."

"So does it mean something to you?"

"Perhaps. I think 'Perry' may be a phonetic version of the Persian word '*peri*.'"

"So what does that mean?"

"In Persian mythology there is a kind of angel called a '*peri*.'

"Okay."

"But it is a dark angel, a demon perhaps. It is associated with suffering and death."

"So you think Malaku has Teal tagged as his angel of suffering and death?"

"Yes, that is what I think."

"And what about that other word, 'Abella'?"

"I think again it is a phonetic version of a Persian word."

"Which one?"

"*abele*."

"And what does that mean?"

She stepped closer to me and riveted her eyes on mine.

"Smallpox," she said.

Chapter Eleven

By nine o'clock the following morning Agent Sassani and I were in a windowless meeting room at Bush International Airport. We were seated across a utilitarian conference table from a man she had introduced to me as Vasily Kirilov, a Russian. He had agreed on the phone the night before to fly in on the red-eye from wherever he was living on the east coast to meet with us. Agent Sassani said she had been part of an interrogation team that had debriefed him when he sought political asylum in the United States some years earlier. Before we were finished I wondered if he belonged in a real asylum.

He had a crooked back, possibly the result of childhood scoliosis. This made him appear to be lurching even when he was sitting down. His head was two large for his body, and to make matters worse it was topped off with a thick shock of black hair, brushed back and up Woody Woodpecker-style. His sharp little rat teeth were the color of wet charcoal. He could pass for a ferret at a ferrets' convention.

On the way to the airport Agent Sassani had said I was free to ask him all the questions I wanted. She wanted me to be satisfied that I knew the full seriousness of the situation. "When you hear this man's story," she had said, "you will understand how important it is for me to talk to Ms. DeLong." I took this as a carte blanche to bore in on nice Mr. Ferret.

"Tell me again what the Biopreparat was," I said. Next to me Agent Sassani was taking notes on a yellow pad. I could hear shrill whine of jet engines out on the tarmac. I looked around the room. It was completely bare except for the table and chairs, a white board on one wall, and large NO SMOKING signs on the other three walls.

Kirilov took a long drag off a nasty looking Turkish cigarette, exhaled the smoke with unabashed sensual pleasure, and resumed his story, all the while smiling at me as though I were the class dunce.

"The Biopreparat was the Soviet biological warfare program," he said.

"Where you said you worked," I said, trying to keep the skepticism out of my voice.

"Where I did work, my friend."

"The Soviet Union tanked years ago. Its biological warfare would have tanked right along with it."

"Don't be naïve."

"You mean its old programs were carried along in the post-Soviet era?"

"You must have been a Rhodes Scholar." He gave me a condescending little grin.

Agent Sassani must have picked up on my tone of voice because up to this point she had been relatively quiet, letting the man she had introduced as Dr. Vasily Kirilov tell his story. Now she placed a restraining hand on my forearm.

"You can believe Dr. Kirilov, Mr. Quinn. I have known him for many years. That is why he flew all the way here from New York to meet with us."

I blanked my face and got the conversation back on track.

"Okay," I said, "now tell us again about Vector."

Kirilov snuffed out his cigarette on the edge of the table, shook another from a boxed pack with weird writing the front and back and lit it with a cheap Bic lighter. He leaned back in his chair and blew a smoke ring toward the ceiling.

"Vector was located in Western Siberia. One of the dark places of the earth, I assure you."

"What went on there?"

"The actual experimentation with biological agents. It was the field office, you might say of the Biopreparat."

"And where was the Biopreparat."

"In Mosow."

"Why not keep it all under one roof?"

"Because Moscow was full of Western intelligence agents. The program was in direct violation of a half-dozen treaties banning biological weapons. It might have been outed at any time. Better put it in Siberia, where no self-respecting spy would dare to venture. No yummy embassy parties there, you know."

"That was the only reason?"

"Oh, heavens no. If some of the biological agents we were working with ever got out in the atmosphere, it would have made Chernobyl look mild. Might have even put some of our dear leaders in the crematorium somewhat prematurely, which might have been a good idea at that."

"What kind of biological agents?"

"The usual kind , you know."

"No, I don't know."

"Well, there was Ebola, anthrax, bubonic plague, Marburg, Lassa, Machupo."

Just hearing the names of these dread diseases, some of which I had heard of and some of which were completely new to me, made my skin itch.

"And what about smallpox?" Agent Sassani asked.

"Yes, smallpox," Kirilov answered. "The greatest scourge of them all. How many millions over the years has it claimed?"

"We don't know. Tell us," I said.

He shrugged, raising his eyes to the ceiling as though to clear his mind of his immediate surroundings. "Well, now let's see. The ancient Athenians had a smallpox outbreak during their war with Sparta. That's why they lost, you know. Alexander the Great and much of his army were victims. Ditto for the Roman Emperor Marcus Aurelius. Queen Elizabeth the First was stricken as a child. She survived, but the episode left her bald and horribly scarred. This was almost certainly the reason she remained the Virgin Queen. Then there were the unfortunate inhabitants of the New World when the Spanish arrived carrying the smallpox virus with them. Twenty million victims? Fifty? Who knows?"

"You worked with smallpox at this Vector place?" I asked.

"Yes, but not as a bio-chemist. I'm an engineer by training. I received my PhD in engineering."

"So how does an engineer fit into this picture?"

"To solve the problem of delivery."

"Delivery?"

He flicked ash on the floor. "Yes. You see it's not all that very hard to produce the base biological agents. Take smallpox, for instance. All you really need are chicken eggs and a way to control the temperature. The virus grows splendidly in chicken eggs. You can produce kilos of agent in this manner, even in a relatively primitive facility. But how do you disseminate the agent to the target population? This is the problem of delivery."

"And exactly what was the problem with delivery?" Agent Sassani asked. "I should think it would be straightforward. Just shoot it in a missile or something."

Kirilov nodded in her direction. "We started with standard munitions. We developed artillery shells that could be loaded with agent. We also developed aerial bombs that could be spiked the same way. But the obvious problem with these devices is that when they explode the heat and blast tend to damage the agent inside. This is not such a big concern with chemical agents, these are inert. But a biological agent? These are living organisms, you know. How to disseminate these? Yes, that was the problem of delivery."

"What about aerosol dispensers?" Agent Sassani asked.

"They can be effective, but they are entirely dependent upon wind currents, even air currents inside large venues. Effective, yes, but undependable. At best to be used with some other form of delivery."

"And did you solve the problem, sir" I asked.

"By the oldest known delivery system known to man: a human delivery system."

"You're kidding."

"Not at all. There is plenty of precedent for it. Your own George Washington would send individuals known to be infected with the smallpox virus to mingle with British troopers. A very effective ploy, I might add."

"That was then, this is now," I said. "We have laws against that type of crap, international treaties, too."

"So sue me, to coin a phrase."

I glared at the little ferret; he smiled sweetly back. Finally I took my eyes off him and studied the tips of my fingernails. I tried to control the familiar ball of red-black anger bubbling deep in my chest. Agent Sassani resumed the interrogation.

"How was the human delivery system supposed to work, Vasily?"

"Our view was that one infected person, positioned in the right place at the right time, could infect enough other persons to start a chain reaction, literally to 'go viral', and in short order transmit the virus to millions of others. Just a matter of weeks."

"What would be a 'right place', Vasily?"

"Some place with a big crowd, of course. At first we favored sporting events, particularly indoor ones. We know how you Americans love basketball, for instance, but we couldn't find any Russians willing to go to a basketball game. Giant black men are objects of contempt in Russia." He giggled, as if he had said something funny.

"So what did you conclude?" Agent Sassani asked.

"Some type of public transportation might work best, a plane or a train, a bus maybe, where passengers are in close proximity for some period of time, and where they might disperse to many parts of the target country upon arriving at destination."

I swallowed my anger for the time being and cut in. "Who

in the world would volunteer for that type of mission? That would be suicide from the get-go."

Kirilov gave out with his sickly sweet smile. "That was the rub of it. No one would raise his hand for that assignment, especially since we had developed a particularly nasty form of the smallpox virus we called the 'black pox'. Oh, we developed a vaccine to go along with it, but nobody was sure it was one hundred percent effective."

"What made this black pox so special?" I asked.

"The traditional smallpox virus, the garden variety you might say, causes high fever, dehydration, and the familiar outbreak of nasty looking pustules all over the body. It's the fever and dehydration that kills you. The pustules just leave you scarred for life. But sometimes the fever breaks and the victim survives."

"How often, 'sometimes'? I asked.

"Hard to predict, but the historical average mortality rate for smallpox is about sixty percent."

"And what about this 'black pox?"

"Well, let me say first that technical term for it is 'hemoragic' smallpox."

"Okay."

"This indicates that in addition to the traditional smallpox symptoms, the victim suffers severe loss of blood, usually through the anal cavity, although often there can be uncontrollable bleeding through the nose, throat and ears. For added suffering, the pustules are larger and more aggressive, sometimes growing together to form giant pustules all over the victim's body. It results in an ugly, bloody mess, I assure you."

"And you've seen this with your own eyes, have you?"

"Yes, of course."

"On whom?"

He smiled again, realizing the import of my question. He took another slow drag on his cigarette.

"On condemned felons who volunteered for a redemptive act on behalf of Mother Russia."

"I bet."

"And what is the mortality rate for this form of smallpox, Vasily?" Agent Sassani asked.

He shrugged as he spoke. "One hundred percent."

There was a moment of silence in the room as Agent Sassani and I gathered our thoughts. Kirilov lit another cigarette and ran half-hooded eyes over Agent Sassani's face. She was making notes on her yellow pad and did not appear to be aware of the rude appraisal of her person. I noticed again that the fingers of her left hand drummed lightly on the tabletop as she wrote with her right, as though she were keeping time with her own thoughts. "Okay, bud." I said. "You guys ever figure out how to use a so-called human delivery system?"

"Yes, of course. The solution was simple."

"So what was it?"

"Basically, use two people."

"Oh?"

"Yes, one we designated the 'control', the other the 'angel'."

With the word 'angel' Agent Sassani stopped writing, as though struck by a sudden jolt of electricity, and looked up. "Can you explain that, Vasily?"

"Yes. The control person, armed with a usable amount of the black pox agent, something we had learned to freeze dry by the way, would infiltrate the adversary country and select from the target population some individual to whom he would administer the agent unawares and then, when the person was infectious, place on a crowded vehicle, preferably one with a large number of passengers. We called this infected individual the 'angel'. And even though the average incubation period for the black pox is only 72 hours, the control could infect the angel, place him or her on a bus, and still flee the target country before the outbreak."

"Why call this person an 'angel'?" I said.

"After the 'Angel of Death' in *The Book of Exodus*. Charming, no?"

"Oh, sure," I answered. I felt the red-black balloon in my chest rise a little higher. It must have shown in my face because I again felt Agent Sassani's restraining hand on my forearm.

"If you and your people were considering pulling this stunt in the United States," I said, "you had another thing coming. We are all vaccinated against smallpox when we register for first grade."

"You are sadly mistaken, my friend," he replied. "The United States stopped vaccinations against smallpox over fifty years ago. Any vaccinations given then have probably worn off. And for those who have never been vaccinated, they are completely at risk."

"That would be children, right, bud?"

"Yes, that is right," he answered. Then he added icily, "bud."

Agent Sassani stepped in again. "I remember right after 9/11 there was a lot of talk about US vulnerability to a smallpox attack. Didn't the government contract for a large supply of vaccine?"

"That is right, my dear. But would it be effective against the black pox? Doubtful. Besides, it is one thing to manufacture a large quantity of vaccine, it is quite another thing to distribute it in timely fashion. Remember Hurricane Katrina? How long did it take the government to get medical and other aid to the victims? Do not bet on your government, my friends."

I knew something about betting, and about the government, and on this point I knew he was right. I kept quiet. Agent Sassani went on.

"Vasily," she said, "do you remember the story you told us back when we were debriefing you about the man with the scarred face?"

"Of course. Quite a story wasn't it? It was the only thing that ever seemed to frighten you."

"Vasily, did this man with the scarred face have anything to do with this human means of delivery you've been describing?"

He gave her a long and studious look. "How did you guess?" he said finally.

She made a slight shrugging motion with her shoulders. "I have . . . other information. Now tell us about this man, Vasily."

Kirilov leaned back in his chair again, blew a smoke ring toward the ceiling, and spoke without looking at us. "About fifteen years ago we had a new arrival at Vector. You have to understand, Vector was a closed community. Everybody knew everybody. We all had advanced degrees in medicine, or biology, or related sciences. And the security was very tight. Only Russians were allowed to work there, no Europeans or Asians." He paused.

"Yes, go on," she said.

"So one day a new man was introduced into our little world. It was a mystery to us at first. He was neither a scientist nor an engineer, nor a Russian for that matter." He paused and blew another smoke ring.

"What was he?" I asked.

He glanced briefly at Agent Sassani. "An Iranian," he said.

"How did he crash the party?" I asked.

"He had special qualifications."

"Oh?"

"Yes, he was the only person we ever knew of to have survived a bout with the black pox. Oh, it left him hideously scarred-up, and maybe not just a little insane, but he had survived. It was either a freak of nature or an act of God, take your pick."

"This guy have a name?"

"Yes, but I forget it. I remember, though, he rather modestly began referring to himself as Malaku. That's the name of the Angel of Death in the Quran, you know."

"Why did he do that?"

"Because since he had miraculously survived the black pox, he felt chosen by God to bring death to the infidels on behalf of Islam."

"How did he get infected in the first place?"

Kirilov snuffed out the butt of his cigarette on the table top and lit another. "He was an Iranian army officer. His special warfare unit was detailed to launch a biological attack on a Sunni village in eastern Iraq. Iranian's are mostly Shi'ite, you know, and Shi'ites feel as though there is a year-round open season on Sunnis."

"I know more than you think about Muslims, sir," I said. "Tell us what happened."

"Well, the attack was a success. Everybody in this village of about two hundred was infected and eventually succumbed. But this was an attack launched with wind-aided aerosol devices. There was blow-back on the Iranian unit, and they were all infected, too. Only this Malaku fellow survived."

"Where the hell did these Iranians get the biological agent?"

"From us, of course. Then, as now, we Russians considered ourselves the patrons, if you will, of Iranian technology. Look how much support we have been giving to the Iranian nuclear effort."

"But why would you give a dangerous biological agent to them?"

"Call it field testing."

"Two hundred civilians died, sir."

"You have to break a few eggs to make an omelet."

"I never saw anything reported about this."

"This took place in a very remote village, up in the mountains. It was as primitive and hidden as any place in the world, basically beyond the pale of civilization. The people who lived there were little more than animals. Who would know? Who would care?"

I felt Agent Sassani's hand on my forearm again, but it was getting harder to choke down that red-black balloon.

"Vasily," Agent Sassani said, "weren't you concerned the Iranians would acquire the formula for the agent?"

"No. The agent was pre-sealed in the aerosol dispensers. And our advisers with their unit kept close tabs on the canisters."

"Any of your guys caught in the blow-back?" I asked.

"Yes, but they were properly protected in a sealed observation car,"

"Too bad."

I lowered my eyes and concentrated on an invisible spot halfway between me and the mad scientist on the other side of the table. I had had just about enough.

"Tell us now, Vasily," Agent Sassani said, "how did this Iranian soldier get to Vector?"

"It was simple, enough. Our ground observers observed his progress through the stages of the disease and realized right away that if he survived he would be the perfect control agent in a human delivery system."

"Why?"

"Because once you've been infected with the virus and you survive, you're immune for life. This soldier could handle vast quantities of the agent every day, even manufacture it in primitive conditions, and never become re-infected."

"And just what would it take to manufacture it?"

"Not much, really. A seed amount of the agent, fertilized chicken eggs, an incubator, a low-speed centrifuge to harvest the product, a refrigerator for storage, and of course a test subject."

"A test subject?" I asked without looking up.

"Yes, of course, someone to test it on."

"Of course."

Agent Sassani went on. "So your field agents just brought this fellow back to Vector and started training him as a control agent?"

"Not exactly. First he was vetted by the security forces, for over a year, I recall. He checked out okay, and what's more they found he had an intense hatred for America and all things American. That made him especially desirable to us, of course, because you can well imagine who our principal target population was."

"What did you do with this fellow, Vasily?"

"Well, my dear, we did our best to train him for the mission, how to handle and manufacture the bio-agent and so forth. We hoped of course we would never have to launch such a terrible undertaking, but our intelligence attaché schooled him just the same in basic espionage techniques such as covert immigration, assumption of false identities, blackmail, extortion, creation of diversions, even seduction. At first he did well, but problems developed."

"What kind of problems?"

"I suppose what you might call psychological problems."

"Did it ever occur to you," I chimed in, "that all of you were crazy to be involved in crap like that?"

Kirilov ignored me, but Agent Sassani had squeezed my forearm just in case. "What do you mean 'psychological problems', Vasily?"

He smiled at her. "Well," Kirilov said, "this fellow was very taken with himself. Oh, he was extremely intelligent, don't get me wrong, but he just went off on this Malaku thing."

"What do you mean?"

"He began to act out, wear robes and sandals like a regular whirling dervish. Yes, and he grew a beard, too, and started carrying a dagger. He even had made this sort of elaborate, scrolled battle ax in the style of those carried by Saladin's hordes. It was a frightful looking thing with a curved blade and a spike on the end, like a pike, but shorter and handier. He made a study of fighting with the damn thing, and eventually became quite expert with it. He scared the hell out of everybody, let me tell you."

"Anything else?"

Kirilov cleared his throat.

"Yes, this madman was ferociously strong, and he had a ferocious sexual appetite to go with it. He felt entitled to any woman he wanted,"

"Why was that, Vasily?"

"I suppose because he thought he was God's special agent."

"There were women around this place?" I asked.

"Of course: wives, lab technicians, even some scientists."

"He hit on them?"

"Yes, and very forcefully, to put it politely."

"Put it impolitely, so we're all on the same page."

"All right, my friend. He raped them."

"How many?"

"At least three we knew of."

"You let him get away with it?"

"He was a very valuable asset."

"What about the women? Weren't they valuable assets, too?"

"Yes, but none of them had survived the black pox. So we tried to civilize this fellow, even eliminate his odor."

"His odor?"

"Yes, the infection had done something to his apocrine sweat glands. These are the glands that produce body odor, you know. During intercourse the gland is stimulated. In his case, the stimulation was hypoactive and the result was an awful stink. His female victims complained about that as much as the assault itself."

"Was the treatment successful?"

"No, in fact his condition became worse. Everyone began referring to him as 'that stinking devil.' Behind his back, of course."

"What happened to this guy?" I asked.

He shrugged. "Eventually we had to get rid of him."

"What did you do, have him snuffed?"

"We preferred to say we had him reassigned."

"Reassigned? Where?"

Kirilov chuckled. "To eternity."

I shook my head, leaned back in my chair, and closed my eyes. My head throbbed, as though I was wearing a shirt with a too-tight collar. I wanted out of that closed, smoke-filled, nasty little room and away from that nasty little man. But there was more to come.

"Vasily," Agent Sassani asked, "is it possible this man is still alive somewhere?"

Kirilov roared with laughter. "No possible way, my dear. I assure you, he is very, very dead."

"Did you actually see him killed?"

"Of course not. That was done by the security section. They didn't invite witnesses to those occasions."

There was a brief interlude, a sudden silence. I opened my eyes and watched as Agent Sassani reached into her wood bead bag and removed a large manila envelope. She slid out an 8X11 glossy and showed it to me. It was the surveillance photo of the man coming out of the Blue Parrot.

"Have you seen this man, Mr. Quinn?"

"Yes."

"Where?"

"On a boat deck in Galveston."

"When?"

"A couple of nights ago."

"Was he alive?"

"Yes."

She slid the photo across the table to Kirilov. "Is this the man who called himself Malaku you knew at Vector?"

Kirilov took a casual drag off his cigarette, exhaled with self-assured sensual pleasure, and smiled. The smile vanished in a flash when he saw the 8X11. "I don't believe it!"

"Believe it, bud," I said.

He shook his head and rubbed his eyes. "It cannot be!"

"But it most certainly *is,*" Agent Sassani said. "Is this the man, sir?" For the first time her tone of voice sounded less than friendly, prosecutorial even.

"Yes, yes, that is him. Older now for sure, but that is the man. Look at those facial scars! Where did you take this?"

"That is not important, Vasily. Now, I have one more question."

"Yes, of course," he said, the composure gone from his voice now."

"When this man left Vector is it possible he took a sample of the smallpox virus with him, freeze dried or something?"

"No! No! Absolutely impossible!"

"Just like it was impossible for him to still be alive?" I asked.

After the interview we escorted Kirilov to the gate for his flight back to New York, passing through security checkpoints like visiting royalty on the strength of Agent Sassani's FBI credentials. He had been visibly shaken when we left the conference room. Our good-byes had been brief and formal. I was glad to be rid of him. Now Agent Sassani and I were walking back across the terminal to the garage where we had left her beat-up Crown Victoria parked.

"Remind me," I said, "what does Najwa's husband do at the cancer hospital?"

"He is in the procurement section."

"Procuring what."

"Equipment, I believe."

"Such as incubators and low-speed centrifuges?"

"Yes. This is surely what Malaku wanted from him. How Fasil came under his influence I have yet to find out."

"Try money," I said. "It's the universal influencer."

"I will look into it."

"Does it sound to you that Malaku is off somewhere manufacturing this black pox stuff?"

"I'm afraid it does, Mr. Quinn."

"Have you talked to Fasil?"

"No, Mr. Quinn. He has disappeared."

We walked on, not talking, each of us plumbing our own thoughts.

"So what's next?" I asked after a while.

"I must talk to your friend, Teal DeLong. Now that you have heard Dr. Kirilov's story and you see what's involved here, will you introduce me to her and persuade her to cooperate with me? She is in the grip of a very dangerous man. Will you help me help her?"

"I'll do what I can."

We drove directly over to the Delong mansion after leaving the airport. Neither of us spoke until we were almost there. Agent Sassani broke the ice.

"Mr. Quinn, I will give you the option of foregoing this particular chore. I have been thinking. Perhaps it will cause you trouble. You might lose your job with Senator DeLong. You said so yourself. I was too hasty last night to insist you come along."

"Thanks," I said, "but I better stick with you on this. You may have trouble even getting into the house to see Teal. I can probably talk you in."

"I appreciate your assistance," she answered, then added, "but just the same I think it may cause you trouble later."

"No prob," I said, but I silently wished I was wearing a flak jacket. "Anyway," I added, "I should be thanking you for giving me an alibi for the night Soos' was taken out. Sooner or later that'll catch up to you. Why did you do it?"

She shrugged as she wheeled around a stalled eighteen-wheeler. "As I explained before, I do not think you are a murderer, sir; a killer perhaps, given your military background. There is a difference. And as you can understand from our interview with Kirilov this morning, we have very little time to spare here. Something very bad is about to happen. I sensed that even before I saw Robin's diary, starting with the time I saw this so-called Malaku come out of the Blue Parrot. I knew I had seen that face before. That night I remembered I had seen in it connection with our investigation of the attempted assassination of the Saudi Ambassador. I was stationed in Washington then. And I mentally connected that to the story I had heard from Kirilov when we debriefed him. When I showed the surveillance shot to Najwa and heard her story and how this man had been addressed by Fasil as Malaku, I knew who we were dealing with."

"That's pretty good detective work."

"So if I don't intervene in that situation back at your ranch, I lose a lot of precious time. You get arrested, you get a lawyer. The lawyer tells you not to talk, so you keep existence of Robin's diary to yourself. You know how it works. So, I take a little short cut. Now I have the diary. I know what this is all about. It is about a biological attack with smallpox. I will stop it. How, I just don't know yet. But I will stop it."

"I hope so, ma'am," I said, "but I still think somebody's going to use your little short cut against you."

"So be it. The important thing is to stop this maniac."

We didn't talk the rest of the way.

A hefty black house maid named Bernice answered the door at the DeLong house. She had worked for the senator since he was first elected to public office and was a virtual member of the family. Her hair was peppered with gray but she claimed she could still hit a softball over the centerfield fence. She could, too; I saw her do it once. She told us that Teal wasn't there.

"Her car is here," I said, pointing to the white BMW in the circular drive.

"Miss Teal done left with some friends 'bout an hour ago, Mr. Jeff." There was conviction in her voice but her eyes avoided mine.

"Bernice," I said, "I would never accuse you of lying, but in this case I think you're being a little weak on telling the truth. Please go tell Teal we want to see her. Don't make us come back with a warrant," I said, remembering the cheesy line the deputy had used on my front porch what seemed like a long time ago.

She hesitated, pursing her lips, shaking her head. Finally, she said, "Ya'll come on in. I'll go tell Miss Teal get her raggedy ass down here."

We waited in a front room somewhat over furnished with Oriental antiques. A large woodblock print of a tiger adorned one wall. It looked ready to devour the closest two-legged meal it could find, but it seemed tame by comparison when Teal marched into the room, eyes blazing. She didn't ask us to sit.

"What do you want?" she demanded.

"This is Special Agent Parvin Sassani of the FBI," I said. "She would like to talk to you."

"Oh, is that so? About what?"

"About what we talked about the other night."

"You're a piece of work, Jeff. I blow you off and you call in the FBI."

"This isn't about me."

"Then who's it about?"

"It's about you."

"Oh, fuck off." She turned her head and ran her eyes up and down Agent Sassani. "And take this raghead meter maid with you."

Agent Sassani took the blow without a flinch. She spoke in a soft tone of voice. "We're here to help you, Ms. DeLong. Do not be angry."

"Don't tell me what to do," Teal said. "And what makes you think I need your help?"

"We believe that you are being used by a very dangerous man."

"And who would that be?"

"The man calling himself Malaku. I think you know that this is the man that had you abducted some years ago in Africa. I think he has a hold on you of some kind. Perhaps something you confided to him under duress while you were in captivity."

"You don't know shit, lady."

Agent Sassani kept boring in, even moving a half-step closer to Teal. "This man intends to use you to do something terrible, something that could result in your death and the deaths of untold others"

"Use me as what, frog face?"

"As his *peri abele*."

"His what?"

"That is Persian. It means a certain kind of angel."

"Oh, just what kind?"

"I cannot tell you at this moment. It is a confidential part of my investigation at this time."

"I see. You threaten your way in here, tell me I'm in some kind of danger. Then you play hide-and-seek with what it's all about."

"You will have to trust us, Ms. DeLong."

"I wouldn't trust you with my dog's poop."

Teal turned back to me. "Is this the woman who said you were with her the night you killed Soos. Crowley told me what she said."

"I didn't kill Soos."

"That's not the way I heard it.'

"You heard wrong."

She clucked her tongue and cocked her hands on her hips. "And by the way, have you seen my brother? No one's seen Travis since that night you butchered his bud."

"Haven't seen him," I said, "and I didn't kill Soos."

"I think you have. I think you took Travis somewhere and murdered him after you murdered Soos. Did you butcher him, too?"

"Teal," I said softly, "that's enough."

"It's damn well true and you know it. You killed Soos and you killed my brother and now you come here with this poor excuse for an FBI agent and tell me I'm about to be killed, too. Get Out! Just get out, before I call a real cop. And by the way, Jeff, too bad you turned out to be such a coward. If you had manned-up the other night, we wouldn't even be having this discussion. Good-fucking-bye!"

And that was that.

Agent Sassani offered to drive me out to my ranch. I accepted because I needed a shower, fresh clothes untainted by Turkish cigarette smoke, and a long walk out in the country. More than anything, I needed to be alone. She didn't say anything else until we were almost out of the city.

"That young woman needs help," she said.

"What she needs is a spanking," I answered.

We never made it to my ranch. We had just passed the Houston city limits when Agent Sassani received a call on her cell phone. She talked softly but I could make out words such as "when" and "where" and "we'll meet you." She turned to me.

"Do you remember that young state trooper that was on duty at the crime scene at your ranch?" she asked.

"You mean Hector Gonzales? Sure. Why?"

"He thinks he's found Travis DeLong."

"Where?"

"By a cabin on Lake Conroe."

"What do you mean 'by'?"

"He is lying dead next to it."

Lake Conroe is in Montgomery County only about thirty miles due north of downtown Houston, but it took us the better part of an hour to drive there from where we were. Houston is an economic boom-town and as a result the traffic is clogged day and night. I didn't mind the delay; I dreaded what we were going to find.

The cabin was on the north shore in a secluded, pine shaded, upscale resort development. I knew it well: it was owned by the DeLong family. I had spent the night there once on a DeLong family outing. There was nothing secluded or romantic about it now. Montgomery County sheriff's cruisers practically formed a corral around the property. Deputies had strung yellow crime scene tape from tree to tree on the periphery and from several improvised posts impaled in the loamy sand on the waterfront side of the lot. Fly-clusters of curious neighbors loitered just outside the tape, craning their necks at the scene around the cabin. Rubberneckers in fishing boats and ski boats hugged the shoreline. It isn't every day that a corpse turns up in a neighborhood like that.

We parked along the private roadway. Even though it was an exceptionally warm day, Agent Sassani opened the trunk of her car and pulled out the same navy blue nylon jacket with the letters FBI emblazoned on its back in giant white letters. She tugged it on and started toward the cabin. She motioned for me to follow.

The deputy guarding the driveway entrance didn't give us any trouble, but he did give Agent Sassani the usual sideways glance. He ignored me.

Most of the lawmen were standing in a semi-circle around an elongated dirt pile about five yards from the east side of the cabin. They were all uniformed Montgomery County deputies, except for one Hispanic male in starched and creased jeans, a starched white dress shirt, ostrich leather boots, and a white straw western hat. When we got closer I recognized Trooper Gonzales.

"What's going on, Trooper," I asked as we stepped up to the group.

He turned and placed his hands on his hips and gave us a silent once-over. He raised one eyebrow, but that was all. He nodded in the direction of the dirt pile.

The dirt came from a shallow grave about six feet in length and about three feet deep. A corpse lay in the grave. It looked as though it had been there a long time. The skin that remained was stretched tight against the bone, the eyes eaten out by worms. Its dark hair was matted with mud. The sweetly sick smell of death that every combat veteran has imbedded in his darkest memories hung in the air.

"This your boy Travis DeLong?" he asked me. "There's no ID on the stiff."

I looked closer at the remains. "Nope. Travis was a blonde." I felt sorry for the dead man, but I felt relieved for myself. This wasn't going to be my bounce after all.

"Know who it is?"

Agent Sassani spoke up. "It is Fasil."

"Najwa's husband?" I asked.

"Yes."

Trooper Gonzlaez raised his hat with one hand and ran his fingers through his thick black hair with the other. "Who is Fasil?"

"May we talk in private, Trooper?" Agent Sassani asked.

That might have been a law enforcement faux pas if the other lawmen had heard her say that, but they didn't. Right at that time the county meat wagon was ushered onto the scene and the deputies were arguing among themselves about who had to help load the body onto the gurney. The three of us stepped over about ten yards to the shade of an ancient pine tree.

"Okay, who is Fasil?" Trooper Gonzalez asked again.

"Fasil is the husband of a woman who is a witness in a federal investigation," Agent Sassani said.

"Is that all you can tell me?"

"That is all I can say."

"You can't tell me why he might be stretching out dead on Senator DeLong's lawn?"

"Not without potentially compromising my investigation."

He carefully positioned his hat back on his head and chewed lightly on his lip. He narrowed his eyes slightly when he spoke again. "This the same investigation you cited when we found that headless guy the other day at Mr. Quinn's ranch?"

"Yes."

"That why you have Mr. Quinn with you now?"

"Yes."

He lowered his eyes and watched the tip of his boot make a little circle in the dirt. He spoke without looking up. "You're making it awfully hard on me, ma'am, if you don't mind me saying so. I don't think Mr. Quinn here is a killer, but there's folks who don't see it the same way. They'll make trouble for him and you if they can. Trouble for me, too."

"Yes, I know," she said. She stepped closer to Gonzalez and placed her hand on his arm. "Look at me, young man."

He raised his eyes.

"This is a matter that involves thousands, maybe millions of lives," she said softly. "If word gets out prematurely, even by accident, the man we're looking for may do something terrible before we can capture him, and all these lives may be lost. I have to ask you to trust me on this."

Gonzalez blinked once or twice and he frowned, but he eventually nodded his head. "All right, ma'am, have it your way. Is there anything I can do?"

She squeezed his arm slightly. "Yes, keep looking for Travis DeLong. Let me know when you find him. Now will you excuse me?"

Agent Sassani stepped over to the crowd of deputies to officially identify the corpse. Gonzalez and I kept talking.

"Do you mind if a call you Hector?" I masked.

"Go ahead, boss."

"How did you happen to be here, Hector?" I asked. "This is a little off your regular beat, isn't it?"

"A little, Mr. Quinn. But you said yourself that if I helped Ranger Crowley find Travis he'd take all the credit."

"So?"

"So I took some personal time to look for him myself. My supervisor knows all about it. Ranger Crowley doesn't have many friends in the Department of Public Safety."

"I believe that. How did you find the cabin?"

"I saw a picture of it on Travis' Facebook page. He had a big-ass fiesta out here at Easter with lots of hot *chiquitas*. I guess he couldn't resist showing them off on the internet. He posted that the cabin was on Lake Conroe. The rest was easy."

"How did you find the grave?"

"That was easy, too. I was in the Marines over in Afghanistan. I know a grave when I smell one."

"Good man, Hector," I said. "You'll make Texas Ranger someday."

"Maybe, boss, maybe. *Vamos a ver*. We'll see."

Agent Sassani came back to join us. "Mr. Quinn, I know I offered to take you out to your ranch, but I feel I must go directly to the safe house and tell Najwa about her husband. Perhaps Trooper Gonzalez can take you home."

I shook my head. "No, Hector needs to finish this business here. Besides, he doesn't need to be seen doing me favors. I'll go with you. You can drop me off at Mickey's after we've seen Najwa."

"You would like to see her? Why."

"To convey my condolences and—I don't know—make up for my being rude to her the other day. It's been on my mind."

"Very good, Mr. Quinn."

Hector clasped a hand on my shoulder. "Good luck, boss."

"Thanks."

I didn't know how much I was going to need some good luck.

It was another hour's crawl through traffic to get to the safe house. The late afternoon sun was like a steam iron on the side of my face. The Crown Vic's air conditioner was low on Freon, so it only made it worse when I turned up the dash fan.

"I should think the government could spot you a better car," I said.

"They could," she said, "but I like this one."

"Like the color, huh?"

"No, I like it because it's old and beat up. If I wreck it, nobody cares. I am not a good driver. I only learned to drive when I was twenty. It does not come naturally to me. I prefer to ride horses. At that I *am* a natural."

Images of my dead wife astride Sergeant Pepper flooded my mind and my thoughts drifted back to happier times. After a few seconds I snapped out of it and got back to the precarious present.

"How did that come about? A horse woman—that's about the last thing I would have figured you for."

"My father was a great horseman. In fact, he commanded the last company of cavalry in the Iranian army. He began teaching me to ride before I could even walk. I was a bit of a tomboy, I am afraid."

"He teach you about horse diseases, too?"

"Yes, why do you ask?"

"Derwood told me you could tell our rescue horse has laminitis just by feeling the top of its hooves."

"In those days in Iran we didn't always have up-to-date veterinary diagnostic equipment, like x-ray machines, so we had to rely on a great deal of traditional methods. Horses have been raised and bred in Persia—that's the ancient word for Iran—for thousands of years."

"You were close to your father, weren't you?"

"Yes, very, and even closer with my mother."

"What happened to them?"

"It's a long story."

"I'd like to hear it."

"Someday, perhaps."

The traffic thickened up after that and we didn't talk any more. I concentrated on my apology to Najwa. I wanted to be smooth but I didn't want to come across smarmy. Agent Sassani must have read my mind.

"Mr. Quinn, Najwa will appreciate whatever you have to say. She is not used to men showing kindness to her. Yes, she will appreciate it very much."

"Roger," I said, and turned back to my thoughts, which alternated among the words I wanted to say to Najwa, memories of my wife, and imaginings of this very unusual woman next to me riding some exotic Middle-Eastern horse. It was an absorbing mix. That's why I didn't see the smoke right off.

It came to my attention when Agent Sassani off-handedly said, "Some poor family will be homeless tonight."

I looked up. "How come?"

She nodded her head in the direction of a brown-black cloud of smoke in a residential area about a half-mile away. "That smoke over there. It's from a house fire, don't you think?"

I studied the gray-black whisps. "Probably. Industrial fires usually give off a green-black smoke. That looks gray-black, like smoke from a campfire."

"You know, Mr. Quinn, that smoke looks pretty close to where we're going."

"How close?"

She didn't answer. It was as though an alarm had gone off in her head. She floored the accelerator. I was wearing a seat belt, but still I had to brace myself against the dash as she tore down the streets and squealed on two wheels around corners.

It *was* the safe house. She skidded to a stop at the curb and we both jumped out. A small crowd of Middle-Eastern looking women in various stages of undress were frantically stomping around in the yard, crying and pulling at their hair. A few were hugging each other hysterically. Agent Sassani went from one woman to another, "Where's Najwa? Where's Najwa?" No one knew. Just then a woman's scream came from inside the house.

"Has anyone called the fire department?" Agent Sassani screamed.

One of the women said "yes." And indeed someone had because I could hear fire truck sirens closing in. By now curious neighbors had come out and were shuffling toward the scene as though drawn by magnets. The truck sirens had alerted little boys on bicycles that something big was happening; they were ripping down the street in squadrons of two's and three's.

I tried to gauge how far away the trucks were, a few blocks maybe. I thought at first they might get there in time. Although the inside of the house was lit with an ominous red glow, so far I had seen only smoke on the outside. That changed suddenly when a thick tongue of flame rocketed through a side window in a whoosh, scattering window glass like shrapnel and spooking the crowd back across the street. Now the smoke was curling out in thick black curds. The fire trucks weren't going to make it in time. I grabbed Agent Sassani by the arm and shouted, "I'm going in after her."

"No, it is too dangerous."

"No time to argue. I'm going in."

She raised her eyes and held them on mine. She nodded. "Here, take this for the smoke." She took the black scarf that had once been my blindfold out of her purse, stepped around behind me, and tied it around my face up to my eyes. When she was finished tying it off, she spun me gently around and took my hands in hers and squeezed them strongly. "Be careful," she said. I nodded and charged toward the front door, which by now was framed in a ring of fire. That's all I remembered.

Chapter Twelve

I am in scuba gear, going hand-over-hand down an anchor rope, the water getting colder in layers, the sunlight from above the surface ever more diffuse. Fish and water creatures of every kind swim up to my mask, peer into my eyes, and finding nothing of interest, swim on. I breathe deeply from my air tank. Cool air, rich with oxygen, fills my lungs. I want to follow that rope deeper and deeper, where the water is even colder, the light even softer. I breathe deeply again and feel the rush of oxygen into my blood. Then there is a gentle shaking.

I wake to see not the eyes of some exotic fish peering at me, but those of Mickey Simski, although they did have a certain fishy aspect behind his thick horned rim glasses. His nose was about three inches from something strapped around my face.

"Mick, do you know that up close you look like a goggle-eyed perch?" I said.

"That's what Beth says, too. How you feeling, *jefé*?" he asked.

"How do I look?"

"Like one of those movie zombies fresh out of the grave."

"That's how I feel. Who shoveled all the dirt in my mouth?

"That's the aftertaste of all the smoke you inhaled."

"Remind me to quit smoking."

"It's from the fire, not those Cuban cancer sticks you light up when you think no one's looking."

"What fire?"

"At the safe house yesterday. Don't you remember?"

I hit the start button on my brain and looked around. I was in a hospital bed with an oxygen mask over my face, and coughing with every other breath. "Oh, yeah," I said between hacks, "how's the girl, what's-her-name?"

"Her name is Najwa, Jeffrey," a woman's voice said from somewhere outside my vision. "And she will be okay, we think. She's in a room down the hall." I knew the voice, but I couldn't place it.

"Where exactly am I?"

Mickey raised his face away. "Memorial Hospital."

I recoiled from the fiery images starting to register in my memory. "The burn unit?"

"No, but it might have been if you'd been in that goddamn house ten seconds longer. It went fireball just after you brought the girl out."

"I like dramatic finishes."

"Well, I hope you don't like the clothes you were wearing yesterday. There wasn't anything left but the stink. Beth buried them in the backyard this morning. All that's left are your boots and hat."

"That's all a cowboy needs these days, that and food. Mick, I'm hungry, and no hospital food."

"How about pizza?" Mick said. "There's a twenty-four hour fast delivery pizza joint just down the street. I'll write you a prescription. That way your insurance company can pick up the tab."

"You're a disgrace to the medical profession, Mick, but while you're at it write me a prescription for a gallon of Pepsi."

"Will do. When you're through chowing down I'll release you and drive you over to the house. Beth is already fluffing a pillow for you in the guest room."

"No way. You don't have to take me home with you. As soon as I get this mask off I'll call Derwood and have him bring me some fresh clothes. Then he can drive me out to the ranch."

I coughed twice.

Mickey shook his head. "I can't believe the State of Texas gave that tobacco chewing redneck a driver's license."

"They gave you one, didn't they?"

I heard the unseen woman laugh. I twisted off my oxygen mask to see Special Agent Sassani standing by a small couch and floor lamp next to the lone window. A black and gold headscarf was wrapped almost entirely around her face so that only her eyes showed. She lowered the scarf somewhat.

"How's what's-her-name?" I asked again, my memory still fuzzy.

"Najwa's fine, Jeffrey. She's down the hall."

"No burns?"

"Well, her hair is a little crisp, but she will be fine."

"Glad to hear it."

Agent Sassani turned to Mickey. "Dr. Simski, I must leave for the office now, but I would like to invite you and Mrs. Simski to my house for dinner Sunday evening. I feel I owe you so much for your hospitality the other night. It is a tradition in my native country to return hospitality as soon as possible. It is unlucky not to do so. My investigation is on hold for a day or two until I get some crime lab reports back, so there is this little window of time. I am not a bad cook, if you do not mind Persian cuisine."

Mickey looked at me. I shrugged and he looked back at Agent Sassani. "We'd be delighted, of course, but don't feel obligated. What about our smoke jumper here?"

"If he would like to come, yes," she said, looking away as if she was either unsure of her invitation to me, or unsure of my response to her.

"Sure, why not?" I said.

She turned her head back in my direction. "Then it is

agreed," she said. "I will text you later and give you my address. Goodbye."

She wrapped her scarf around her face again, walked across the room, opened the door and left without further comment. I looked up at Mickey.

"How long has she been here, Mick?"

"I don't know, *jefé*. She was here when I came in about ten minutes ago."

"What time is it now?"

"Just after eight in the morning."

"She must get up early."

At that moment the door opened and a nurse backed into my room pulling a wheel chair. At first I thought it was in connection with my discharge, but when she turned the chair around I saw it was holding a little girl, six or seven years old maybe, blond-haired and twinkle-eyed. She was wearing pink pajamas, a plaid house robe, and bunny ear slippers. A spray of multi-colored balloons was attached to her forearm by a ribbon.

"Excuse us," the nurse said, "Abigail is going home this morning and wants to say goodbye to the nice lady. Oh, the nice lady is gone!"

"What 'nice lady', nurse?" Mickey asked.

The nurse's face flushed. "Oh, Dr. Simski, I didn't know you were here. I'm sorry, we'll leave."

"No worries. What 'nice lady'?"

"Abbey, I mean Abigail, was our runaway angel last night. I went to her room about three this morning to update her chart, and shazaam! Her bed was empty. She wasn't in the bathroom, either. There was a general panic, I tell you. Everybody on the ward floor was looking for her."

"Where did you find her, nurse?"

"Right here in this room. She was curled up on that couch with a lady with a beautiful headscarf around her head. She was reading Abbey a story out of one of her story books. They looked like they were having a lot of fun."

"How did she come to be in here?"

"Abbey said she couldn't sleep, so she grabbed one of her story books and kept going into rooms until she found someone to read her a story."

"I see," Mickey said. "What happened next?"

"Well, we were a little uncertain about this woman until she showed us her FBI credentials. She asked us to let Abbey stay until she fell asleep. So we did. We put her back to bed about a half-hour later. Did we do wrong?"

"No, nurse," Mickey said. "You did fine."

The nurse turned her eyes to me. "I hope we didn't disturb you last night, sir."

"Nope, they don't call me Rip Van Winkle for nothing." I looked down at Abigail. "Did you like that lady who read you a story?"

"Yes, sir," Abigail said. "She was real nice. Is she real nice to you?"

"I don't know, she hasn't read me a story yet. I guess I'm not cute enough."

"Oh, no sir, you're very cute, Mr. Winkle."

We all laughed. The nurse wheeled the little girl out. Mickey phoned in my pizza order and my discharge instructions. Then I briefed him on the meeting with Kirilov at the airport the day before and the discovery of the dead Fasil out at the DeLong lake cabin.

"So what are the symptoms again of this hemorrhagic brand of smallpox those crazy Russians developed?" he asked.

"Super-high fever, pustules that grown so big they run together and look like one large blister, and severe bleeding out the tailpipe. Anyway, that's what I remember."

"This guy they found, he show any signs of pox?"

"Not that I saw. I'd say he died by severe shortening."

"Shortening?"

"He was holding his head in his hands like he had just taken it out of his sock drawer."

"Our friend Malaku at work again?"

"Not too many homicidal meltdowns have a decapitation MO, Mick."

"Why'd he take out this Fasil guy?"

"I don't know, but he may be trying to eliminate anyone who actually knows who he is. From what Najwa said when I first met her, her husband knew the guy. Fasil worked in the procurement section of the cancer hospital. I'm betting Malaku used him to get equipment like incubators and centrifuges to enable him to gin up a stew of this black pox crap. When he had the gear, he didn't need Fasil anymore. So he offs Fasil and gets a little hack and chop practice in while he's at it."

"Why bury him at the DeLong place?"

"I think he was sending a message to Teal: do what I say or you're next. He had to dump the body where the message would be sure to get through."

"I bet those hick cops up in Montgomery County had never seen anything like that."

"They were flipping coins to see which of them could start their summer vacations before the meat wagon showed up. Nobody wanted to help load it."

"Any idea where Travis is?"

"No, but a state trooper named Hector Gonzalez is out looking for him. He was one of the troopers out at my ranch the other day. Not a bad sort. Thinks for himself."

Mickey nodded thoughtfully. "Hmmmm. You know, the fire marshal found an incendiary device at the rear of that safe house. You think Malaku was going after Fasil's wife, too?"

"Why not? He'd want to be thorough. Snuff everybody who knows who he is."

"I thought safe house locations were secret."

"This guy was trained by the KGB or its successor. He'd know how to dig information like that out. The Muslim community in Houston is pretty tight. Lots of people probably know where the safe house is. All he'd have to do is ask around. Hell, it's probably on the internet. Everything else is."

The pizza came. Mickey sat on the side of the bed and we had a pizza breakfast together. Usually he's talkative at mealtime, but he had turned silent, his face and eyes empty of meaning. He finished eating and washed his hands in the sink.

But before he went out he came over to the bed and looked down at me.

"Sounds like that nice lady was your guardian angel all night, *jefé*."

"Sounds like it."

"She could have had the hospital police post a guard."

"She's probably the do-it-yourself type."

"It could be something else entirely."

"Like what?"

He arched an eyebrow into a question mark. "Jeffrey now, is it?"

"Knock it off, Mick."

I spent the next two days at the ranch putting back in order what the Malaku, Soos, and the cops had torn apart. I poured lye on the large, dark spot in the horse barn where Soos had exsanguinated. I let it dry then shoveled out the affected dirt. I did this three times. Horses have a keen sense of smell; in the desert they can smell water over a hundred miles away. I didn't want Sergeant Pepper to return home to the smell of death in her own living space.

In the cool of the mornings I did some serious roadwork: walking at first, then jogging three miles along the county road and back, sprinting the last quarter mile. It left me gasping for air, my lungs aching, my heart pounding against my rib cage. When I was finished running, I did as many sets of pushups and stomach crunches I could stand. I would have topped off my workouts with some old fashioned wood chopping, but the cops had taken my axe as evidence.

They had also taken the .30-06 out of my truck, my laptop, my hunting knife, even my rod and reel. Black graphite fingerprint powder had been dusted on every door, countertop, piece of furniture and windowsill. The floors, walls, and bedding had been sprayed with Luminol. No respect whatsoever had been given to my property or my person. It was like having been stripped searched and my cavities probed with a dirty finger.

I cleaned up the mess as best I could. That kept me busy.

On the second day Derwood brought me a take-out box of fried chicken and biscuits. We sat and ate on my back gallery.

"Wrap your mouth around these biscuits, Quinnie," he said. "They'd make grandpa chase grandma up the stairs with that friendly bulge in his overalls."

I winced at the thought but nevertheless chopped down on a biscuit he had plastered with butter and honey. "Pretty good," I said, "but let's nix the erotic imagery."

"The what?"

"Skip it. How's Sergeant Pepper?"

"Comin' right along. We're looking at October first for her to foal. Been thinking about names?"

"I've been pretty busy."

He looked up and past me out to the road. "I think maybe you're going to be a lot busier here in about half a minute," he said through a wad of chicken and biscuits in his open mouth, "if that's who I think it is."

I turned and looked out to the road. Senator DeLong's black Cadillac SUV was just turning into my gravel drive. I got up, took a deep breath, and walked out to wait for him by the horse lot fence. He ground the SUV to a halt in the gravel barely three feet from my boots, a cloud of white chalk dust following just behind. The senator opened the driver's door and jumped out. He got right in my face.

"What do you mean coming into my home with some rag-head cop and accusing my daughter of being involved in some kind of criminal plot?" His breath was heavy with alcohol, which I knew from experience wouldn't help his attitude. "In my house, goddamn it!"

"Nobody accused anybody of anything. And the woman is an FBI agent."

"Then what the hell were you doing there?"

"Senator, we think Teal is being used. Her life may even be in danger. We were there to try to help her."

"Help her, my ass. Bernice says you threatened to get a warrant, that's why she let you in. Who the hell tries to help someone with a warrant?"

"Listen, to me sir."

"No, you listen to me. You stay away from my daughter. You stay from my house. You stay away from my boat. You just stay the fuck away!"

No use. I changed the subject. "Have you seen Travis, sir?"

That was like pouring gasoline on the proverbial fire. His head all but exploded. "We're looking for him. Some sheriff's deputy in Conroe called and said they thought they found him in a grave near a cabin I own up there. It was some other guy. So far they've kept it out of the news. You know anything about that?"

"I know it wasn't Travis?"

"How do you know?"

"I was there. I saw the body. I saw the head, too. It wasn't pretty. And it wasn't Travis."

His eyes widened with amazement. "First, they find a headless guy right over there in your barn, and you show up. Then they find a headless guy at my cabin, and what-do-you-know, you show up again. You seeing a pattern here?"

"Not really." I kept my face flat.

"Well, I sure as hell do. You know, Quinn, I trusted you. I welcomed you into my home. I all but welcomed you into my family. You know what I'm going to do now?"

"What is that, sir?"

He stepped closer and jabbed his finger in my chest. "I'm going to break you, boy. I'm going to break you if it's the last thing I ever do." With that he wheeled and stormed back to his SUV. But he wasn't finished. He turned around, his face distorted with anger and hatred. "And I'm going to break that goddamn raghead FBI agent."

As he was driving away I saw a hawk swoop down in my neighbor's pasture, spear a field mouse with its claws, and lift the mouse away with a flap of its powerful wings.

Chapter Thirteen

Sunday night I picked up Mickey and Beth in my truck. Riding three abreast in the cab and cutting up, we drove over to the address in a middle-class section of Houston that Agent Sassani had texted me earlier that day. It was an unseasonably cool and dry evening and we were all in a good mood. Nobody said it, but I had had a close brush with death. We were all enjoying that rush of euphoria that comes with slipping from the grasp of the grim reaper. Underneath the euphoria, however, was the sobering knowledge that you only get to slip away so many times, and that I had used one of those times up. The plan was for us to have dinner at Agent Sassani's house, after which I would sleep over at Mickey and Beth's house and boogie back to the ranch in the morning. I had an overnight bag in the truck. Other than that, I didn't know what to expect.

Agent Sassani's house was in a modest but well-kept neighborhood west of downtown. All the houses had well-trimmed green yards, but her yard also had a flower bed of forget-me-nots and desert roses. They looked carefully tended.

She answered the door in a beige pants suit and a black headscarf hemmed with gold thread. There was a trace of lipstick, too, and a light dusting of makeup. She was wearing low heels, beige ones that matched her clothes. Her toenails were painted red. It was pretty conservative by almost any measure, but I wondered if this was crowding some invisible line for her. I fretted about whether to compliment her on her looks. I decided against it; I didn't want to step over wherever that line was. She smiled and welcomed us in.

"Please come in, all of you," she said. "And tonight please call me Parvin. No need to be formal here."

The interior of the house was like the exterior: neat, modest, well kept. The floors were polished hardwood, the walls a soft-white. A plush red Persian carpet hung on one wall as a tapestry, framed pictures of a man and woman hung on another. The man was in military uniform and seated on a horse. I took this to be Parvin's father. The woman had long, thick black hair, and was strikingly beautiful. She was seated at a piano in an evening gown. I took this to be her mother. Both photos had that strange, unreal tint of black-and-white prints that had had touches of color added after-the-fact in the photographer's studio. This gave them an air of antiquity.

The furniture was sparse. There were a couple of overstuffed corduroy chairs and lots of ottomans. The dominant piece, however, was a black lacquered baby grand piano in the center of the front room. Rafts of sheet music were stacked on top of it. I remembered Agent Sassani's habit of drumming the fingers of her left hand as she wrote with her right. Pianists often do that.

Beth saw the piano too. "Will you play something for us after dinner?" she asked as Parvin escorted us to the little dining room.

"Yes, of course. Do you like boogie woogie?"

We all laughed because we thought she was kidding.

Agent Sassani served up a fine dinner of veal kabob, rice, and several vegetables I didn't recognize. The place settings were of delicate china and polished silver. Tea was served out of a hand painted pot she said came from a remote region of Persia. Throughout she kept up a lively conversation, mostly asking Mickey, Beth and I about our childhoods and family lives. She never talked about herself. After we had finished the main course, she said gaily, "I know what Texans like for dessert." She went to the kitchen and came back with a tray loaded with coffee, a delicate Persian pastry she called *piroshki*, and a whole half gallon of vanilla ice cream. We ate it all.

Afterwards we went into the living room to hear her play the piano. She hadn't been kidding about boogie-woogie. She led off with a piece called "Errol's Boogie", a jazzed up boogie-woogie by the great jazz pianist, Errol Garner. Then she played Oscar Peterson's version of "Night Train." All of this was done from memory; the sheet music remained untouched on the top of the piano.

"Where did you learn to play?" Beth asked.

"My mother taught me."

"In Iran?"

"Yes, she taught music at the university there."

"Is she still teaching?"

For the first time that night Agent Sassani seemed less than forthcoming. She answered with a terse "no." It was clear this was a subject she didn't want to talk about. I shifted my gaze to the picture of the woman on the wall and wondered.

Her mood lightened again when she pounded out a version of the "Basin Street Blues", singing it, too, lowering her voice at least an octave in imitation of Louis Armstrong. It wasn't a very good imitation, but it didn't matter. She was having fun. We all were.

"I get the impression you like American jazz," I said to her.

"Yes. I get that from my mother. She loved that kind of music. She always wanted to go to New Orleans to hear it played. That's where jazz started, you know."

"She never got there?" I asked.

"No, I am afraid not."

"What about you?"

"I'm afraid I haven't either, but I've always wanted to go. What about you?"

"Many times. When you grow up in Houston, southern

Louisiana is like next door."

Yes, we were all having fun, but the fun didn't last.

Halfway through a rendition of "Stardust" Mickey's phone buzzed. He excused himself and trotted off into the kitchen to take the call. A few minutes later he joined us again, a look of concern clouding his face. The music stopped.

"Jeff, you remember telling me at the hospital about the symptoms associated with this smallpox variety they cooked up over in Russia? You know, the super-sized pustules and everything?"

"Sure."

"Well, after you were released I put out an alert on a physicians-only blog for anyone presenting with those symptoms."

"Okay."

"Well, I just got a call from a doctor in Gun Barrel City up near Dallas."

"And?"

"He says some guy was brought into his clinic this morning who's developing those symptoms, and fast. He doesn't give him long, a day or two at the most."

"Does he know who the guy is?"

"He says his wallet contains a driver's license."

"Who does it say?"

"Travis DeLong."

"Is he positive in the identification?"

"He says the guy is too disfigured to tell just from the driver's license picture."

I turned to Agent Sassani. "You want me to go with you? I can identify Travis no matter how disfigured he is."

"Yes, please."

That ended the party. We determined that Mickey and Beth would take my truck back to their house. Since I had brought an overnight bag, I could stay at Agent Sassani's in a spare bedroom so we could leave together early next day for the four hour drive up to Gun Barrel City. But I thought we'd better get someone on the scene fast. I asked Agent Sassani if she had her cell phone handy.

"Do you have Hector Gonzalez's phone number in there?" I asked.

"Yes, ever since the day out at your ranch."

"Why not call him and see if he can get up there right now. He's been using his own time to look for Travis. He's never said so, but I think he's trying for Texas Ranger. It'll be a feather in his cap if he's first on the scene. Why not give him a break?"

"Yes, of course. I'll call him."

Mickey and Beth left in my truck. I sat down in an overstuffed chair as Agent Sassani made her call. A few minutes later she sat back down on the piano bench, her back to the keys. She folded her hands in her lap and focused her eyes on some invisible spot on the floor.

"Is that a picture of your mother on the wall, Agent Sassani?" I asked.

"Please call me Parvin, Jeffrey."

"Okay, Parvin, is that a picture of your mom?"

She raised her eyes to mine. "Yes, my mother Sharzad."

"Your mom was very beautiful, if you don't mind me saying so. And you resemble her greatly."

She turned her head and studied the picture as though seeing it for the first time. She turned back to me. "Yes, she was very beautiful. Me? I don't know."

"Were you close to her?"

"Yes, very. She was a concert pianist and a professor of music at the university in Tehran. I loved to hear her play. When I was young I would lay beneath her piano bench like a puppy. I liked watching her feet work the pedals, like she was stamping out a fire. I thought that was the funniest thing I ever saw."

"When did you start learning to play?"

"At age six. My mother was my instructor. I was something of a prodigy, I have to admit. After every practice session she would hold me in her arms and tell me how proud she was to have such a daughter."

I smiled, biting my lower lip, shaking my head almost imperceptibly at the thought of this exotic woman as a child at the piano, practicing her scales like little girls everywhere.

"What happened to your mom, Parvin?"

"She died."

"I'm sorry. How did it happen?"

"Are you sure you want to know? It is a very sad story."

"Yes, I want to know."

She turned to the piano and began to play a slow and haunting classical piece, the first she had played that evening. "This is Chopin's Nocturne in E minor. Very beautiful, no? He was only seventeen when he wrote it. I was only seventeen when they came and took my mother. Every time I play it I think of her."

"They who?"

She stopped playing. "The guardians of the so-called revolution. The Islamic Revolution in Iran."

"But why?"

"They said because this music corrupted the young."

"Chopin?"

"Yes, and Debussy, and Granada, and Beethoven. All the music she loved to teach at the university. Some clerics even said the piano itself was a forbidden instrument. They warned her to stop teaching this music, but she defied them and continued on."

"Why in the world would they want her to stop? What harm could the music do?"

"Jeffrey, the regime in Iran is a tyranny. It is not love of God that motivates them, but love of power. They may talk about God, but it is power they lust after. For those in power the freedom of the individual to think is the ultimate danger. Sooner or later, if enough people are left free to think for themselves, their power will be challenged, maybe even taken from them. So the individual must not be left free to think."

"I never thought of music as thinking."

"Perhaps it isn't exactly, but it allows people under a tyrannical regime to sense that there are other ways of looking at life and celebrating it in music. Such a sense might indeed cause them to start thinking, and that is where the danger lies for the regime in Iran. Anyway, this was what my mother thought and why she continued to teach the music she loved. It was her way of resisting the regime."

"What happened to your mother?"

"Eventually they came and got her. You know how I found out?"

"How?"

"I came home one day from school and found her bloody bed-sheets in the trash. That's the last remnant of her I ever saw."

"I'm so sorry. What did you do?"

"My father was already dead. So I was left alone. I had a brother, but he was away. So I rebelled. I quit school. I ran the streets of Tehran. I smoked pot. I did other things. I refused to wear the *chador*, you know, the head-to-toe black garment. You may not believe it, but there were many such children in Tehran and the other cities. There are probably still some, little street rebels against the regime. I was one of them."

"How long did you get away with it?"

"Not long, a year maybe."

"What happened?"

"I was finally arrested and sent to the Qasr."

"What's that?"

She lowered her eyes for a moment, then raised them locked them on mine.

"It was a prison, Jeffrey."

"*You* were in prison?" I wondered if the shock on my face showed. If it did, she didn't react to it. She went on matter-of-factly.

"Yes, prison, a prison for dissidents."

"What was that like?"

"It was like hell on earth. I think you know about that. The worst of it for me was that every day we were required to kneel on the stone floor of the prison and recite long passages from the Quran. If you fell or tried to get up, you were beaten on the backs of your legs with long poles. I was beaten many times, but I was lucky."

"Lucky?"

"Yes, one woman who had been a school principal was put in a sack and stoned to death."

I winced. "How long were you there?"

"Eleven months and three days."

"How did you ever get out?"

"My brother came. He had made lots of money smuggling people out of Iran right after the revolution. He was able to secure my release with the payment of a bribe and get me out of the country."

"You told me you had lived in Brussels. That's how you came to be there?"

"Yes, there is a large Iranian expatriate community there. I was granted asylum."

"How did you get by?"

"I was very talented as a pianist. I enrolled in university at Louvain. Soon, I was giving concerts. And perhaps in those days I was very beautiful, but never as beautiful as my mother."

"Were you still rebellious, from your religion, I mean?"

"Wouldn't you be? I lived freely. In the mornings I rode bareback in the Parc Leopold. I laughed at the idea of ever wearing the *chador* or even just the black scarf."

"So what happened?"

Her face took on a sudden air of determination. "When those airplanes crashed into the World Trade Center I knew I had to do something. What had happened to me was evil, what had happened to my mother was evil, evil in the name of religion. A wise man once said that in order for evil to triumph it is only necessary for good men to do nothing. I think that goes for good women, too, perhaps especially Muslim women, since the evil we suffer is daily and systematic. I believed I was a good woman in spite of my rebelliousness. So when the call went out for recruits to the FBI who know foreign languages, I applied. They snapped me up. I speak Farsi, Arabic, English, French, Italian, and Spanish. These are the languages commonly spoken in Brussels."

"So you became a terrorism fighter?"

"No, I became a fighter against the *jihad*. I think it is important to be specific about what I am fighting, what we all are fighting. Saying we're fighting 'terrorism' is kind of vague, like saying we are fighting bad breath or tooth decay."

"I thought you had to be American to join the FBI?"

"You do. I believe I told you, but my father was an officer in the army. This was under the Shah. When my mother was pregnant with me, my father was sent on an exchange program to the United States. Can you believe it? I was born at Fort Benning, Georgia. My father applied for my dual citizenship. He loved the United States. He always said it was the last, best hope for the world."

"What happened to your father?"

"Another sad story, I'm afraid."

"Tell me."

"As I believe I told you, my father was the commander of the last regiment of cavalry in the Iranian army. They were still using horses in those days to go up into the mountains in search of *janis*."

"*Janis?*"

"You know, bandits. *Jani* is the Persian word for them."

"I see. Is he the one who taught you about horses?"

"Yes. He loved horses and taught me everything I know about them, although not everything he knew. He not only knew how to ride them, but how to doctor and care for them. He's the one that showed me how to check a horse for laminitis. The tradition of raising and caring for horses goes back thousands of years in Persia."

I smiled. "You ever have your own horse?"

"Yes. He bought me one and kept it at the army stables with the service horses. He took me riding at least once a week. He was a wonderful teacher, very patient and gentle with me, like my mother."

"I bet the horse he got you was an Arabian."

"Yes, how did you know?"

"Derwood said you told him."

"Oh, yes, Derwood. I remember."

"Your horse have a name?"

"*Parvane*. That means 'butterfly' in Persian. That was my mother's nickname for me because it is so close to my own name. So I gave this name to my horse, too. I thought that was clever."

"So, what happened to your father?"

"In time all the army officers under in the shah's regime were discharged, although many suspected of being personally loyal to the Shah were murdered outright."

"You're father?"

"No, not at first, he was simply discharged after a few years, when I was about ten or eleven. But one day not long after he was walking down the street in Tehran when he saw two revolutionary guardians beating an old woman selling vegetables from a horse drawn cart. They were beating the horse, too."

"But why?"

"She wasn't wearing the *chador*."

"That can't be true."

"Yes, it is true. He tried to intervene on the woman's behalf, but they overpowered him and took him away. We never saw him again. Some friends of ours who happened to be walking down the same street told us what happened."

"I'm sorry to hear this, too."

Her face became reflective. "You know, Jeffrey, when I first read your file, the part where you intervened with the police on behalf of the young man whose dog had been shot, I thought of my father. I knew right away you were not a bad man, prison or no prison."

"I appreciate that. What happened to your horse?"

"Eventually all the horses at the army barracks were determined to be symbols of the Shah's regime, so they were taken to the holy city of Qom and slaughtered."

"No way."

"Yes, it is true."

"Your horse, too?"

"Yes, my beautiful *Parvane.*" She lifted her hand and brushed away a wet gleam in her eye with a finger.

"So, basically, you were left an orphan?"

"Yes."

"Do you miss Iran?"

"Sometimes, it is a beautiful country. But I love America, too. There is so much freedom here, although I think so many do not appreciate it. Perhaps you have to live under a tyranny for a while to truly appreciate freedom."

"So you're happy here?"

She paused and lowered her eyes. Then she looked me in the eye. "Yes and no. I am like a woman caught between two worlds. I am neither completely here or completely there. I do not feel sorry for myself, though. I think this is the fate of all expatriates, no?"

"Have you always been stationed here in Houston?"

"No. For most of my career I was stationed in Washington."

"How did you come to be here?"

"I requested a transfer out of Washington."

"How come?"

"For personal reasons."

With that she stood up, clasped her hands together in reverse fashion, and stretched her fingers. "If you are tired of my talking about myself, I can go clean up the kitchen."

"I'll help you, but I do have one more question, if you don't mind."

"Okay, Jeffrey. This seems to be the night for it." She sat back down. "Ask away."

"Why does that twerp down at your office, Biderman I think his name is, have it in for you?"

"Oh, him. He's just a nuisance."

"He's a pretty insulting nuisance."

"Sticks and stones, Jeffrey."

"Yeah, but why?"

"Okay, if you must know. For a long time he has tried to

get me to go to bed with him. I say 'no'. He keeps asking. He tells me he'll make my life hell around the office until I say 'yes'. He knows I'll never file any kind of complaint, so he humiliates me every time he gets a chance."

"So why don't you file a sexual harassment complaint on him?"

She paused, her eyes turning inward as if searching for a forgotten idea. After a second or two she turned her eyes to me and smiled. "I do not file complaints against people. That's a form of whining, and I don't like whiners."

"No fair using my own words against me. There has to be another reason."

"There is. I won't file a harassment complaint because I would have to fill in the little box on the form that says 'name of victim'. I will never allow myself to be a victim, even on paper. I have no desire to be a member of the Sisterhood of Victimhood. The world has enough victims. No, I will deal with Biderman in my own way and in my own time."

"Like thwarting a big terrorist attack? Becoming a star?"

"Maybe. In any event, I have a plan."

"Plans can crumble like cookies. I wrote the book on it."

"This one, I assure you, is cookie proof, if I decide to follow it. Any other questions?"

"Yes, plenty of them, but I don't want to wear out my welcome with you. Let's clean up the dishes and hit the sack. We've got a big day ahead."

A little later I was shown to a spare bedroom with just a single bed, a chest-of-drawers and a floor lamp. I slept very little. Around two in the morning I heard muffled cries coming from Parvin's bedroom. Several times I heard her shout, "I don't want to." I got out of bed, slipped on my trousers and a shirt, and eased down the hallway. I opened her door as softly as I could. In the moonlight filtering into the room through the blinds I saw her thrashing around in the bed, her skin glistening with sweat. Then she cried out, louder this time. This was no time for intercultural etiquette. I went in and nudged her gently to wake-up. She sat up with a start.

"Bad dream, partner," I said, "you were crying out."

She blinked her eyes rapidly several times. She was wearing a long-sleeve cotton nightgown and her hair was tied up in a bun. My presence seemed to reassure her, not affront her.

"Want some water?"

"Yes, please."

I went into the bathroom that opened off her bedroom and poured her a glass of cold water. I wetted down a wash rag with cold water to go with it and went back to her bedside. I held the water glass to her lips while she drank. I sponged off her brow and wrists with the rag.

"What were you dreaming about?" I asked.

"The same dream I have had ever since I was a little girl."

"Oh?"

"When I was five or six I began having this dream, not every night, just every now and then."

"What did you dream?"

"About nothing, really, just a dream about a little point of light in the blackness, way off in the distance, like a distant star. But somehow it scared me."

"That's it?"

"No, each year as I got older the little point of light in my dream kept getting bigger. That scared me even more. Eventually, I told my mother about it."

"What did she say?"

"She took me in her arms and said, '*Parvane,* this light means you are special. According to old Persian tradition it means you are an angel. You were sent here to earth to do something special. When this light grows very big, it means you will very soon go back to join the other angels.' And I would say '*Madar,* I don't want to go join the other angels, I want to stay here with you.' And then she would hug me tighter and cry."

"That's beautiful, Parvin. But don't worry, you've got a lot of years ahead of you."

"Yes, you're right, of course. It was just an old fable my mother told me to help me get back to sleep."

I sat on the side of her bed and held her hand until she drifted back to sleep. When she was sleeping soundly, I eased out of her room and pulled the door shut.

I didn't go back to my own room, though. I went into the living room and sat down in the over-stuffed armchair I had been sitting in earlier. I surveyed the room that just a few hours before had been full of music and gaiety. Now it seemed as dark and somber as a church at midnight. I found myself thinking about the fable Parvin's mother had told her about being an angel. The angels and demons thing again. I wondered if fables like that were such a good thing to lay on children, even just to comfort them. I had come to believe that plain and simple facts were the best comforters in the long run. Facts are solid; facts are trustworthy; facts grip the road. Give me facts, all the facts, and nothing but the facts. And there was one plain and simple fact that struck me very forcefully that night: it had been a long, long time since I had had a conversation like that with a woman.

Chapter Fourteen

Gun Barrel City is in East Texas, about seventy miles southeast of Dallas. It's a tough little town out in the old cotton patch. Physicians with medical degrees from prestigious institutions like Harvard, or Johns Hopkins, or even The University of Texas rarely choose to practice there. Most of its few doctors hail from obscure medical schools. The majority come from overseas. Such was the case of Dr. Rao.

"Are you the people from the FBI?" Dr. Rao asked. He was a wiry, dark little man, with horn-rim glasses similar to Mickey's. He was wearing a white smock and white trousers, both of which were a little dingy and not a little frayed at the cuffs from many, many washings. But he was sweet enough. I liked him.

"That is correct," Parvin said. She showed him her FBI credentials. He didn't ask for mine.

"Good," he said. "The state trooper said you'd be coming first thing in the morning."

"This trooper named Gonzalez?" I asked.

"Yes, sir. I believe so."

"How long has he been here?"

"Oh, let's see. It's ten o'clock now. He got here about two

this morning. I'd say about eight hours."

"Good grief. Let's go see the man," I said.

Dr. Rao led us down the hallway of his little community hospital. The walls and ceilings were painted mint green to minimize the unsightliness of the inevitable smudging all medical facilities seem to acquire. The floors were functional gray linoleum. There were no bells and whistles of any kind that I could see. This was rubber-meets-the-road essential medical care. He talked all the way as we walked to what he called the observation room.

"They brought this fellow in about nine the night before last," he said.

"Who is 'they'?," Parvin asked.

"Some farm kids who had been here in town for a movie. They said he was wandering along the side of a county road."

"How did they get him here?"

"They loaded him in the back of their pick-up," he said, "and brought him directly to the emergency entrance."

"Anybody touch him?" I asked.

"No, sir, these kids were pretty savvy about diseases, living on farms and all. Lots of animals develop diseases, so they knew not to touch the unfortunate man. They put on work gloves and masks before touching him. This was such an unusual case the ER called me at home and asked me to come in. When I got here the first thing I did was to confiscate those gloves and masks and have them incinerated."

"You know what we're dealing with then?" Parvin asked.

"Yes, back in India we have a traditional deity for it, Shitala Mala, the goddess of . . ." He lowered his voice and whispered, "smallpox."

"And you've had him in isolation since that night?" I asked.

"Yes. That trooper wanted to go in and question him, but I wouldn't let him. I even locked the door to the observation room so he couldn't slip in there when my back was turned. He seems terribly determined."

"Indeed he is," I said.

"What about yourself?" Parvin asked. "Have you touched

the man or been exposed to him?"

"Yes, but I had smallpox as a child. I'm immune, or at least I hope I am. This stuff is really nasty. I've never seen anything like it."

We found Hector Gonzalez in full uniform standing next to a glass window that gave onto a small hospital room. He shook our hands when we arrived, but said nothing. He just nodded to the sad creature lying on a bed on the other side of the window.

It was Travis all right, although I wouldn't have recognized him if I didn't know him so well. His face and body were swollen with infection. Large, white pustules covered his entire length. Two pustules above either eye had grown to giant size and coupled together to form one giant pustule that made it look as though a white jellyfish had taken up residence on his face. The sheet beneath his buttocks was crusty with dried blood. I shook my head. *A pox on you, sir,* he had cursed me.

I looked at Parvin. "That's him," I said.

"No doubt, Jeffrey?"

"None."

Parvin turned to Dr. Rao. "Does anyone else know about this?"

"No, but following standard protocol, I sent a blood sample to the state health department in Austin this morning. If it comes back positive for smallpox, I'll have to report this to the Center for Disease Control," Dr. Rao said.

"Do what you must," Parvin answered.

When we were back outside we conferred briefly with Hector Gonzalez. He was visibly shaken by what he had seen.

"All right, Hector," I said. "You see what this is all about."

"I do now, boss. If word of this gets out to the public, there could be a real panic, like that Ebola scare up in Dallas not long ago."

"Trooper," Parvin said, "there is a man on the loose who is responsible for what you saw in there. He is a foreign agent. Here let me show you his picture." She opened her purse and pulled out the well-worn picture of Malaku coming out of the

Blue Parrot. "Take this picture. If you see this man, do not attempt to arrest him. He is very, very dangerous. He is the man who decapitated those two fellows whose corpses you have seen. We wouldn't want that to happen to you."

"So what should I do, ma'am?"

"Call me, young man. I'll call in reinforcements."

"Anything else?"

"Yes," I interrupted. "I bet the reason that Travis was found wandering around up here is that this guy has a lab or something nearby to produce smallpox virus. Try to find it, but if you do, don't go in there. Call Agent Sassani."

"You got it, boss. What would a lab look like? Where would I find it"

"Try chicken farms. The virus is grown in chicken eggs. There are a lot of chicken farms in this area. That's probably why Travis was brought up here: to be used as a guinea pig close to where the virus was being produced."

"How would I know if it's a lab?"

"There'll be a lot of unusual medical equipment like centrifuges and incubators, that kind of stuff. That's about all we can tell you."

"If this stuff is on the porch in plain view, no prob. But if I have to go inside somewhere, I'll need a warrant."

Parvin placed her hand on his forearm. "Do not get yourself in trouble, young man. If you need a warrant, call me."

"Will do." He turned back to me. "How do you think that sick dog in there got loose?"

"That's a good question." I cut my eyes to Parvin. "What do you think?"

"I have no idea."

I looked back at Hector. "Have you notified the DeLong family?"

"Not yet. I was waiting for you to make a positive ID. Do you want to notify them?"

"They wouldn't believe me if I did. You better do it."

"Got it, boss."

He nodded and shook our hands. He'd make a good Texas

Ranger, I thought, as we were leaving. I wished him a silent good luck.

"While we're here in East Texas," I said to Parvin when we were back in her car, "let's go see somebody. He's about an hour's drive from here."

"Who?"

"You ever wonder how I got Robin's diary?"

It was high noon when we headed southeast into a world of red dirt, doublewides, dualies, and Dixie. An hour later a light rain shower was peppering the windshield as we pulled into a parking space in front of the old art deco courthouse in Henderson. If Sheriff Tuck was old school, his office was even more so. The black-on-white sign above the pebbled glass door said simply "Sheriff's Department." The deputy named Alton who had banged on my door the night Robin killed herself showed us into the Sheriff's office. He took a long, lingering look at Parvin as he did so. He formed his lips into a little "o" and winked at me.

Sheriff Tuck listened carefully as Parvin and I laid out all that had passed. Once or twice he shifted his weight in his chair, but otherwise he remained motionless. When we finished, he took out a faded old bandana and wiped his brow.

"I'm getting too old for this," he said. "You pretty sure that was Travis DeLong that was in that hospital up in Gun Barrel City."

"No doubt about it," I said.

"Senator DeLong know about it yet?"

"I don't think so."

"Well, when he finds out, somebody's tits are going to be in one hell of a ringer." He turned to Parvin. "Excuse me, ma'am. I didn't mean to be rude. I wasn't referring to you at all."

"I am not offended, Sheriff."

He went on. "And you say Teal DeLong really is involved in this what-ever-it-is? Plot? Just like poor Robin wrote in her little book?"

"Yes, sir."

"She participating of her own free will?"

"She says this Malaku guy is blackmailing her."

"You believe her?"

"I know I want to believe her."

"You've sure stirred yourself up a hornet's nest, son."

"Roger that. But don't forget it was you who told me to look into what Robin had written in her diary."

"Indeed, I did, son. Indeed, I did." He paused, his face reflective, as if thinking to himself or perhaps recalling some long-forgotten incident.

I looked around his office. Like all old men's offices, it was filled with bric-a-brac and mementos of his career: framed newspaper clippings, various citations and awards, a pair of rusty iron handcuffs, and a single action Colt revolver displayed in a glass case. A glassy-eyed eight point buck was mounted on the wall behind him. The afternoon sun was leaking through the blinds of the window, leaving slats of sunlight across the deer's snout. The room smelled of old age and years of routine.

The sheriff came back to us. "Smallpox, you say?"

"Yes, sir," I answered.

"I was a brig-chaser in the Marines during Viet-Nam," he went on. "When one of our young boys decided he had had enough of jungles and rice paddies and Victor Charlie and decided to take a little unauthorized vacation, my partner and I would have to go out and find him and haul him back to the brig. I reckon that's how I got my start in law-enforcement, hauling scared young kids to the brig."

"You've got to start someplace, Sheriff," I said.

"I know, but Southeast Asia ain't no fun place to start anything. We traced one young lance corporal to Lang Son. He'd sought refuge there with some Catholic nuns running a little hospital. What he didn't know was that it was a hospital for smallpox patients. He caught the damn stuff and was dead in two weeks."

"Yes, sir?"

"The point is that I've seen with my own eyes what smallpox can do. So my question is what do you want me to do now?"

"Back us up, Sheriff, if push comes to shove," I said.

"You mean help you take on Albert DeLong when he lowers the boom on you both."

"That's about it, sir."

He leaned back and folded his hands across his watermelon belly. "I don't know what I can personally do—all of this is outside my jurisdiction—but I know a fellar in Austin that might be some help to you down the road."

"Who's that, sir?"

"Another law enforcement fellar. Used to work for me."

"Used to?"

"Sure did. The best deputy I ever had, smart and absolutely fearless."

"This the guy who used to twist an ear now and then?"

"That's him. I was sorry to have to run him off."

"You mean you fired him?"

"No, no, just sort of suggested a man with his talent needed a bigger stage to perform on. He got the idea."

"How can he help us now?"

"Oh, he landed on his feet alright. Got himself a job in law enforcement over in Austin. He's done pretty well. I'll look him up if things get a little tight for you."

"We'd appreciate it."

He lifted his ponderous weight from his chair and walked over to the window. He picked up a little yellow sprinkler bucket with 'Grandpa' written in black script on the side and began watering some flowers in trays along the sill. When he had finished he took out the old bandana and wiped his brow again. He stared out the window for a while. Then he turned to Parvin.

"I ain't never met no Muslim before. You get hot wearing that black scarf in our hot Texas summers?"

It was a long drive back to Houston down old Highway 59, behind what they sometimes call the Pine Curtain region of Texas. It is a vast area of third and fourth growth pine forest bisected with red-dirt logging roads, elevated oil and gas pipelines, and high voltage power lines. The forest is occasionally broken with stump-water swamps lurking with alligators and snapping turtles. Water moccasins coil themselves on the tops of semi-submerged logs, and gray clouds of mosquitoes float in the air like smoke. The major industry in the area is logging. Convoys of logging trucks move up and down the highway day and night. The old-fashioned truck stops catering to this trade often have mom-and-pop cafes as part of the service. The food in these joints is always bad and the décor worse. Parvin saw one of these as we rounded a curve.

"Let's stop and eat, Jeffrey," she said. "I'm hungry. Aren't you?"

"Not that hungry."

"Are you sure you were a SEAL? I thought you guys were trained to eat anything, even ants and roaches."

"Find me a roach and I'll eat it."

"Oh, don't be difficult."

She slowed down and turned off the highway onto a white chalk parking lot in front of the café. A dozen or so logging trucks were scattered around the outskirts of the lot. Another dozen or so dualie pick-up trucks hugged a little closer to the café entrance. The interior was just as I expected. Wooden booths with red leather seats patched with duct tape lined three walls. Chrome trimmed tables with linoleum tops were arranged in no particular order around the interior. Framed publicity stills of the likes of John Wayne, Randolph Scott, George Jones, Elvis Presley, and Dolly Parton hung just about everywhere on three walls. The fourth wall was covered with side-by-side Texas and Confederate flags, pinned to the wall with rusty thumbtacks. The air smelled of Marlboros, Redman, and fried chicken grease. An antique Rockolla jukebox blared out a scratchy recording of Merle Haggard's *Mama Tried.* A full lunch crowd of loggers and assorted rednecks crammed the little place. When we came in, they virtually stopped talking and stared at us open-mouthed for a full thirty seconds. One-by-one they drifted back to their lunches as we were shown to a booth at the rear of the room.

If Parvin was fazed by the atmosphere, she didn't show it. We both ordered hamburgers, fries, and iced tea from a bouncy little waitress in blue-jean cut-offs and a black t-shirt with LUV U spelled in sequins on the front.

"Do you think Sheriff Tuck will help us if we need him, Jeffrey?" Parvin asked while we waited for our food.

"No chance."

"Why not?"

"He doesn't want to get involved. That's why he palmed Robin's diary off on me in the first place."

"He seems like a good man."

"Maybe he is, but you said yourself that all that is necessary for evil to prevail is for good men to do nothing. I'd say he's one of those do-nothing good men."

"But he's a law officer."

"He's a politician first. He wants to win one more election, serve out his term, and then retire. No need to stir up his constituency over a long-shot case involving Senator DeLong's baby daughter."

"What do you know about his constituency?"

"Look around you, you'll get the idea."

"They just look like working people to me."

"Folks like this used to burn crosses in the yards of their neighbors, if the neighbors happened to be black."

"Times have changed, no?"

"Maybe, but human nature hasn't changed."

"You're a cynic, Jeffrey."

"I've earned the right to be."

"You have to give everybody a chance to do the right thing, Jeffrey."

"Like you did with Teal?"

"No, Jeffrey, like I did with you."

Our lunch was served at that point and we paused in our discussion while we ate, but a question was bubbling in the back of my mind. I wasn't sure she could or would answer it. Nevertheless, when we had finished eating and each were having a second glass of iced tea, I went ahead and asked.

"What happens next with your investigation?"

She patted her lips with her napkin. "I need to create a report and submit it to the Special Agent-in-Charge of our office. If he thinks there is something to it, he'll refer the case to the Joint Terrorism Task Force. That's the special inter-agency team that handles serious terrorist threats. That's when the wheels really start to turn and resources are committed."

"What resources have been committed so far?"

"Just me."

"One riot, one ranger, huh?" I was referring to the occasion during frontier days when the mayor of El Paso had requested the governor to send in a company of Texas Rangers to quell a riot. When the train carrying the answer to the request arrived at the station, the mayor was distressed to find only one ranger on board. "One riot, one ranger," was the ranger's famous reply.

"Yes, I've heard that story. I suppose it fits."

"So, what's this guy's name, the Special Agent-in-Charge?"

"Special Agent Rawlings."

"What's he like?"

"He's very professional, Jeffrey, completely above-board. No funny business."

"Not like Biderman?"

"Not a bit like him."

"No bumps or warts?"

She began to answer, paused and seemed to think for a few seconds, and then laughed under her breath as she went on.

"Well, he is a little ambitious perhaps."

"How so?"

"He wants to be transferred to the Seat of Government."

"What in the world is that?"

"J. Edgar Hoover used to call FBI headquarters in Washington the Seat of Government when he was the Director."

"There's a window into a man's mind," I said. "Do you trust this guy Rawlings?"

"Oh, yes, absolutely. We all have our little ambitions, you know."

I let it go at that, but I filed the name Rawlings in my memory. We finished lunch. I left an extra-large tip for the cute waitress and paid the check at the register. Then we boogied down to Houston. We didn't talk further until we were on the periphery of the city.

"Do you miss it, Jeffrey?" Parvin asked, not taking her eyes off the road.

"Miss what?"

"Being in the Navy."

"I did at first. For a long time after I was discharged I had a recurring dream, a nightmare really, that I was falling through space, just falling and falling and falling."

"What do you think it meant? this dream."

"Mickey said it was a psychological reaction to having the structure of my life taken away, so that there was nothing there to support me. I thought that was a pretty good explanation."

"Do you still have this dream?"

"Not as often. Why do you ask?"

"Oh, no reason. Just wondering."

Parvin dropped me off at Mickey's around seven in the evening so I could pick up my truck. Even though it was still sweltering hot, Mickey and Beth were in their front yard weeding out the circular flower bed surrounding the trunk of an ancient pin oak. Parvin got out with me and walked over to shake hands with them. "Thank you again, my friends," she said. Then she turned to me and hugged me lightly, pressing her cheek next to mine for what seemed like a very long time. "And thank you for saving my friend," she whispered in my ear. With that, she turned and walked back to her car without looking back. I turned to Mickey and Beth, whose eyes were as wide as physically possible for human beings. Mickey shook his head.

"I told you," he said.

That evening I poured myself a mason jar of sweet tea, sat down in the big wicker chair on my back gallery, and watched the sun set in a panorama of colors that shaded the horizon in turn from orange, to blue, to a purple so deep it reminded me of a bruise. I literally had nothing else to do. My horse was hidden twenty miles away, my hired man was on paid leave, and I already had tidied up my house as much as I could after the events of the last few days. I was too wound up to read or to listen to music, and I never watch television when there's a beautiful sunset to take in. So I sat there and drank my tea and tried to put my thoughts in order as the sky darkened.

Eventually the sky turned completely black and the stars came out. The night I had walked along the Galveston seawall with Teal these same stars had reminded me of freshly polished diamonds strewn across a black velvet sky. Now they reminded me of shards of glass, sharp and pitiless, embedded in the living skin of the universe. My thoughts turned to Teal. Most of us like to believe that the past can be forgotten and left behind, even washed away entirely. That's what Teal had thought. But some of us have a better sense that the past is always with us, a penumbra of memories and regrets that travels with us day and night. And if there is something bad in that past, especially something that remains un-atoned for, a fear that the day of reckoning could come at any time travels along with it. I wondered if all these years Teal had carried that fear somewhere behind her beautiful blue eyes. That thought brought to mind the most unusual character I encountered during my year in the belly of the beast: Eyes Eggleton.

His real name was Joseph Eggleton, but everyone called him Eyes. The superficial reason for this nickname was that he suffered from Grave's disease, a medical condition associated with a thyroid deficiency that left his eyes enlarged and protuberant, like boiled eggs with the corneas and pupils painted on their surfaces. But there was a darker and more sinister reason. Eyes was serving a half dozen consecutive life terms for child molestation. His victims had mostly been six and seven year old boys in the first grade class he had taught in San Antonio. In prison parlance that made him a "short-eyes," a man with an unnatural attraction to "shorts," i.e. little kids.

Most cons have bitter memories of their childhoods, which are often marred by sexual abuse and parental neglect. Short eyes are living reminders of that unhappy era in their lives, so short eyes become the special object of hatred and contempt from the other cons. A short-eyes is a pariah among pariahs, and he gets treated accordingly by the other inmates.

Eyes Eggleton was no exception. In the five years he had been in the Eastham Unit he had been beaten, spat upon, splattered with urine-filled balloons, and even sodomized with a broom handle by a squad of Aryan Brotherhood goons. But this was all in the present. He could handle the present; it was his past he worried about. He never said what was in his past that worried him so, but we all assumed it was something to do with his pedophile proclivities, something that could sooner or later send him to The Walls.

The Walls, situated in downtown Huntsville, is the main unit of the Texas prison system. It gets its name from the thirty foot high red brick walls that surround the city block-square facility. It's here where prisoners are processed in and out of the system, and, ominously, it's here where executions are carried out. The prison graveyard is just outside The Walls.

Most cons deal with their personal demons with contraband drugs, or a gut-grinding homebrew called *pruno*, or sexual hook-ups with other cons. Not Eyes, though. He had a unique way of dealing with the demons from his past. He created for himself an invisible fantasy creature that he claimed followed him everywhere. The creature, he claimed, was an enormous carrion bird, something of a cross between a vulture and a marabou stork. It had a sharp hooked beak and feathers as black and shiny as onyx. He named the creature Harvey, after the invisible rabbit in the old James Stewart movie. Harvey, he said, would leave him alone as long as it was fed, but if it got hungry it would peck out his eyes in retribution for his past sins. So Eyes made it a point to purchase little cellophane bags of peanuts at the prison commissary and grind the contents into peanut dust. He would toss the dust over his shoulder at lunch or dinner, as some might toss salt for good luck. "Got to feed Harvey, got to feed my bird," he would say to anyone who raised an eyebrow at the spectacle. Eyes was crazy and everyone knew it.

I had very little contact with Eyes until mid-August, when we were both assigned to a crew tasked with harvesting cucumbers in a vast nine-hundred acre cucumber patch about twenty miles southeast of the Eastham Unit. The patch was on a section of bottom land bordered on three sides by a dense and practically impenetrable swamp formed by the backwaters of the lower Trinity River. It was a hellish maze of algae covered green water, willow islands, water oaks, swamp blackgum, thorn bushes, Spanish dagger, kudzu, duckweed, and beggar-tick. Alligators, snapping turtles, and water moccasins were the principal inhabitants, although stories had circulated for years about feral hogs the size of hippopotamuses having moved in. I suppose there must have been birds and waterfowl, too, although I never saw or heard any. Back in the 1970's three prisoners had tried to escape together through the maze. They gave themselves up after less than twenty-four hours in the bush.

Escape attempts were always a possibility when convicts were bussed out of a secure facility to work in an outlying field, so of course there were mounted guards. There was also a pack of bloodhounds kept in an open cage on a trailer near our bus. But the dogs were just for show, as I soon learned.

The mounted guards included the fearsome Roper McDade, so named because before he became a prison guard he had worked the rodeo circuit as a calf roper. He was old and fat and bent now, with a bulbous nose and ears like club steaks, but he could still ride and rope. Other guards might try to discourage a fleeing convict with a warning shot in the air from a cut-down shotgun or a Winchester 30-30. Roper would chase him down on horseback and lasso him with the lariat he always kept in hand when on station. Then he would drag him a ways "to straighten out his thinkin'." I once saw him lasso a Mexican con hot-footing it to a waiting car, and drag him by his ankles, screaming and twisting, for a quarter mile through the cucumber vines. The Mexican may have had his thinking straightened, but he couldn't walk straight for a month.

So it happened one cloudless day I was working a stretch of cucumber vines, kneeling in the furrow on one side of the vines, sweating from every pore, smelling my own odor, picking cucumbers from the ground-hugging vines and plopping them into the ten gallon galvanized pail I dragged behind me like a ball-and-chain. Eyes was on the other side of the same vine, doing the same. In the harsh sunlight his white flabby skin had the color and texture of a boiled ham. His weird eyes always gave him a frantic countenance; this day he looked positively manic.

"I've got to make a run for it, Quinn," he whispered.

"Don't be a fool, Eyes," I whispered back.

"Got to do it, pal."

"Roper's right over there. You want to be dragged through the vines?"

"I ain't got no choice."

"How come?"

"The commissary's been out of peanuts all week. I ain't fed Harvey in three days."

"You'll never make it."

"I gotta try."

"Don't do it."

He shook his head. "You're not like the other cons, Quinn. You shouldn't even be in this hell-hole. For what? Punching out a no-good cop?"

"A cop is a cop, according to the law."

"The law sucks. You shouldn't be here."

"Well, here I am."

"Okay, okay, but before I leave I want to do something for you."

"Like what?"

"You've always been square with me, not like these other mutts around here. No mean stuff. So before I take off I'm going to tell you where some of the bodies are buried. Maybe you can use the information to make yourself a deal, get out a little early, like cutting class or something."

"What bodies?"

"Of some of those kids I diddled, what do you think? There's a lot those prosecutors don't know to this day."

"I don't want to hear this."

"Get smart, Quinn."

By this time we had worked our way almost to the end of the row closest to the tree line. Out of the corner of my eye I could see Roper McDade eyeing us suspiciously from atop a big chestnut stallion, running a gloved hand over the lariat lying across his lap. He walked the horse over to where Eyes and I were kneeling and working. The leather saddle creaked and groaned under his great weight.

"You boys going to flap your gums or pick cucumbers?" he asked. He cleared his throat and spat out a giant hocker to the side of his horse.

"Just being happy in our work, boss," Eyes said.

"Well, let's have a little less happy and a lot more work," he answered. He turned the horse and rode away slowly, but from time to time he would look back over his shoulder at us.

"Now's my chance, Quinn," Eyes whispered, a little more loudly now.

"You'll never make it, Eyes."

"Got to try. I ain't fed Harvey three days now. It's gonna peck out my eyes if I don't get away and find it some peanuts. I can feel it breathing down my neck right behind me. I ain't never felt it that close before."

"You're crazy, Eyes. There isn't any bird behind you, and no bird is going to peck out your eyes. It's all in your mind."

"See you, Quinn."

With that he was up and running. Roper saw him bolt but even at full gallop couldn't catch him before he disappeared into a curtain of kudzu hanging from the trees at the edge of the swamp. Roper reined-in his horse in a spray of dirt and torn cucumber vines. He spat again.

"Goddamn pervert," he said. He shot me a dirty look. "You know he was going to rabbit, Quinn?"

"I thought I had talked him out of it. I tried, anyway."

He fixed a doubtful eye on me. I wondered if he was considering lassoing me and dragging me through the vines in Eyes' stead. But he just spat again and turned his horse toward the roadway.

"Going for the dogs?" I asked.

"Hell, no. We wouldn't turn no dogs loose in that crap. There's snakes and no tellin' what all in there that'll kill a dog as quick as they'd kill a man. And them dogs is registered bloodhounds. They're worth a damn sight more than that fuckin' pervert. No, sir. We'll go in later on some ATV's and fetch him. He ain't goin' to get very far."

He rode away and I went back to picking cucumbers. And that's what I did for the next three days, marveling all the while how human beings can create fantasies and illusions that spell their doom as certainly as any real-world hazard. I was certain in my conviction that in order to secure peanuts for an imaginary bird Eyes had launched himself on a fool's errand, and a fatal one at that. On the fourth day Roper McDade rode up to where I was working. He reined in his horse a few feet away and spat.

"We found ol' Eyes this mornin'," he said.

"Where?"

"About a mile in. Didn't get far, did he?" We reckon a water moccasin got him. His leg was swole up like a bull's penis."

"How did you find him?"

"Followed our ears. When we turned off the ATV's to listen for footsteps or splashes, we could hear some feral hogs a-sloppin' on somethin'. Quiet as a graveyard in there, so you can hear for a long ways off. We knew we had him before we ever even saw him. Tell you the truth, though, I wish I hadn't seen him."

"How come?"

"Them hogs was slurping up his innards like they was spaghetti. Damndest thing I ever saw. I'll be remembering that 'til they throw the dirt on me."

"Nasty, huh?"

"Yes, sir, and that weren't all."

"Oh?"

"Before them hogs got to him some bird got in there and pecked out his eyes."

These were dark and bitter memories that always put me in a dark and bitter mood. I feared I was in for a long night of unwanted memories and unhappy reflections on the burdens of the past. But then a kind of miracle happened. A thousand fireflies lit up my backyard all at once, flickering on and off, zigging and zagging with happy abandon. There is something reassuring to me about fireflies, something that says after all the universe is wonderful and warm and full of fun. I found myself wanting Parvin to be there to see them, too. I wondered if there were fireflies in Iran. I wanted to talk to her about that. I wanted to talk to her about a lot of things. I fell asleep in the big wicker chair, the side of my face still feeling warm where she had held her cheek earlier that day.

Chapter Fifteen

I awoke just after sunup the next morning. It was Tuesday, the third week in June. It was cloudy and cool. A front had blown in overnight from West Texas, carrying with it not only cooler air but also fine particles of red West Texas dirt that settled on my truck in a reddish layer that would soon turn to a permanent reddish crust if I didn't wash it off, or so I told myself. So I made myself a pot of coffee, poured a cup, and got to work. Over the next few days I would do a great many chores like that. I slapped another coat of white paint on the horse lot fence; I changed the oil in my truck; I repaired a section of barbed wire fence at the rear of my property; I replaced the screen door to my kitchen; I changed the oil in my truck again. I did anything to keep busy because the truth of the matter was that I was high and lonesome. I had lost my job. I was under suspicion for committing a violent crime that could send me back to prison for most of the rest of my life. Now I was dry docked in my own home with nobody to talk to and nothing important to do. I did not want to burden others with my loneliness, so I resisted the urge to call Mickey for lunch or even call Derwood to truck down to Bellville to check on Sergeant Pepper. Most of all, I resisted the urge to call Parvin. She had her investigation to wind up. She didn't need me bugging her. So I just sucked it up and tried to stay busy. In the back of my mind, however, a thought was taking shape, like a vision of a cool blue lake taking shape in the mind of a man walking across a desert. I questioned whether I had the nerve to try to turn the thought into reality. I was to find out soon enough.

Parvin called around ten in the morning on Friday.

"How is it going, Jeffrey?"

"I'm about to change the oil on my truck for the third time."

"At loose ends?"

"I would be if I could find the other end."

"It sounds like you could use something to do."

"Affirmative."

"Then I have something for you."

"Oh?"

"Remember I told you that when I finished my investigation I had to prepare a report and submit it to the Special Agent-In-Charge?"

"That's right, a guy named Rawlings."

"Well, Monday is the day I submit it. There will be a conference at the office. Agent Rawlings asked that you be there."

"What? Why me?"

"He may want to question you."

"How come?"

"You saw Malaku. Teal more or less confessed her involvement in this situation to you. You identified Travis. Let's face it, Jeffrey, you're the central witness."

"Does this guy know I've been in Huntsville?"

"Yes. He says it doesn't matter at this stage."

"What about the episode in my barn with Soos?"

"You're in the clear."

"You sure?"

"Yes. The crime lab report came back negative on your axe as the murder weapon. There wasn't a trace of blood on it. It was the wrong size, too. The weapon that killed Soos was bigger and heavier, judging from the slash marks."

"You actually had it tested? I mean, was there any doubt in your mind?"

"I had to check the box, Jeffrey."

"I see."

"There was something peculiar about the axe though. You know whose fingerprints besides yours were on the handle?"

"If they weren't mine, then I don't know. Malaku's maybe?"

"No, they were Soos's. What does that suggest to you?"

I thought about that for a moment. "It suggest to me that Soos grabbed my axe and tried to fight off Malaku with it. And that he lost."

"Precisely."

She went on to brief me to the extent she could on the highlights of her report. She sounded very excited, proud of the work she had done. And as far as I could tell she had done a very thorough job. She had found out that Fasil had indeed worked in the procurement department of his hospital, that he had made several unauthorized orders of incubators and low-speed centrifuges, and that these items were now missing from inventory. She also had found a number of large, unexplained cash deposits into his personal bank account. Old-fashioned greed appeared to be his motive for aiding and abetting Malaku. He wasn't the first to lose his head over money.

Now the test of my nerve. "Is your report all complete," I asked, "all done and tied up with a little red bow?"

"Yes, Jeffrey, all done. Now I can relax until Monday."

"Then I have a suggestion."

I took a deep breath and told her what I had in mind. There was a long silence on the other end of the connection. Almost immediately I regretted having said anything. I was about to say goodbye and power off when she answered.

"Yes, I could do that," she said.

I picked her up at her house at seven the next morning, a Saturday. The sky was clear with a southerly breeze and very low humidity. It was a perfect morning by Gulf Coast standards. By eight-thirty we were on a Southwest Airlines flight to New Orleans. We barely talked on the way to the airport and not at all when we were in the terminal. I waited until our plane was far out over the Gulf of Mexico before I cut to the main question.

"I'm surprised you agreed to go," I said.

"I'm surprised you asked."

"I bet it's not every day that a murder suspect invites you on a road trip."

"It's a first for me, all right."

"So why did you?"

"Did I what?"

"Agree to come with me?"

"I have my reason."

"Want to clue me in?"

"Later, Jeffrey. So tell me, why did you ask me to go?"

I ran several flip answers through my mind, but decided to play it straight. "I like talking with you."

"We don't have to go to New Orleans to talk."

"You haven't had *beignets* at the Café du Monde."

"So that's it? You invite a lady to travel three hundred miles by jet just to talk over a plate of doughnuts?"

I studied her face. The corners of her eyes were crinkling and she was softly biting her lower lip.

"No that's not it, not entirely."

"What is it then?"

"I'm not sure really. Can we leave it at that? And in case you're wondering, I don't have any big ideas. I reserved separate rooms at a hotel in the Quarter."

"Good. I can cancel my reservation at the Airport Hilton."

I laughed. "You've been ahead of me from the jump, haven't you?"

"Yes, and I'm still ahead of you."

Indeed she was. I didn't care. Today she was more dressed down than I had ever seen her, just blue jeans, a loose-fitting short sleeve white blouse, and a white scarf bordered with gold leaf. Her face looked fresh and rested and innocent, angelic even. I looked out the airplane window. The treacherous waters of the Gulf looked as cool and inviting as a spring in a desert oasis.

We landed just after nine o'clock and took a shuttle to our hotel in the French Quarter. It was a vintage structure with plantation shutters, a marble staircase, and a baby grand piano tucked between two potted palms in the lobby bar. We checked our bags with the desk clerk and ventured out into a bright muggy morning to explore the historic, time-worn, decadent, and fatally romantic city that is New Orleans.

First thing, we walked over to Canal and Carondelet and boarded the streetcar that runs the length of St. Charles Avenue all the way to Audubon Park. No doubt this is the most famous streetcar line in the world. They know about it in Tehran.

"I saw this streetcar in American movies so many times when I was growing up, Jeffrey," Parvin said. "I feel like I'm in a movie myself."

"Let's hope this one ends better than most," I said.

The streetcar rattled and clanged down the track under the massive oak trees that line the esplanade, past ante-bellum houses with columned galleries and leaded glass front doors, past the gothic structures of Loyola and Tulane Universities, through time itself it seemed. To the innocent eye very little has changed in New Orleans for a hundred and fifty years. I knew better. I knew about the wave of crack cocaine induced crime that settled in the nerves and sinews of the city like a virulent form of lupus some years ago, and from which it has never fully recovered. But I kept this to myself. Parvin was an FBI agent; she probably knew the statistics in an abstract way. But she had never known the old New Orleans. Why ruin her fun?

We got off at Audubon Park, took a quick tour of the zoo, and then walked back toward the Quarter on Magazine Street. We stopped for a sidewalk vendor lunch of boiled shrimp and dirty rice, which we ate standing up under a two-hundred year old oak tree.

By one o'clock we were back in the Quarter. We made the

antique shops on Royal, browsed through the French Market, and explored an old Jax brewery that had been converted into an upscale shopping mall. Parvin stopped and stared at the window display in one of the dress shops in the mall while I checked out a bookstore. We went back outside and just wandered around for a couple of hours. Parvin took it all in: the scrolled iron balconies on the buildings, the smell of fresh fish displayed in bins of ice in the little mom-and-pop grocery stores, the lush plumage of banana trees and crepe myrtles in the courtyards accessed through narrow alleys that remind you of the Casbah. She took it all in like it was her last day on earth. Around four o'clock a rain shower drove us into the outdoor pavilion of the Café du Monde. I ordered us a plate of *beignets* and two mugs of chicory coffee.

"Good heavens," she said, biting into a fresh *beignet,* "if I lived here, I'd come here every day."

"And you'd weigh four hundred pounds. You want to tell me now your reason for coming down here with me? You said you had a reason."

"Later, Jeffrey."

She finished her *beignet*, napkined off the trace of powdered sugar on her upper lip, and took a final sip of chicory coffee. "Jeffrey, I'd like to go back to that mall in the old brewery for a few minutes. Do you mind waiting here?"

"Go ahead. This is the best place in the world to wait on anybody."

As soon as the rain stopped Parvin left for the shopping mall. I ordered another plate of *beignets* and another mug of chicory coffee and settled back to watch the goings-on across the street at Jackson Square. The sidewalk artists had returned from their temporary rain shelters under the colonnaded eves of the surrounding buildings and were setting up their easels along the outside of the iron fence that encloses the square. Couples and families, invariably dressed in shorts, t-shirts and running shoes, strolled around, periodically checking fold-out maps or taking pictures with their cell-phones. From time to time a horse drawn open carriage carrying more romantically inclined tourists would rattle by. It was an innocent enough crowd; the real carnival in the Quarter doesn't start until after dark. But my own personal carnival was about to begin.

Three heavy-set, middle-aged women in shorts and Chicago Bears t-shirts, carrying Styrofoam cups filled with God-knows-what, came in and were seated at the table next to mine. I had seen them around the Quarter all afternoon and had steered us clear of them. Now they were three feet away, laughing and talking loudly, and gaping around as if to discover something interesting on which to focus their attention. They discovered me.

"Hey, good looking," the chunkiest of the women leaned in my direction and said. She had breasts that sagged under her t-shirt like half-empty water balloons. The varicose veins in her legs reminded me of the dark canals on Mars. "Where you from?"

I forced a smile. "Texas."

"We're from Chicago."

"I never would have guessed."

"What are you doing here, sugar?"

"Waiting for a friend."

"What a coincidence. We're looking for a friend."

"That's nice."

"We're sweet to our friends."

"Good for you."

"That's because we're angels."

"You're what?" I could hear a barge horn out on the river.

"Angels, as in Like Your Own Daughter Angel Care. You never heard of us?"

"Can't say that I have."

"We do home health care. It's a big company. There's always a lot of ads on TV."

"I don't watch much TV."

"Oh, honey, you need to. Stay up to date."

"I'll try to remember." I smiled and turned my head back toward Jackson Square, checked my watch, yawned, looked at the ceiling, checked my watch again, all in vain.

"We're in New Orleans for a training seminar and a little R&R," the woman went on.

"Glad to hear it."

"We're especially here for the R&R. Know what I mean?"

"You're in the right town for it."

She leaned further in my direction now, shifting her weight in her chair, stretching her t-shirt tight against her sagging breasts. She spoke in a hoarse whisper that carried like a cattle call. "Angels do it with their wings on, you now."

"Say what?"

"I said angels do it with their wings on." She gave me a big smile, showing yellowish teeth smudged with red lipstick. The other two women began giggling, sucking on their lower lips to keep from laughing.

"What exactly is 'it', ma'am?" I asked, keeping my face blank.

"You know, 'it.' She lowered her hands to her lap and began poking the index finger of one hand into a little circle made by the thumb and forefinger of the other. The other two women began laughing out loud now. Patrons at the surrounding tables shook their heads and rolled their eyes. A young woman gathered up her two small children and boogied for the exit.

"I see," I said. I pushed back my chair and started to stand up.

"Oh, don't go, sweetie," the woman said. "We haven't even ordered yet. What do you recommend?"

"I'd better not say."

"Don't be bashful, honey. What do you recommend?"

I was on my feet now, but she reached out and grabbed my arm. "Come on, be a friend. We're just having a little fun. Maybe we can have some more fun later, if you're a good boy. What do you recommend?"

"Try Weight Watchers," I said.

Nobody was laughing now. The three women stared at me open mouthed, the color rising in their throats like flares just before a firefight. But before things got out of hand Parvin returned, a large shopping bag in hand. She gave the ring-leader a killer look and slipped her free arm in mine. "Let's go, Jeffrey," she said. She led me out.

"What was that all about, Jeffrey?" she asked as we strolled-arm-in-arm along the sidewalk bordered by the Jackson Square fence. I described what had happened.

"These women were hitting on you?"

"Like sharks on a side of beef."

"And you told them to try Weight Watchers?"

"It was a totally honest recommendation."

"Don't you think that was a little rude?"

"I wouldn't call it rude."

"What would you call it?"

"I'd call it fighting fire with fire."

We arrived back at the hotel around five. The afternoon sun had broken through the clouds and was turning the entire Quarter to a Turkish bath. I hit the shower in my room and twisted the water dial to extra-cold. I stayed there a long, long time. I expected to take Parvin to dinner at Commander's Palace that evening at eight, but at around seven o'clock she called and said she would meet me there. I assumed she had some FBI calls to return, so I dressed and took a cab to the restaurant in time to secure our reservations. I arrived in a coat and tie just as the sun was sliding behind the tree line in a soft orange glow.

Commander's Palace is situated in the Garden District, not far from the streetcar line we had ridden earlier that day. It's a grand old Victorian structure that offers unusually fine dining, as well as the opportunity to mix with old New Orleans money, if that's what you're interested in. I was interested in the food, but Parvin was running late so I sat down in the waiting area and watched the money walk in instead. There was a lot of it: women in Neiman-Marcus dresses and fistfuls of diamonds; women in West Coast get-ups aped from the latest music videos; women in fashions they had probably acquired the week before in Paris or New York. They came in with the kind of men my father used to lend millions to at the bank by day and take millions from in poker games by night. It was quite a parade. About eight-fifteen a cab pulled up outside and discharged a woman dressed simply in a sleeveless black dress, a coral necklace, and black patent leather heels. The dress was modestly hemmed just above the knees and cinched at the waist with a black cloth belt. The ensemble was classic, conservative, something Jackie Kennedy might have worn. But it wasn't Jackie Kennedy wearing it. It was Parvin. She walked from the cab to the entrance with her usual athletic stride. I noticed she was strongly built, heavy-breasted, and not a bit wobbly in the heels she was wearing. But mostly I noticed that there was no headscarf tonight. The thick black hair flowed back from her head like the mane of a wild mare. I couldn't take my eyes off her. Neither could anyone else.

"Quite a transformation," I said as we were being seated at our table.

"Women's liberation, Iranian style."

"From the mall today?"

"Yes, while you were fighting fire with fire with those women in the Café du Monde."

"You going to tell me why?"

"Yes, in a bit, but let's eat first. A lady gets hungry tramping around New Orleans all day."

"How about a cocktail first?"

"Let's make it two glasses of wine."

We had two glasses of house red, talked about the sights we had seen during the day, and mulled over the menu. A trio of black jazz men with muted trumpet, clarinet, and guitar strolled among the tables playing it soft and mellow. Parvin's hair seemed to sparkle with tiny lights reflected from the candle on the table. We ordered dinners of pecan crusted redfish and barbecued shrimp. We got down to business while we ate.

"Okay, partner," I said, "clue me in."

"You mean the American dress?"

"That's what I mean."

"You don't like it?"

"I like it fine, I just don't understand."

She put down her fork, touched the corners of her mouth with her napkin, and took a deep breath. She sat straight up and folded her hands in her lap. She leveled her eyes on mine.

"Jeffrey, you remember when we were talking at my house I said I felt like a woman caught between two worlds?"

"Yes, of course."

"Well, tonight I did not want to feel that way. I have never felt more American than I have today. I wanted to dress the way I feel. Is that wrong?"

"Not to me. What makes you feel so American?"

She shrugged. "I don't know exactly. I think it's a sense of freedom."

"New Orleans specializes in personal freedom. You should check it out during Mardi Gras."

"I don't mean it that way, in just letting go."

"How do you mean it?"

"I mean it just the opposite, I think. I mean it in the sense of having control over your own life. If you have not lived under a tyranny, it is hard to imagine this. But to control your own life, that is freedom. Just letting go isn't freedom. You have to stay in control. I am taking control of my life beginning today."

"Don't you feel in control at the FBI? You certainly seem like you do."

"It is very frustrating, Jeffrey."

"How so?"

"The FBI is a very large organization, Jeffrey, over thirteen thousand agents, so it has many rules and regulations. And worse than that are what they call "policies."

"For instance?"

"Well, the one that drives me crazy is the one that says we are never to use the word *jihad* in our training or our work. Can you imagine that? The hardliners of Islam are promoting *jihad* all over the world, but we are not allowed to use the word. How can you fight an enemy you refuse to name? It is like punching at the wind. In the long run you will lose a fight like that."

"Who came up with this policy?"

"It came from the very top."

"You mean 1600?"

"Yes."

"So, what's your solution?"

She paused, took a sip of water, and went on. "I am leaving the agency."

"What?" I almost came out of my chair. I must have spoken a little loudly, too, because several patrons at nearby tables twisted their heads in my direction. I lowered my tone. "You're doing what?"

"I am leaving the agency."

"But why?"

"Because of what I just said. The bureau is fighting a losing battle. It will not name, nor is it allowed to name, its enemy. It will lose. I know what will happen."

"But it needs agents like you if it ever has a chance of winning."

"Yes, it does, but does it appreciate agents like me? Does it appreciate an agent like me when I am appointed to the Unconfirmed Raghead Sightings detail? Even if this is done in jest by the office Romeo, it is very degrading. And it shows a lack of seriousness about the fight we are in. I am usually shunted off to what they consider secondary cases, to work on my own to see if there is anything there to get worried about. They don't much care what I do, as long as I don't step on any important toes. So I take a few short cuts here and there to dig out the truth, like I did with you. If I happen to come up with something promising, they cut me out and send it to the Joint Terrorism Task Force. I am like the Indian army scouts in the old western movies. I am free to locate the enemy war parties on my own, but then I have to call in the cavalry."

"You do sound frustrated. Do they know yet?"

"Not yet. After I submit my report Monday to the Agent-in-Charge, I'll give my notice, probably by the end of the week. I am very proud of my report. I am sure it will impress the Agent-in-Charge. I want to go out on a high note."

"Is this what you meant when we talked at your house about having a cookie proof plan to deal with Biderman? Just make your statement and get out?"

"Yes, that is a good way to put it. Make my statement and get out."

"You've been working up to this for a while, haven't you? I remember you're asking me about what it was like when I separated from the Navy"

"Yes, but I only made my final decision today. That's why I feel so American. Americans have many faults, but they are decisive, are they not?"

"We used to be, at any rate. I'm glad I was with you."

"I am, too."

"They'll miss you."

"Yes, they will."

"What's next for you?"

"I intend to study music."

"What? Where?"

"I have been accepted at the Julliard School."

"But that's in New York, isn't it?"

"Yes, in Lincoln Center."

I thought about that for a few seconds. I laid my hands flat on the table between us when I spoke. "I understand there is an acute shortage of classical pianists in Texas. In fact, I understand the governor plans to call a special session of the legislature to address the problem."

She reached out and placed a hand on top of mine. "You're a sweet man," she said.

"What comes after Julliard?" I asked.

"I don't know yet. I think perhaps I am a little too old to begin a concert career. Teach somewhere, perhaps."

"That's pretty vague."

"Yes, but I like the idea of vagueness. When you are locked into a career that no longer sustains you, the worst part is the very predictability of it all. Yes, I like the vagueness of what comes next. It's like opening a fresh book."

I took a sip of water and turned my table knife over and

over on the tablecloth. "Well, a lady has to do what's best for her."

She placed her elbows on the table and cupped her chin with her hands. "It's not all about me, Jeffrey. Did you ever read a book about a future society in which special fireman squads go around burning books whenever a stash of them is discovered?"

"You mean *Fahrenheit 451*?"

"Yes, that is the one. My mother had it in her library."

"How does that apply here?"

"Well, in the book there is a secret society of book lovers who want to preserve the best books, so each of them undertakes to memorize a certain section of a forbidden book, know it by heart so to speak so that it can be preserved by passing it along by mouth to later generations. You know, books by Milton and Dante and the like."

"I remember reading that."

"I like to think I will do the same for music, the music my mother loved so and passed along to me. I'd like to know some of it by heart, and perhaps pass it along to someone else to know by heart someday. That's why I want to teach, high school preferably. I am afraid of what might happen if the *jihadists* actually takeover."

"You think there is any real risk of that?"

"Do not underestimate the furious determination of these men."

On that somber note, we ordered light desserts and coffee. I had one more question to ask, perhaps the most important as far as I was concerned. I struggled with how to ask it, and then just blurted it out.

"Why me?" I asked.

"What do you mean, Jeffrey?"

"I mean, why me? You know my history. You know the trouble I've been in. You know what will happen to you if the Bureau finds out we're here in New Orleans together. Talk about Lady and the Tramp."

"You're no tramp, Jeffrey. You're a good man, an educated

man, who was blindsided by fate. Your trouble was not of your doing."

"My doing or not, I'm a branded man and always will be."

She smiled. "Not with me you're not."

"But that doesn't answer the question. Why did you agree to come down here with me? You said earlier you would tell me."

"I will, but first tell me why you asked me here."

"I like talking with you, that's all. No big ideas."

She nodded. "Okay, now I will tell you why I agreed to come. I needed someone to talk with about this big change in my life, and I like talking with you. I think it is because you are a good listener, someone who takes an interest in what others are saying."

"I gave you a hard time at first."

"Understandable, given all you had been through."

"I still feel bad about it. You should have heard Father Blanton chew me out over it, too."

"That nice old priest? I liked him. And I bet you listened to him, too, in you hardheaded fashion. I think this is a natural thing with you. I've known men who were not that way."

"Anybody special?"

"Yes. I had a rather lengthy relationship with a professor of Middle Eastern studies when I was stationed in Washington, an Iranian like myself. He was quite brilliant. He was famous in his field, too. He often appeared as a guest on television news shows. You may have seen him."

"I don't watch much TV. This the personal reason that caused you to transfer out of Washington?"

"Yes."

"What went wrong?"

"Nothing, really. I just woke up one morning and realized that whenever we were together he only talked about himself, or about some book project he was working on, or some grand theory he was spinning up. He never even once asked me about my mother or father."

"Sounds like a charmer."

"Oh, he could charm you if he thought it would help his career. And there's something else."

"What would that be?"

She shook her head slightly. "He would never, ever race into a burning house to rescue a woman he barely knew." She laughed and went on. "In fact, he would never, ever race into a burning house to rescue his own mother, let alone me."

I lowered my eyes and took a sip of coffee. "Don't get the wrong idea about me. I don't know what got into me that day. When there's trouble, I usually run and hide under the bed."

She shook her head again and smiled at me with her eyes. "You do not. When there's trouble, you're always the first to step forward, like you did for that boy whose dog was shot."

"You see what it got me."

"Yes, but you would do it again, wouldn't you?"

I tried to change the subject. "What about that little light you have nightmares about? Seen it lately?"

She shrugged nonchalantly. "Haven't seen it for a long time."

I paid the check with a nice tip and asked the waiter to call for a cab. There was one more place I wanted us to go.

Preservation Hall is on Peter Street in the French Quarter, in a building once owned by a freed black woman back in the 1800's. Now a non-profit group maintains the building as a place to perform traditional music. It's about the last place on earth where you can hear genuine, un-dubbed, down and dirty New Orleans jazz. Parvin and I took in the last show of the evening. She listened transfixed as a band of old-timers riffed through such classics as "St. James Infirmary", "Bill Bailey, Won't You Please Come Home", and "Just A Closer Walk With Thee." The beat was a little off, and the piano hadn't been tuned since the Civil War, and the singer couldn't carry a tune in a mop bucket, but it was the real thing and it was a lot of fun.

"My mother would have loved this place, Jeffrey," Parvin whispered.

"What about you?"

She squeezed my arm for an answer.

After the show I hailed a passing horse-drawn carriage for the short trip back to the hotel. Parvin didn't make it even that far. She fell asleep, her head on my shoulder, after only a block or two. I was glad. She missed the rogue's gallery of pimps, hookers, pickpockets, drug dealers, Murphy artists, drunken college kids, and general melt-downs that parade up and down Bourbon Street at night. This wasn't the memory I wanted her to take away from New Orleans.

When we arrived at our hotel the lobby and bar were quiet and empty. Besides the desk clerk the only other person in sight was a lonely looking bartender in the lobby bar. He was polishing wine glasses with a white towel and watching the clock. He would probably go off duty in a matter of minutes. I started to guide Parvin to the elevator, but she pulled me aside into the bar. She sat down at the baby grand piano we had seen when we checked in early that day and began playing Chopin's Nocturne in E minor. The bartender, who up to this point had paid us no more attention than if we had been two stray dogs, looked at her as though suddenly she was the most interesting thing in his life.

"The tune that always makes you think of your mother?" I asked.

She kept playing as she spoke. "Yes, but now it will always make me think of you, too."

When she finished playing she stood, planted a demure kiss on my cheek, and said goodnight. She walked by herself to the elevator and went up to her room. I stood there like Kaw Liga the Wooden Indian without the faintest idea of what to do. The bartender looked at me, arched his eyebrows, and went back to polishing wine glasses.

After a few minutes I went up to my room. I stripped and took a shower to wash off the heat and grime of the evening. That done, I lay down on top of the bed sheets and tried to wind down enough to go to sleep. There was nothing for it. My entire body seemed to course with electricity, my eyelids jittered with electric charge. I couldn't keep my eyes closed for more than a few seconds. I stared at the ceiling in the dark. Then a sliver of moonlight slipped through a crease in the window drapes and cut across the room with the intensity of a naval searchlight. My hearing, too, was dialed to a super-sensitive level. I could hear the late night crowd on Bourbon Street, a barge horn out on the Mississippi, a police siren over in the projects. These noises all sounded as if they came from the room next door. I turned over and covered my head with a pillow. The outside noise was gone, but now I could hear my heart thumping against my ribcage.

Eventually I fell into an uneasy sleep, one roiled by a weird dream. In my dream a freight train was stopped on a siding in a grassy, rolling savannah. One of the freight cars was a flat-car, on which sat an uncovered animal cage. Inside the cage was a tawny colored panther, no doubt on its way to a circus or a zoo. The animal was agitated, restless, scudding around the cage at an ever increasing pace. As the details of my dream clarified, I could see the source of its discontent: a grass fire was raging over the ridge, filling the night sky with a pulsating orange glow and sending acrid smoke into the panther's cage. Antelopes, buffalos, giraffes, wildebeests, and other animals streamed across the railroad tracks, terrified of the fire. The fire line crested the ridge and snaked down the hillside. The big cat became frantic now, slamming its hard-muscled body against the bars of the cage in a desperate effort to escape.

I woke in a sweat, the sheets around me twisted and damp. I slid out of bed, tugged on my trousers and shirt, and went out. I walked barefooted down the hall to Parvin's room and tapped on the door. She answered after only a few seconds, cracking the door just wide enough for us to see each other. Her hair was still down. She was wearing a short sleeve cotton nightgown that reached only halfway to her knees. Her breasts look swollen and hard under the thin cotton fabric. Nothing was said. She took a deep breath, veiled her eyes, and bit softly on her lower lip. Then she opened the door wider and let me in.

Chapter Sixteen

On Monday I arrived at ten sharp at the FBI office in Houston. I wore my Sunday best: khaki's, a white shirt with a black knit tie, a charcoal tweed sport coat, and my most expensive Stetson. I sat in an interior waiting area as Parvin made her case in an adjacent conference room. I was prepared for a long wait. But in less than ten minutes the door to the conference room opened and she walked out, slowly, her head hanging.

"How'd it go, partner?" I asked.

She spoke without looking at me. "I have been suspended."

She trudged away, like some beautiful and exotic creature thrust into sudden and unexpected captivity.

I burst into the conference room. Biderman and some older dude with thinning hair and yellow teeth were sitting together on one side of a long mahogany table. I took the older guy to be Rawlings, the Special Agent in Charge. They didn't look all that surprised when I crashed in.

"What the hell did you do to that woman?" I demanded in a voice that wasn't designed to convey love and affection.

"Hello, Mr. Quinn," the older man said. "We've been expecting you."

"Answer me," I said. "What did you do to that woman?"

"We suspended her," the older man said.

"What for?"

"Oh, let's see: violating just about every rule in our field manual, failing to report her daily activities, interfering with a state murder investigation, and last but not least associating with a known felon. That would be you."

"What do you know about any association with me?"

"She spent the weekend with you in New Orleans, didn't she?

As a matter of fact, she spent the night with you, didn't she?"

"You're bluffing," I said, but I knew it was me trying to run a bluff against a high hand.

"No, sir, we are not bluffing. We had you two under surveillance the whole time."

"I didn't see anybody."

"Oh yes you did, you just didn't recognize our surveillance team."

I thought about that for a moment. "The three fat old bags in the Café du Monde."

"Excellent. My, what a quick learner you are."

I tried to go on the offensive. "This is a load of crap. She's been out digging up the facts of a terror attack while you two have been in here with your feet on your desks."

"What she has been digging up, sir, is a lot of libelous dirt on the daughter of a United States Senator." To emphasize his point, he flipped gingerly through the pages of Parvin's report on the table before him as though they were so many toxic waste products.

"So, DeLong got to you, did he? He said he'd break her. What'd he do, promise that he'd put you in charge of the New York office, make you the next director of the FBI, if you threw her under the bus?"

"I have had no direct contact with Senator DeLong, Mr. Quinn."

I thought for a second. "Of course not. You have Biderman here to run those kinds of errands. Well, DeLong said he'd break me, too. I won't be so easy."

"Oh?"

At that moment Texas Ranger Conway Crowley and two men in SWAT gear slid through the door behind me. "You're under arrest, hotshot," Crowley said. "Bring joy to my heart. Resist a little."

I knew better than to do that; I'd be snuffed right there in the FBI office for resisting arrest. I stood motionless as the two SWAT guys frisked and cuffed me. When they were finished, Crowley stepped up behind me and pulled my Stetson down over my ears. He stood me up straight.

"Gentlemen," he said, "I present to you Jeffrey Quinn, King of the Cowboys."

I was transported back to my home county, where I was charged with second degree murder of Jesus Raza. Because of my prior conviction, I was denied bail. I was going to be in lock-up for a good long time. My attorney, a celebrated defense lawyer from Houston, whom Mickey retained for me because my bank account was frozen, wasn't optimistic about getting me out.

"What are my chances of bonding out?" I asked him.

"I don't know, but it's a big number," he said across the scarred wood table in the windowless attorney-client conference room, "a big negative number, given the judge we're dealing with."

"Why? Who's the judge?"

"A visiting judge from West Texas. He's here temporarily so the local judge can go on vacation."

"What's the word on this guy?"

"From what I hear he's a law and order type on steroids," he told me. "He once had a neighbor's dog picked up on a bench warrant and put to sleep for peeing on his yard. Think what he'll do to you."

"Give it a try, will you, partner. My cell mate is a three hundred pound recidivist who keeps blowing me kisses."

"Will do."

But the bond hearing wasn't scheduled until the end of the

week. During that time Mickey came to visit me every day.

"Have you heard from Parvin?" I asked.

"Sorry, *jefé*. We've called. We've been by her house. It's like she's dropped off the face of the earth."

"Maybe she has." There was gloom in my voice, and no doubt on my face, too.

"She'll turn up, *jefé*. Keep the faith."

"Sure."

But it's difficult to keep any kind of faith in jail. Most people know about jails from what they see in the movies or on television. It's a place where down-on-their-luck fellows are dressed in coarse but clean work clothes, fed cafeteria style on tin trays, and allowed to turn in at ten o'clock. When together they swap stories about their lives on the outside, commiserate about their respective troubles, and form lasting friendships. At worst, it's a grim, silent place where men are left alone to ponder their misdeeds. Nothing could be further from the truth.

First, there is the noise. The noise is constant, grating, unnerving. Steel doors are constantly being banged open and slammed shut. Jailers bark orders to inmates, who in turn shout back obscenities and threats. Trusties schlep mop buckets up and down the hallways at all hours of the day and night. Inmates with radio privileges keep them on full-tilt-boogie 24/7. It's never classical music from Monterrey; there's a reason some call rap "prison music." Even on those nights when the din is subdued, there are muffled grunts and groans coming from nearby cells that you prefer not to think about.

Then there is the smell. The smell is a combination of feces, urine, sweat, body odor, cigarette smoke, disinfectant, and a dozen other odors that men in confined quarters seem to produce systemically. But the worst smell is the smell of fear. Those who have been in combat know this smell. Some vets say the smell is a harbinger of death; those who emit it are on the short list for a body bag.

But worst of all is the paranoia. In jail you are never, never alone. You shower, shave, dress, urinate, and defecate in full view of other men, most of whom have file jackets that read like episodes from the writings of the Marquis de Sade. You have cellmates who hang on your every word, not because they enjoy your company, but because they are looking for some scrap of information they can use against you to help their own cases or lighten their own sentences. There is no band of brothers in jail. There is only one positive about jail: it gives you time to think. This I did around the clock until I had the game figured out.

My bond hearing began on Friday morning, July third. Two sheriff's deputies brought me in shackles to the courtroom, plopped me down at the defense table as though I were a box of frozen meat, then went and sat in the empty jury box and tried to stay awake.

Court proceedings on the days before holidays are usually short and perfunctory. Everybody wants to light out ASAP and get the good times rolling. That Friday was no different, except that the party was already underway. Everyone on the other side was in a good mood. The district attorney, who had designs on higher office, was glad-handing everyone in the courtroom who might be a newsman or a potential voter. Crowley and Biderman were seated next to one another near the aisle. They made no effort to hide their glee at my predicament. Even the judge, a wiry little man with a bald head the color of a fertilized chicken egg, was happy that day. Maybe he had run over a dog on the way to the courthouse.

My attorney put on a good case, I thought. Mickey testified about my war record and my loyalty as a friend. Beth testified I was gentle with children and animals. Father Blanton testified about my willingness to let the parish kids keep a rescue horse at my ranch, and that I often attended Mass. He didn't say how often. Even Derwood testified. He said over and over that I was a "good ol' boy" and "a damn fine poker player."

The judged drummed his fingers and balanced his checkbook as all this evidence was presented. The district attorney didn't cross-examine any of my witnesses, nor did he call any of his own. My train had already left the station and everybody knew it.

At the conclusion of my attorney's case the judge banged his gavel and issued his ruling without even looking up. "Request for bail denied." No surprise.

But it was to be a day of surprises.

The first surprise was when a uniformed Hector Gonzalez appeared in the courtroom doorway, followed by Special Agent Parvin Sassani. She looked pale and bloodless as a ghost. She asked to be allowed to testify. I was against it because I thought she might say something hurtful to herself, but my attorney thought it might help. "Can't hurt, might help," he said in a voice that had the ring of desperation. He asked to reopen our case. The district attorney didn't care one way or the other.

So Parvin was allowed to take the stand and give her testimony. She was dressed in a long black robe that buttoned in back and a black headscarf. Her usual robust look was gone. Today she looked scruffy and shrunken. I noticed dirt and grime on her clothes. She met my eyes for a moment but quickly glanced away. After she was sworn in, my attorney began asking her the standard questions about whether I was violent or posed a flight risk. She raised her hand and stopped him.

"I did not come here to answer questions," she said, "I came here to issue a warning."

The judge stopped balancing his checkbook long enough to say, "Just answer the questions, madam."

She turned to the judge and spoke calmly. "No, sir, I will issue my warning and you will listen. You all will listen."

It's almost certain the judge had never been spoken to like that. He dropped his pen and looked up from his checkbook, his mouth wide open. Parvin continued on before he could recover himself and call for the bailiff, a white haired old gent of about ninety.

"A man has come to the United States," Parvin began, "to kill Americans, thousands, perhaps millions of Americans. He will introduce a scourge into your midst that you will not be able to control. He will do this today, perhaps tomorrow, but he will do it. Time is short to stop him. You must stop what you are doing and act now, or else your time will run out."

The district attorney suddenly snapped to, perhaps seeing a chance to enhance his reputation as a law and order tough guy by humiliating a suspended FBI agent. He jumped on her like a hyena on a crippled wildebeest.

"How do you know? Are you a clairvoyant?" he asked. This was the first question he had asked any witness all day.

"I know because this man told me."

"Oh, when?"

"Three days ago."

"If it's so damn urgent, why haven't you said anything until now?"

"I have been unable to."

"Why?"

"I was . . . physically disabled."

Parvin winced as she straightened up in her chair. She set her jaw and fixed her gaze on her questioner.

"So who is this mysterious man?"

"He is a member of the Iranian Quds force. He has been sent here by the Iranian regime to set a plague on America."

"Why would they want to do that?"

"To sow death and confusion."

"And why would they want to do that?"

"When these men chant 'Death to America', they mean it."

"Oh? And after he told you all this, what did he do."

"He raped me, then . . ."

"Then what?"

"He beat me. After he was finished, he left me chained me to a pipe in a garage."

The district attorney laughed out loud. "Oh, sister, you take the cake. Why should we believe anything you say? Why should we believe this mysterious bad guy raped and beat you?"

For an answer Parvin stood up. She slowly and painfully

unbuttoned the buttons down the back of her robe and turned around. Her back was crisscrossed with welts and bruises and torn skin and dried blood, like Najwa's had been, only worse. What looked like savage bite marks covered her shoulders, neck, and upper back. After a few seconds she fainted, just like that, probably from blood loss. The judge motioned for the bailiff, who helped her up and over to a bench by the side of the courtroom.

It was a dramatic moment, a powerful moment, but it made little impact on the judge. He banged his gavel and again said my motion to grant bail was denied. At that point I didn't care anymore. I could not control churning in my stomach when I looked at Parvin.

Then the second surprise burst into the courtroom.

Sheriff Tuck wobbled in, accompanied by a tall, powerful black man of about fifty. The black man carried himself with the most imposing military bearing I had ever seen in any man, and I had known admirals, generals, and two presidents. The man was in Texas Ranger uniform, hat and all. He was carrying a black three ring binder and a large manila envelope in one hand and was swirling an unlit cigar in his mouth with the other. He left Tuck in the middle of the seating area, walked up to the little swinging gate in the wooden partition that separated the courtroom from the seating area, and let himself through. The judge's little white haired bailiff sprang up.

"You can't approach the court without permission, sir," the bailiff said, "and you must remove your hat and take that cigar out of your mouth."

"Shut up and sit down, grandpa," the Ranger said. He beckoned to the judge. "I want to see you in your chambers."

"This is most irregular, sir," the judge said. "Why should I see you in chambers?"

"Because I have a writ."

The judge look flustered, but he rose up and led the Ranger back to his chambers. The district attorney tried to follow, but the Ranger shook his head.

"Not you, junior."

"You can't present a writ to the court in a criminal case without the state's attorney being present."

"Watch me."

"I strongly protest."

"Well, don't go bald over it."

As soon as the big Ranger disappeared in back, Sheriff Tuck came and sat down behind me. He put a big meaty hand on my shoulder.

"Hang in there, son," he said. "Everything's going to be alright."

"I'm hanging on as best I can. Who is that guy?"

"You remember I told you I had a former deputy who had gone over to Austin and made a career in law enforcement?"

"Yep."

"Well, that's him, Bradley Johnson. He's Captain of the Texas Rangers now."

"Well I'll be damned. What's that binder in his hand?"

"Your friend over there mailed it to me a few days ago. Just got it yesterday. She attached a note saying it was a copy of something she had turned in at the FBI office, and that if something went wrong get over to that former deputy who knew how to twist ears. I took it over to Austin as soon as I got it. I knew you were jammed up down here."

"Thanks, cap. What's in the manila envelope?"

"Oh, that? That's the writ. Sit tight. You'll be out of here shortly." He patted me on the shoulder.

Sure enough, in less than three minutes the judge hustled back to the bench, banged his gavel, and said, "The court reverses its earlier ruling. The Defendant is released on his own recognizance. Good day." He scampered out of the courtroom without even banging his gavel again.

Captain Johnson made his way back leisurely from the judge's chambers, lighting his cigar with a gold plated lighter. He stopped at the bench where Parvin was sitting barely upright, her eyes wide as she tried to comprehend what was happening. "You the FBI agent who sent this report to Sheriff

Tuck?" He held up the black three ring binder.

"Yes, sir."

"Good work."

"Thank you."

"The FBI suspended you, huh?"

"Yes, sir."

"Don't worry, you're working for me now." He patted her gently on the cheek and turned away.

He walked past me toward the partition gate, still not looking my way. As he passed the counsel tables the district attorney started to rise, but Johnson flicked cigar ash on his papers and told him, "Sit down, junior." The DA did as he was told.

Johnson passed through the little swinging gate and up to where Crowley was sitting.

"Okay, Crowley, let's have 'em."

Crowley looked genuinely befuddled. "Have what, sir?"

"Your star and your sidearm."

"You can't do that!"

"I'm doing it."

"I have rights!"

"All the rights you have today, Conway, are in the toe of my boot, if you want them."

"So what did I do? Can't you tell me at least that?"

"Sure, I'll tell you. We've known for a long time what you did to your ex-wife, but we could never find her. We found her last week in Louisiana at her sister's house. Two Rangers are escorting her back from New Iberia to Texas even as we speak. They got one hell of a statement from her. You just won't believe what's about to come down on you. Satisfied?"

Crowley got up reluctantly and handed over his badge and weapon. He beat it out of the courtroom even faster than had the judge.

Now Johnson turned his attention to Biderman, next to whom Crowley had been sitting. "You Biderman?"

"That's right, Captain, and may I remind you I'm a federal agent and not subject to your authority."

Johnson took a long drag off his cigar and blew a cloud of

smoke into Biderman's face. "That's right, son, so we'll do this the old fashioned way. Get the hell out of here before I whip the white off your ass."

Biderman hesitated, as though trying to decide if Johnson was bluffing. He must have seen something in Johnson's face he didn't like because he didn't hesitate long. He hustled out of the courtroom.

Finally, Johnson came to my table. He peered down at me from behind the cigar that he was now swirling in his mouth. "You Quinn?"

"Yes, sir."

"I've heard a lot about you."

"Oh?"

"A SEAL, huh?"

"That's right."

"My son's a SEAL. Lord, I hope he doesn't turn out to be a troublemaker like you."

"He's young yet."

He saw I was still in shackles. He turned to the two deputies sitting in the jury box who had brought me into court. "Cut this man loose. C'mon, shake a tail feather. We don't have all day."

After I was un-shackled we congregated in the jury room: me, Parvin, Mickey, Beth, Sheriff Tuck, Captain Johnson, and Hector Gonzalez. Parvin was sitting on the jury table. I talked with Johnson and Gonzalez while Mickey and Beth dressed Parvin's wounds with Neosporin and bandages from a drugstore across the street. Sheriff Tuck was daintily rubbing the back of her hand to comfort her and softly saying over and over, "Now, now."

"I heard you tell the judge you had a writ," I said to Johnson. "What was it, a writ of habeus corpus or something?"

"No, sir, no time for that. So I served him with a Writ of How Come-Us."

"A what?"

"A Writ of How Come-Us. Here, let me show you." He opened the manila envelope he was still carrying and pulled out a large color photograph. It depicted our judge dancing in a nightclub somewhere. The judge was dressed in drag, a white dress with black polka dots. His dance partner was a young man about twenty, whom the judge was lustily kissing as they danced.

"I showed the judge this," Johnson said, "and asked him How Come-Us you be kissing that young man full on the lips, your honor? Does your wife know about this? What about your constituents? Wouldn't this make a splash of a front page for the newspaper back home? Besides, don't you know polka dots are definitely out this season? It didn't take him long to see the light on your bond request."

"Isn't that blackmail?"

"I think of it as a form of ear twisting. Got to get their attention first, you know."

I laughed and shook my head. "Roger that. Where did you get the snapshot?"

"A freelance videographer in Austin took it on New Year's Eve. She videos a lot of parties around Austin. When she isn't freelancing, she works as a photographer for the Department of Public Safety. Whenever something interesting turns up, she shoots me a copy."

"Did she know who this guy was when she took it?"

"Oh, sure. This judge is famous for his holier-than-thou approach to judging. Gives a lot of speeches on the Bible and the Law. He's a deacon of his church and a Boy Scout leader, too. The sort of stuff you see in this picture is no big deal in the city, but out in West Texas it would definitely upset the church ladies."

"You have more of these kinds of pictures?"

"A drawer full. You never know."

He put the picture back in the envelope.

"How did you find Crowley's ex-wife?" I asked.

"After she beat it out of Texas to get away from Conway, she ended up in New Iberia, Louisiana. She's a Cajun you know and that's Cajun country. Well, she got herself a job at the Sheriff's department doing file work and this and that. She meets this old detective who sounds like a pretty good dude. She tells him her story and he counsels her to let him call us so we can take Crowley off the streets. She says okay. We got the call last week."

"Sometimes the good-guys win."

"No, sir, the good guys always win in the end." His face turned serious. "I've got the whole force out looking for this fucker Malaku. You have any idea where he might be?"

"Nope."

"Senator DeLong's kid Travis was found wandering around in the country up near Dallas. We're thinking he's probably up there somewhere, planning to hit Dallas. What do you think?"

"You're the detective."

He studied my eyes to the point I had to break contact. He put his cigar in his mouth and swirled it around. "Well, if you should happen to hit on an idea, you let me know, okay, son?"

"Yes, sir."

Johnson and Tuck left the room together. Mickey and Beth had not quite finished dressing Parvin's wounds, so I turned to Hector Gonzalez.

"What happened to Parvin?"

"Better let her tell you, boss."

"How did she get here?"

"I found her this morning at that women's shelter that burned. She was out in the garage, all bound and gagged. The son-of-a-bitch had used her own handcuffs to chain her to a water pipe. She was just about dead."

"You take her to a hospital first?"

"She wouldn't go. She wanted to get here as fast as possible. All she did was wash up in a little sink in the garage. When she was ready, I hit the flashers and rushed her out here."

"Good man. How did you come to find her in the first place?"

"I tried to call mucho times on her cell to tell her I thought I had found the lab we were looking for up in Hopkins County. I had gone all over East Texas flashing the photo she'd given me of our suspect. I finally found a throwback rural delivery postman who recognized the face. 'I tell you one thing, sonny,' he told me, 'the ol' boy lives on that run-down farm yonder don't raise chickens for a livin'. He's too damn ugly even for a chicken farmer.' It was just like you said, an old chicken and egg farm. I tried to call her on her cell but she wouldn't pick up or return my calls. So I went down to Houston to find her. They practically threw me out of the FBI office. So, I hit the streets, checking all the Islamic stores and restaurants until I found a Muslim woman who told me I should check out the shelter. She even had the address. So I boogied over there. When I saw the lady's Crown Vic, I figured I had found her. Dead or alive I didn't know. Thank God and the Virgin Mary, she was alive. But just barely, boss, just barely. I estimated she'd been cuffed to that pipe two, maybe three days. But, like I told you, boss, she insisted on coming here first. I think this lady likes you."

I clapped him on the shoulder. "Good man, Hector. You'll make Texas Ranger yet. Better go hook up with Captain Johnson."

He shook my hand and went out. Mickey and Beth were finished dressing Parvin, so I went over and held her head to my chest. I kissed her lightly on the forehead. "See you later, partner."

"Where are you going, Jeffrey?"

"To find Malaku."

I sat her up straight and headed out. Mickey caught me just as I got to the door. "I heard you tell Parvin you're going to find our friend Malaku."

"That's right."

"And I heard you tell Captain Johnson you don't know where he is."

"That's right."

"What about the Dallas area? That's close to where they found Travis wandering around."

"I turned that over in my mind a thousand times when I was in lock-up, Mick. We always thought Travis escaped somehow. But you should have seen him. He didn't have the strength to escape from a paper bag. Malaku set him out on that country road for a purpose. I think he set him there to be found."

"Why?"

"As a diversion. Keep everybody's eyes focused up there, while he takes care of business somewhere down here."

"You should have told Captain Johnson."

"He's a smart guy; he'll figure it out."

Mick fixed his eyes on mine and held my gaze for a long time. "You do know where he is, don't you?"

"I have a pretty good idea."

"What are you going to do when you find him?"

"I'm going to kill him, Mick."

Within the hour I had been processed out of the jail and was back in street clothes. When I walked out of the jail a free man Parvin was waiting for me.

"I'm going with you," she said.

"No you're not."

"What are you going use for transportation?"

I jangled the keys in my pocket. "Derwood is letting me borrow his truck."

"Jeffrey, it's my case."

"You need to get to the hospital."

"There will be time for that later."

I threw up my hands. "Okay, Okay, let's go."

We piled into Derwood's truck, an old Ford F-150 that had gone through two engines already. On the third try it coughed to a start and we were off.

"Where are we going, Jeffrey?"

"Galveston."

"Why there?"

"You remember Kirilov said the ideal way to spread this smallpox virus was on some mode of transportation, someplace where the passengers are closeted together for a period of time so they can all be infected, then head out in all different directions when they reach their destination?"

"Yes."

"Well, today is July third. Teal is scheduled to leave on a Caribbean cruise this evening out of Galveston with a boat-load of kids from all over the country. I'm betting Malaku will be there with her."

"Shouldn't you tell Captain Johnson?"

"I have to tell him what I know. I don't have to tell him my bets."

"You want to do this yourself, don't you?"

"It's the best way."

"But why?"

"Eventually, the Rangers will find this guy. They are very good at their work and absolutely relentless. But once they have him you can bet your former employer will step in and put a federal hold on him."

"Why, Jeffrey?"

"Because the fix is in. DeLong set the hook good and deep in Rawlings, probably by promising to get him out of rough and tumble Houston and into a plum assignment somewhere, maybe even Washington. But DeLong doesn't do handshake deals. He's from the LBJ school of doing business: grab 'em by the *cajones* and their hearts and minds will follow. He's got something on Rawlings that'll keep him on the hook even now. I have no idea what it is, but Rawlings will need to get Malaku into federal custody on whatever federal charge he can dream up and keep him quiet until DeLong can scrub Teal's involvement out of the picture. He's been down this trail before, when he first got Teal out of the jam over the refinery fire."

"How could Senator DeLong keep Teal's name out of it?"

"The first step was to neutralize you. You were the biggest threat. You were with the FBI. You could turn a lot of dials. So you had to go."

"Have me suspended?"

"Exactly. You've probably been under surveillance ever since DeLong swore he'd break you and me both when he was out at my ranch. They've been trying to find something to nail you with all along."

"I never saw anyone watching me."

"Maybe you did and didn't know it. Remember those fat women at the Café du Monde?"

"Those were FBI agents?"

"That's what Rawlings told me."

She shook her head in disbelief. "All that trouble."

"I'm afraid I didn't help you any, talking you into going to New Orleans."

"I went on my own accord, Jeffrey. I wanted to be with you. I had been so lonely for so long."

I reached over and squeezed her hand. She sat there for awhile, thinking before she spoke again. "Why should you worry about Malaku now? Won't he eventually go to prison anyway on a federal charge?"

"I thought about that a lot when I was in lockup. Maybe he'll go down for a time, but remember he's not your everyday dirtball criminal. He's not even your everyday dirtball terrorist. He's an agent of a foreign government, a spy. He'll have special value to the feds, maybe as swap bait for some American spy being held by Iran. He could end up going back home in a few years to be welcomed as a hero, like that Lockerbie bomber a few years ago. I won't abide that."

She turned and looked at me, her eyes unblinking. "You're rationalizing, Jeffrey. You want to kill him because he represents all the evil that has befallen you since your wife was killed."

"Maybe so, but you said yourself that all it takes for evil to triumph is for good men to do nothing. Well, I intend to do something right here and now. I'm going to put this creep out of business once and for all."

"Isn't this how you got into trouble before, taking things on yourself when you beat up that policeman?"

"If I hadn't, that kid at the service station might be as dead as his dog. That thought is what kept me from going insane when I was inside."

"If you feel this way, why didn't you shoot Malaku on the

Persephone that night?"

"Because that was a set-up. Teal sent him there so I would shoot him. I don't play patsy for anybody."

She turned away from me, twisting her hands in her lap. "I don't want you to go back to prison, Jeffrey."

"And I don't want Malaku to slip away, now or later. You want out?"

She didn't answer right away. She took her smart-phone out of her wood-bead bag and logged on. She flipped silently through a few screens. Finally, she spoke in a voice that was firm and unwavering. "The Galveston Port Authority website says the ship is due to cast off lines at seven o'clock. Hurry, Jeffrey, we'll have just enough time to make it."

I stepped on it, but at the edge of town I stopped at a Coffee Jack's Feed and Tack. I raced in. First, I went to the implement section and picked out the item I wanted. Then I went over to the firearms department and picked out a cheap pseudo-leather rifle case, one with a flared end to accommodate a scope. I paid for two items, placed item one in the rifle case, and raced back out. I slid the rifle case onto the seat next to Parvin and fired up the truck. We were back on the highway in less than three minutes.

Our ride down to Galveston on the Gulf Freeway in the holiday traffic might go down as the wildest pick-up truck ride ever seen on a public street. I weaved in and out of traffic. I drove on the shoulder. I drove on the grassy right-of-way when the traffic became completely jammed. A cop in Friendswood south of Houston got on my tail, but I shook him by going down the wrong way on an entrance ramp to the freeway. On the way Parvin told me what had happened to her. This is my best recollection of her story.

After her suspension the previous Monday, she had gone directly home and locked herself in her house. She closed the blinds and the drapes and turned off all the lights. She turned off her cell phone, the computer, the television, and the radio.

If she had been able to waive a magic wand and cause herself and all trace of her existence to be expunged from the face of the earth, she would have done it. She parked herself in one of the large chairs in the living room, perhaps even the one I had sat in that night which seems so long ago, and sat motionless in the dark. She sat there a long time. All day? All night? All the next day? She didn't remember.

Winston Churchill suffered from depression; he called it his "black dog." Well, the black dog was on Parvin, devouring her spirit in gnarling gulps. Her humiliation was complete. She pondered suicide as a way to escape her shame.

It was the following Monday morning before she had the will to do anything other than nibble a few crackers. She made herself something substantial to eat and resolved to fight off the black dog. The best way to do that, she believed, was to do something constructive, indeed something for somebody else so she could forget her own worries. She decided to go to the burnt-out women's shelter and see what she could salvage of the residents' belongings. She no longer felt American; she felt she had been rejected by America. So she dressed in a traditional Persian robe and black scarf. On the way over to the shelter she mailed her copy of her report to Sheriff Tuck, with a note explaining her circumstances and a request to forward it to the former deputy who liked to twist ears.

She arrived at the shelter around noon. One look at the house told her any salvage efforts there would be useless. What devastation the fire hadn't caused was completed by the high-pressure hoses of the fire trucks. The house was a pile of wet, black, char. She decided to look through the detached garage in back. It hadn't suffered any damage.

She had just entered the garage through its side door when a steely strong arm from somewhere behind her wrapped itself around her midsection, and a coarse callused hand gripped her throat. "I have been waiting for you," a man whispered in her ear. The man's breath was rife with funk and made her sick to her stomach. His hand slid from her throat to a pressure point at the base of her neck. In a few seconds she was unconscious.

When she came to, she found herself laying face up on a pile of padded mats they kept at the shelter for the children of the women to practice gymnastics. She also found she was naked. When she tried to move, she discovered that her arms were extended behind her head, her hands handcuffed with her own handcuffs to a water pipe serving an auxiliary wash basin in the garage. Then she saw a man standing over her. He too was naked, his skin as rough and pitted as a reptile's, an erection throbbing from his loins.

"Who are you?" she asked.

"I am Malaku."

"It is a sacrilege to say that."

"It is no sacrilege if it is true."

"Why are you doing this?"

"To prove my power over you and your kind."

"What do you mean 'my kind'?"

"Let me tell you something about yourself, woman. Have you not since childhood had a strange dream in which a little point of light in the darkness grows larger and larger with each dream?"

She didn't want to answer but her face gave her away. Her eyes widened in terror. She gasped for air.

"Then know who you are and know who I am, and know that I am your ancient adversary."

With that he knelt down on the mats, forced her legs apart, and mounted her. The assault was vicious, primitive, not so much sexual intercourse as a rutting. His skin was coarse and scaly to the touch, his odor overwhelming to the senses. She looked him in the eyes once, and turned away in horror. He clamped her buttocks with a vise-like grip and bit her like a wild animal on her neck and shoulders. She prepared herself for death.

When it was over she was not dead, but she wished she were. Her assailant stood up and pulled on his trousers. He looked down on her with a mixture of lust and disgust.

"You are crazy," she told him.

"You think so? Can crazy people see into the future? I will make you a prophecy. In a few days' time I will set loose a terrible plague on this earth. Many will be killed."

"But why?"

"Because that is my mission."

"Why tell me now?"

"Because the worst kind of torment is to know something terrible is going to happen and to not be able to do anything about it. It is the stuff of nightmares. Now, I will leave my mark on you so that you may never forget my power."

With that he turned her over and beat her with his belt, as he had Najwa. She passed out from the pain.

She awoke sometime that evening, for the garage was completely dark. She was still cuffed to the water pipe. Her back throbbed and she was thirsty. The mat on which she lay was sticky and wet with her own blood. She lay on the mat for three more days and nights, slowly dying from loss of blood, thirst and dehydration, until Hector Gonzalez arrived on the fourth morning.

We were crossing the high-arching causeway into Galveston when she finished her story. I gripped her hand; it was cold and clammy.

"Jeffrey, how are we going to stop this man? You will not believe how strong he is. I have to tell you that when I was suspended they took my Glock."

"Look in the rifle case," I said.

She unzipped the cheap zipper on the case, working it twice because it stuck the first time. She looked inside.

"What's the idea, Jeffrey?"

"Parvin, we're in a crooked game, a crooked game all the way around. When you find yourself in a crooked game, you fight fire with fire."

"Are you sure? Think about what Malaku did to Soos."

"I'm thinking about what he did to you."

She turned her head away, her face troubled with thought.

From the top of the causeway I could see an enormous thunderhead building over the Gulf, boiling with black and green clouds, pulsating with inner lightning. It was as of yet too far away for its thunder to be heard on shore, but it was closing fast.

"Jeffrey," Parvin asked, "that little light I dream about?"

"Yes?"

"How over the years it has gotten bigger and bigger?"

"Yes."

"Well, last night it filled my whole dream."

I took her hand again and squeezed it tighter.

The cruise ship was booked full, so when we got there we had to park at the far end of the parking lot. I helped Parvin out of the truck and grabbed the rifle case. We threaded our way through the crowded lot. It had been extraordinarily hot that day; the asphalt surface of the lot was soft and a little sticky. There were cars, school buses, church buses, and trucks of every kind and description. The license plates were from all over: Iowa, Nevada, Tennessee, every state in the union it seemed. Many were from Mexico.

The ship was still at berth, so we weren't too late. Passengers, most of them kids, were leaning over the deck rails and waiving to the crowd of onlookers lining the wharf. Other kids were already playing volleyball and basketball on the foredeck. Crepe streamers and confetti swirled around in the breeze that swept in from the storm front over the Gulf. Somewhere on deck a band was playing The Stars and Stripes Forever. It was a gala and festive atmosphere, a throwback to the grand era of passenger ship embarkations of decades past.

I worried how we would find Malaku and Teal among the throngs on board, particularly if they had already checked into a stateroom. I needn't have. Malaku and Teal were coming across the parking lot from the opposite direction. Teal was dressed in the gray terry cloth dress she wore the last time I saw her in Galveston, and the same outrageous platform shoes. But she looked far less vital today. She seemed glassy-eyed, stiff in her movements, even zombie-like. I wondered if she had been sedated. Malaku was in standard tourist garb: a beige Havana shirt, loose slacks, even a stingy brim straw hat. He was carrying their lone piece of luggage and that large duffle bag I had seen him carry onto the *Persephone*. We intercepted them about twenty feet from the gangway.

"Time's up, bud," I said to Malaku.

He look startled, but not for long.

"I thought we might meet again," he said. "And I see you brought your whore with you."

"I'd appreciate a little respect for my friend. You call her a whore again, and I'll get on you like a chicken on a June bug. You reading me on this?"

He laughed. "You Americans, so good with words, so poor with actions."

"As least we don't cut and run when the flare goes up. I see there's just one piece of luggage. What did you plan to do, park Teal on board with the smallpox virus then bug out for the airport?"

"When she is on board my work is finished."

"Your work is finished now."

"There's nothing you can do to stop me."

"You're already stopped."

"Do you think you two can make me your prisoner by yourselves?"

"We're here under a black flag. No prisoners."

He just sneered. He sat down the piece of luggage and opened the duffle bag, removing a four-foot wood and steel axe. The axe had wicked looking curved blade and a sharp ten inch spike protruding from the top end. I had seen a battle-axe like that before: in pictures of a black-masked man beheading American prisoners in Iraq.

"I have looked forward to meeting you again." he said.

"Don't lose your head," I said, but it was all bravado on my part. That damn axe would have frightened Superman.

Meanwhile, a security guard from the cruise line had come running up, shouting, "Hey, put that down!" He came too close. Malaku swung the axe in a powerful backhand, like a tennis pro on a killer return shot. The blow caught the security guard on the side of the neck and severed his head as neatly as a farmer's hatchet severing the head of a Thanksgiving turkey.

Then Malaku started toward me.

I wasn't quite ready. As I fumbled with the cheap zipper

on the rifle case, Parvin lunged at him like a cat, catching him off-guard. She scratched at his eyes, and bit his hand, and kneed him in the groin. It had little effect. He picked her up by the back of her neck with his free hand and ran her through with the sharpened spike of the axe with the other. She was dead when she hit the ground. At that precise moment I heard a loud ripping noise, as though the heavens themselves were rent to allow her spirit passage. Perhaps it was just a crack of thunder from the approaching storm in the Gulf. I didn't have time to think about it. Parvin's had been a suicidal assault, as she surely knew, but it had bought me the second or two I needed to open the rifle case. I took out the heavy-duty, double-bit, Michigan axe I had bought at Coffee Jack's.

It is the conceit of modern society that man's brutal, primitive nature has long been tamed, at least in what we like to call the advanced industrialized world. Violence, like man himself, so the theory goes, is a creature of circumstances. But perhaps this is not so. Perhaps the primitive lives in all of us, a sharp-toothed, slant-eyed beast, always waiting for the right moment to spring out, ready to slay all in its path. If so, the primitive was on full display that afternoon in Galveston, when two men, each bearing the mark of Cain, did battle in the most brutal, primitive fashion imaginable.

The axe fight itself probably didn't last that long, but I had no sense of time. Malaku slashed at me, swung at me, tried to hook me, even tried to impale me as he had Parvin. It was all I could do to slip and parry his axe blows and maintain my balance. I had little opportunity to mount my own offensive. The fight raged over onto the soft asphalt of the parking lot. Malaku's face became contorted, as though he was deriving sensuous pleasure from the encounter. An unearthly odor radiated from his powerful physique. It made me nauseous. I choked down my breakfast and tried to survive the onslaught.

We sparred and lunged but neither of us drew blood. Meanwhile, a crowd of onlookers had gathered and were actually cheering us on. A crowd, too, has its beast. This seemed to encourage Malaku in his megalomania, for when I stumbled and fell he made a vicious overhead swing at my head. I rolled out of the way. He missed, the axe head swinging down on its own momentum to catch hard in the heat-softened asphalt of the lot. He kneeled and used both hands to try to un-stick it. This was my opening. I stood up, stepped to the side, and brought the head of my axe down hard on his right wrist. He looked with shock and disbelief at the right hand that was still grasping the axe handle, even as the stump of his right arm was spurting blood.

"That was for Robin," I said, "and this is for Parvin."

I swung again, a home-run swing that caught him right at the nape of the neck. His head severed from his body and wobbled across the lot like an out-of-round bowling ball. I thumped the headless torso with the toe of my boot. "I told you not to lose your head."

Epilogue

Throughout the axe fight Teal had stood motionless, like Lot's wife turned to salt. After Captain Johnson and a dozen Rangers arrived on the scene, just moments after the fight had ended, she was transported by special ambulance to Memorial Hospital in Houston and tested for smallpox. The test came back positive. She was placed in a contagious disease isolation unit and watched day and night for the next week by medical personnel garbed in bio-hazard suits reminiscent of moon landing equipment. On the third day she became symptomatic, pustules breaking out all over her body, fever gripping her like a boney hand from hell. As had Travis before her, she bled profusely from the anal cavity. She called repeatedly for water through lips that had become cracked and worn as ancient leather. The worst of it, however, were the two large pustules that formed over her eyes, covering them like a poultice of toxic white putty placed there by some mad faith healer.

"Any hope, Mick?" I asked. Mickey and I were standing together outside the observation window to Teal's room. Mickey had arranged for me to have a special visitor's pass.

"Not a chance, *jefé*," he said. "She'll be gone in a day or two."

"DeLong been up here yet?"

"Every day. You just missed him."

"How's he taking it?"

"So far, so good, but I think he's living on false hope."

"Aren't we all?"

I made it a point to go up to Teal's room the following day at about the same time. Senator DeLong was there, peering down at Teal through the observation window, shaking his head. Suddenly he brought his right arm up and bit hard on the back of his hand. I stepped next to him. He looked at me as though I were a ghost from a prior life, then back down at Teal. "Her eyes, Quinn, her eyes! Horrible! Horrible!" He turned and fled down the corridor, holding his hand over his mouth.

I looked down at Teal. Sometime during the night the pustules over her eyes had burst, leaving behind nothing but empty sockets, just two black holes rimmed with crusted blood. *Look into my eyes, Jeff,* she had told me. I was looking now. Her eyes had been eaten out by the infection as surely as if they had been pecked out by a giant avenging bird. Her past had finally caught her. She died that night.

A quiet ceremony was held for Parvin the following week. A living will she had left specified that in the event of her death she be cremated and the ashes scattered. It did not specify where the ashes were to be scattered, so I requested that they be scattered on my ranch. My request was granted.

Three weeks later, I went to a court hearing in which all criminal charges against me were dropped. The district attorney accepted the finding in Parvin's report that my wood axe had not been the murder weapon in Soos's death. Moreover, DNA tests on microscopic blood particles found on Malaku's battle axe matched Soos' blood. The judge, of course, was only too glad to get rid of the case.

After that I did little that summer. I stopped working out and practically stopped eating. As a result I lost twenty-five pounds and the man in the mirror stopped looking like me. I didn't care.

I unplugged my television and computer and put my cell

phone in a drawer. I left my radio plugged in, but the only program I listened to was the all night classical station from Monterrey. What news of the outside world I received was from Mickey, who drove out to the ranch at least once a week.

Mickey told me that an autopsy on Teal had shown that she was 48 hours into infection with the Russian-made smallpox virus when we confronted her and Malaku. Had she gotten on the cruise ship, she would have infected the entire compliment of passengers and crew within a few days. Truly a *peri abele.*

Senator DeLong had been true to his word about what he would do if something ever happened to Teal. A month after her death he had taken the *Persephone* out of harbor at night, outrunning the harbor patrol and the Coast Guard, and steered into the worst storm in years. No trace of the boat or DeLong was ever found. I had a certain amount of respect for this action, although I recognized the self-aggrandizing element in its melodrama. But he was a politician, what should you expect?

Ex-Texas Ranger Conway Crowley was indicted and convicted on charges of aggravated assault stemming from the beating and pistol-whipping of his wife. He was now serving a ten year sentence in the same prison unit I had been in.

After a thorough investigation by the FBI's internal affairs section, Agents Rawlings and Biderman were discharged from the agency. At last report they had opened a private investigation firm in Texas City, specializing in running down bail-skips and delinquent car loan debtors. They were a long, long way from The Seat of Government.

The FBI even did a sort of bureaucratic *mea culpa* with regard to Parvin, naming her Agent-of-the-Year and establishing a fund in her honor to help the families of other Muslim agents killed in the line of duty. But it still couldn't get its collective mind around the main issue. The press release announcing these steps conspicuously failed to mention she had died fighting the *jihad.*

The new Texas Ranger for our district was former trooper

Hector Gonzalez. From time to time he stopped by the ranch to see me. I enjoyed his visits.

Even Captain Johnson came to visit. We sat under the oak tree in my back yard and smoked cigars for a good two hours. He told me that the reason he and the Rangers were on the scene so fast after the axe fight was that they had been following me from the jump, but lost me temporarily in the wild ride down to Galveston.

"That was the plan all along?" I asked.

"That's right, son. That's why I hit that old fart of a judge with the Writ of How Come-Us. It was clear to me from Agent Sassani's report that we had very little time to stop that fucker Malaku. There wasn't time for legal niceties. I needed to twist an ear or two and set you on your way. I wanted you for my bird dog."

"How come?"

"I knew you were going to go right for that son-of-a-bitch."

"How did you know I would do that?"

"Because that's what I would have done." He took a deep drag off his cigar, exhaled a thick cloud of smoke, and grinned widely.

Mostly, though, I sat on my back gallery in the big wicker chair and watched Derwood nurse Sergeant Pepper through the last stages of her pregnancy. He was a gentle man, especially with horses. He had chosen a trade to match his personality. I wondered if the trade I had chosen reflected my own personality: violent and unforgiving. I hoped it wasn't so, but I had a deep fear about it. And was Malaku the actual Angel of Death he claimed, or just a crazed human being with the blood-taste for killing? If so, was I like him in more ways than I wanted to believe? Was I myself a source of the evil I hated? Most importantly, was I responsible for Parvin's death? These are not the kinds of questions a man wants to be asking himself, not if he intends to live out his full term of years.

Sergeant Pepper foaled at the end of September, a beautiful black filly. I helped Derwood and the vet guide the delivery. I think this simple act, repeated across the ages, was what snapped me out of my funk. Death there was, for sure, but new life always, too. Embrace it.

Two weeks later I threw a party at the ranch on a beautiful fall day blessed with cool air and a blue-gold sky. They all came: Mickey and Beth and their new born daughter, Derwood, Hector Gonzalez, Sheriff Tuck, Captain Johnson, Coffee Jack, Sally the vet and her runaway husband, Dr. Rao, Father Blanton and the kids, together with their spouses and families and neighbors from all around the county. We barbecued hamburgers on the horse feeder grill, drank Cokes and Seven-ups chilled in ice, and danced to a western swing band I hired out of Austin.

But even during the festivities I had an inward turn. I walked away from my guests and stood by the fence surrounding the pasture where Sergeant Pepper and her filly were nubbing the grass, delighting in being alive in each other's company. The scene brought to mind another mother and daughter in a faraway land who had delighted in each other's company, too, the mother telling her daughter she was an angel, until men with a lust for power had destroyed their brief spell of happiness on this earth.

Mickey must have seen me walk away, for a minute or two later he put his hand on my shoulder.

"Been thinking about a name for the filly?" Mickey asked.

"How does Persian Angel sound to you, Mick?"

"Sounds good to me, *jefé.*"

And so we named her. Yet in spite of St. Paul's admonition that angels walk among us, and in spite of the many chilling things I had seen and heard that suggested angels and demons do indeed carry on an ancient war of which we are allowed only partial and fleeting glimpses, I wasn't completely sure Parvin had been an actual angel. My own faith always teeters precariously between belief and doubt. But of one fact I was sure: she had been the best human being of us all.

71507870R00154

Made in the USA
Middletown, DE
25 April 2018